Pi^x

PR

Bad Moon Rising

Donna Julian

A SIGNET BOOK

SIGNET
Published by the Penguin Group
Penguin Putnam Inc., 375 Hudson Street,
New York, New York 10014, U.S.A.
Penguin Books Ltd, 27 Wrights Lane,
London W8 5TZ, England
Penguin Books Australia Ltd, Ringwood,
Victoria, Australia
Penguin Books Canada Ltd, 10 Alcorn Avenue,
Toronto, Ontario, Canada M4V 3B2
Penguin Books (N.Z.) Ltd, 182–190 Wairau Road,
Auckland 10, New Zealand

Penguin Books Ltd, Registered Offices:
Harmondsworth, Middlesex, England

First published by Signet, an imprint of Dutton Signet,
a member of Penguin Putnam Inc.

First Printing, January, 1998
10 9 8 7 6 5 4 3 2 1

 REGISTERED TRADEMARK—MARCA REGISTRADA

Printed in the United States of America

PUBLISHER'S NOTE
This is a work of fiction. Names, characters, places, and incidents either are
the product of the author's imagination or are used fictitiously, and any resemblance to actual persons, living or dead, events, or locales is entirely coin-
cidental.

This is for Cameron Donavon Julian,
who arrived on the best of nights
under a happy, smiling moon.
I look at your beautiful little face
and remember why I dream.

Chapter One

It was a typical spring evening in Manhattan. Drizzling, slushy, overcrowded, and clamoring. Five o'clock and the city's high-rises were spilling their guts into the streets.

Faces tucked into necks, eyes to the pavement, noses and ears quickly reddening with cold, and backs hunched, the people knew to keep their minds to the task of making their way home.

But as Eric Keaton worked his way in the opposite direction, against the tide, eyes turned upward. He attracted second looks.

Tall and lean, he had an easy self-confidence that people responded to. Not even New Yorkers—the most callous, jaded species of life on earth—were immune.

It wasn't something he thought about. Whatever it was that drew attention, he was used to it.

From his youth, still round-faced, the clear, strong lines of manhood as yet unformed in the planes of his features, folks had reacted to the black eyes—more often than not flashing with mischief—or to his wide, earnest grin that was always slightly lopsided.

Now at thirty-six, his features chisled to sharp angles from his aquiline nose, to his prominent cheekbones, and his strong, square chin with its deep cleft. Only the dark eyes and crooked smile remained unchanged. And the charisma. He'd had it then, he had it still. That would never abandon him.

A black leather garment bag slung over his shoulder, he held his briefcase out in front in his other hand, wielding it as a rod to divine a path through the crowded sidewalk, winning pardons with the charm of his smile.

He was a *Savant*—one of a trio of elite investigators who had earned a reputation as superheroes in the never-ceasing wars against crime, terrorism, injustice, and plain old everyday wrongdoing. They got results. They were precise, hard-hitting, right on the money every time, though some charged that Eric, particularly, cared little how many casualties were sustained along the way—how costly or devastating the consequences to the innocent as long as he got the job done. Not wholly true. Not exactly inaccurate either. He wasn't a saint. In fact, if asked, he'd be the first to admit he was driven by demons, not angels.

Still, he wasn't a celebrity. He had a reputation, not a famous mug. Somehow, people just seemed to know, by instinct, perhaps, that he was special; a force to be reckoned with.

It was an enviable talent—this power to influence others with a smile or an apologetic shrug—especially in New York.

A woman, exiting the midtown high-rise Eric was headed for, held the door open, smiling up at him as he passed her by. Closing time, and the building was emptying fast. Those few employees of Liberty Investigative Network Corp. who hadn't yet made their escape, were hurrying to tuck traces of the day's turbulence away in desk drawers, or scampering to the coat closets for jackets and scarves and the occasional pair of galoshes. Several people called out to Eric as he stepped from the gray marble floor of the expansive lobby to the escalator. He nodded or grinned in return, then raised an arm in salute and called out to one of the firm's attorneys in jest, "Hey, Santini, when you sidle up onto that bar stool you're headed for, drink one for me. Hell, slam a whole bottle of Chivas. I'm on my way out again."

Shelley Crown, an attractive corporation veep, glanced over her shoulder as she passed him on the opposite escalator descending to ground floor level and said, "Whose neck are you out to noose this time?"

Eric laughed. "I thought I might try to find the genius who sculpted our lady," he said, his chin jutting in the direction of the sixty-foot-tall statue that had been erected in the exact center of the building. Shelley had commissioned the multifaceted statue symbolic of the firm's pentagon of statutes on which its foundation was based—integrity, humanity, excellence, preservation, and justice. LINC was the largest, fastest-growing, and most prestigious private investigative firm in the world, and its lady was fast becoming every bit as famous.

Despite his razzing, Eric liked her. Had even named her. Janus. Jan for short. There was something about her that inspired pride. Sort of like the Statue of Liberty, only his kinship with LINC's lady was tighter, up close and personal. After all, one of her faces—humanity, he guessed because of the gentle gaze—looked right into his office. He imagined an ally in her who commiserated and empathized. Especially during the past weeks when he'd spent so much time holed up in there around the clock assembling information for his next assignment: the probe of five unresolved slayings tagged by the media as the Rose Murders. And stupid as it might be, he was going to miss ol' Jan.

Several employees laughed at his comment to Shelley. Others called out with offers to do their part in helping the attorney with that bottle of Scotch in honor of Eric's impending departure and newest challenge.

But Eric's attention was already diverted to the third floor where Levi Thornton stood leaning over the banister awaiting him.

He lifted his arm again in greeting, taking the last of the escalator steps two at a time to the top. His grin widened as he saw Levi disappear. They would reunite on the second floor in the men's room. It had been their designated conference room for the past four years. The second floor housed the finance department, and had proven a successful getaway for their private two-man 'board meetings.' At least there, they could talk uninterrupted for more than five minutes. Everyone from the lowliest position to the biggest muckamucks upstairs detested the numbers crunchers and control freaks who regulated budget and spending with choker-chain intensity, so they avoided the second floor as if it were a hospital quarantine ward for highly contagious patients.

Though the two men had spent much of the past ten days together researching their latest assignments—Eric to Kansas City, Levi to an obscure little spot on the globe in South America—Eric dropped his baggage on the men's room floor to embrace his friend. "Hey, man, I thought you'd be halfway to Tingo Maria by now."

Levi laughed, the deep resonant sound filling the tiled room with its richness. "Naw. Pappy notified some honcho at CIA and I got all tangled up in that red tape we're all familiar with. Shit, we know how those guys like to screw around—all in the name of national security and concern for my well-being, of course. Anyway, Pappy's got it set now." He glanced at his watch. "Matter of fact, flight leaves in approximately ninety minutes. I just waited around hoping to catch another of his workouts with you serving as his punching bag." His long, coffee-dark face crinkled with his laughter again.

Eric shook his head, laughing with his friend although a slight furrow of annoyance creased his brow as he walked over to the mirror on the wall to run his hands over his thick, sandy hair. Pappy—Guy Jameson to most—was the man with the power to nix or approve the probes that were taken on by his savants—the three senior investigators who got the prime assignments. Their boss first, he was also their friend, although in recent days, Eric had been hard put to remember this. "Shit, Lee, he's still not hollerin' about the Rose probe? I thought we had that settled two weeks ago."

Levi Thornton's dark face sobered as he stood behind his colleague, his eyes at once clouded. "Well, let's just say he's quiet, but it's a heavy quiet, which we both know means he's not a happy camper, Eric. The Anthonys are his friends, and Pappy's loyal, damn it. That ain't exactly a defect. Matter of fact, it's a quality you and me hold pretty high on our list of 'gots to have' if you be our friend. Comes in handy when the man's your boss, too."

Eric braced his hands on the sink, pausing, head down for a few seconds before he sighed deeply and turned to meet the other man's gaze straight on. "What're you saying, Lee? After pitching the fight of my life for this assignment, you think I should back off of it after all?"

Levi shook his head. "Hell no, man! I think you're as right as rain about this. It's smack up your alley, and you know I believe if anyone can put together a profile on the maniac who's been killing those girls and come up with the perp's identity, it's you."

Eric frowned, folding his arms across his chest. "Then what?"

"Then nothing." Levi turned on his heel, slamming

the wall with the flat of his hand before stopping at
the door. "I'm just telling you to be careful. You were
handpicked, bro. And not by Rosenthal or Giopanni
to dig up dirt for some rich dude on whose dick his
old lady's got her mouth around or to find out what
motherfucker's got his hand in some company's till.
You were recruited as a *Savant* by The Guy himself.
You've always had Pappy's support one hundred percent. You don't want to go messing with that. You're
not just good. You're a friggin' genius. Hell, Pappy
knows that better than anyone. But hey, he's The Guy,
you know? He was catching bad guys and writing pol-
icy for all levels of law enforcement almost long as
you been breathin', but this company is his baby.
LINC ain't Mickey Spillane or Magnum P.I., it's an
international network so big—" He stopped, shook his
head. "Aw, shit, what am I doing? You know this
same as me. Guess I just don't want you losing sight
of Pappy's first loyalty. He cares about you, but he's
LINC before he's Guy Jameson, if you follow."

Eric muttered a curse under his breath before
reaching out to grab his friend's shoulder. "Hey,
man, thanks."

Levi let go of the door handle and turned back to
face Eric. "Just cover your ass, homey. That's all I'm
sayin' here. No point in flushin' your career down the
john for a gig that probably ain't never gonna make
lead story even in the rags. I mean, I know it's bad—
real bad—that someone's been getting away with murder, but let's face it, Keaton, in today's market, a half-
dozen beauty queens getting themselves killed is an
ABC movie of the week. It ain't something Oliver
Stone's gonna be looking to bring to the big screen."

Eric was still scowling, but he surprised the other
man by laughing suddenly. "Yeah, well, a drug cartel
in Tingo Maria isn't exactly going to make it as a
category on *Jeopardy*, Lee."

Levi jabbed him sharply on the shoulder with the well-manicured nail tip of a long, dark finger. "Well, guess the joke's on both of us then, 'cause everybody's heard of the infamous rock star, Jade, and her famous escapades with that dyke guitarist in her band. Now if our Roni finds the hit man Jade's emasculated actor hubby contracted to off the bitch before he succeeds, Roni'll likely grab Jameson's MVP award."

"Most valuable player? Roni?"

"The girl's good."

"The *girl's* a pain in the ass," Eric argued.

"Yeah?" Levi asked, raising a brow and causing a dimple to appear in one of his brown cheeks with the suddenness of his crooked grin. "And how the hell would you know that? You been diddling our Miss La Marc?"

"Fuck you," Eric said, though amusement sounded in his tone.

The tension gone, both men laughing and relaxed, they leaned against the wall for a few more minutes before Levi glanced at his watch again. "Hey, bro, you hang loose. I got me a plane to catch and some drug dealers to rap with."

Exiting the 'conference room,' they retraced their steps to the escalators. Though only twenty minutes had passed, the ground floor was empty below except for a woman watering the potted foliage; Mondays found even the most zealous in a hurry for the tranquillity of home.

Eric set his bags down before drawing his friend against his chest in a tight bear hug. "You just cover your ass down there and don't go foolin' around with any *senoritas.*"

Levi clapped Eric firmly on the shoulders before pulling away, his deep, resonant voice loud and joking as it always was whenever they parted to go their separate ways on potentially dangerous assignments. "Say what? I ain't gonna be doin' no fraternizin' wif no *senoritas*, bro. I got me a hot little mama sittin' home wif three sweet babies jes' waitin' fo' Daddy to bring home the bacon."

"Yeah, well, remember that."

"Can't do nothin' else, man. I'm big, I'm bad, but I loves my lady and babies."

"Yeah, well, Big and Bad, you certainly soundin' black enough to convince me."

Levi stepped onto the escalator, his big white teeth gleaming with the wickedness of his grin. "Case you forgotten, I *am* black. But, while we on the subject, you ain't heard nothin' yet, baby. I'm getting it rollin' and by the time I step off that airplane, I's gonna be the baddest motherfucker drug pusher them Latinos ever seen. By the time we exchanged our *buenos dias,* asshole, and back atcha, they gonna know this nigger can cut a deal, a line of snow, or a double-crossing throat. Whatever it takes, I aims to please."

Eric grinned though his dark eyes failed to reflect even a modicum of mirth. "Yeah, like I could forget your African heritage with your ugly black mug right in front of me, and I know how good an actor you are. I've seen you in action, remember? Just make sure you don't get so far in you don't notice when it's time to get out. Way I hear it, it ain't so much fun once the gunfire starts. 'Specially if you're standin' in the middle. *Comprende*?"

"Yeah, and I'm gonna miss my flight if I don't get going."

"Okay, but don't forget you still owe me a rain check for a Rangers game, and I'm expecting front-row seats."

Levi rolled his eyes. "Oh, man, don't you ever give up? Tell you what. You get on upstairs to the war room and face Pappy so you can get to Missouri and wrap that probe up by the time my plane touches down at Kennedy again, and I'll take you downtown for some real entertainment. You'll forget all about that pussy-ass hockey."

His grin already faded, Eric ignored the last. "Speaking of Pappy and the war room and the MVP award . . . Roni gone yet?"

Levi laughed, "Our Ms. Veronica La Marc? Ball buster, queen bitch, and gorgeous requisite female member of our little real-life mod squad? Yeah, man. She's halfway to Paris by now, her blood-red nails no doubt already filed to razor-sharp claws. Things get rough for you out there in that mine field of Anthony, Missouri, you just thank your lucky stars you ain't a hit man after a rock star named Jade."

"Hey, I thank God every night that Roni and I are on the same side, Lee. *Every* night."

"You and me both," Levi said. He moved toward the escalator before stopping and backing up. There was one more thing he had to get said. Much as he wanted to leave it, some things just wouldn't go unattended.

This time, though, when he spoke, he stared straight ahead instead of looking at Eric. "You gonna be able to handle being in K.C. again? I mean, I can't go off into the wild blue yonder 'less you tell me you ain't gonna be taking side trips digging up the past."

Eric followed the other man's gaze, fixing on the same place in history before he answered. "Don't worry, Lee. David and Bryn are dead and buried, both literally and figuratively. And Kansas City's just a place like anywhere else."

"Uh-huh," Levi muttered. "That's what my granddaddy used to say about an ol' grove outside of East Memphis where folks claimed ghosts danced at night."

Eric raised a skeptical brow. "But you're saying there really were ghosts and your grandfather saw them for himself?"

"Hell, no. What's the matter with you, Keaton? There ain't no such thing as ghosts."

Eric shook his head. "Okay, I'm lost. What's your point?"

"I'm just telling you to be careful. I don't want you stirring up stuff you can't change, but neither should you go pretending nothing ever went down in K.C. What happened six years ago was bad, real bad, and you gotta know it's still gonna get inside you once you're back."

"I thought I was the shrink."

"You are, but you know what they say about doctors who treat themselves, and one thing you ain't is a fool. So, I didn't expect you'd mind lettin' this layman give you some wise counsel."

Eric laughed, clapping his friend on the shoulder. "I hear ya."

"Good, then I'm outta here." Levi walked away, making it onto the escalator this time.

"Hey, Lee, one thing. What was going on in that grove?"

"The KKK hung more'n a dozen black men out there between nineteen fifty-five and sixty. Wasn't no ghosts, like I said, but wasn't just any old grove either. My granddaddy found out the hard way." He grinned, faced straight ahead again, and held a hand up over his shoulder, two fingers raised in a *V*. "Peace."

Chapter Two

Peace was about the last thing Eric expected to find when he stepped from the elevator onto the tenth floor minutes later.

His assistant, Karen, was waiting for him, a broad smile adding youth and vitality to her plain freckled face. "Put it off as long as possible, huh?" she teased, gesturing with a slight turn of her head in the direction of the door behind her that boasted in brass letters of belonging to the office of chief honcho, Guy Jameson.

Eric shrugged. "Ran into Lee on the way in, and we had a brief meeting before he left to catch his plane."

Karen folded her arms, a smug, satisfied grin still in place. "Second-floor men's room. Yeah, I saw him waiting for you. I swear to God, if Roni La Marc knew about your conference room, she'd check herself into the hospital to have her breasts removed and a penis attached."

"Jesus, Roni with a penis! Is there a scarier thought than that?"

Karen chuckled. "Come to think of it, no, but don't let it haunt your nights. Miss La Marc is very proud of herself just the way she is."

"This is true," he said, as she picked up a thick file folder from her desk, placing it in her boss's hands before grabbing her coat from the back of her chair. "There you go. A copy of every scrap we have on the Rose Murders inside. You've been over it all except a clipping from yesterday's edition of the *Kansas City Star*."

"Something heavy?"

Karen shrugged. "Nothing you have to look at this sec. Just a rehash of the same ol', same ol'. Mostly it's a recap of Christianne Anthony's decision to resign her post as product V.P. of their European operations. A company spokesperson is quoted as vehemently denying rumors that Ms. Anthony's decision is in any way related to the Rose Murders. Sort of seemed to come out of nowhere, so I don't know. There may be some smoke leaking out of Anthony headquarters that hints of fire." She paused, leaning against her desk. Her eyes reflected worry she'd managed to hide until now. "Like I said, most of it's old stuff. . . ."

"But?" Eric prodded.

"But you might want to note the reference to the Special Agent your former employer has assigned as the new case agent."

Eric was already opening the folder, his brows drawn together in a scowl.

Michael Sansom. Funny how easily old memories surfaced, how quickly bile rose, and how acrid it tasted on his tongue.

Eric scanned the clipping quickly, then snapped the folder shut and raised his eyes to his assistant. "Thanks, Karen. As usual, you're right on top of it. Don't know what I'd do without you—"

"Yeah, I know," she interrupted with a roll of her eyes. Grabbing her purse from the bottom desk drawer, she closed it with a sharp little kick, then leaned forward to peck his cheek. "Bring in the bad guys."

Eric chuckled, enjoying the familiar ritual of their farewells. "Always."

She indicated a yellow square of Post-it paper on her desk calendar. "You're confirmed at the Kansas City Airport Marriott tonight. Plane tickets are on your desk along with your itinerary, and you better get hustling. Your flight departs La Guardia at eight."

Eric thanked her again, raising a hand in farewell as she walked away. "See ya," he said, watching her absently until she jabbed the elevator button in the hallway.

He glanced down at the folder. He'd read the article more thoroughly on the plane. Right now he had a meeting with Guy Jameson to get to. The one-on-one conference before all on-site probes was standard operating procedure for the *Savants*. The last-minute interviews were generally helpful, insightful, given Guy's good judgment calls and keen eye for detail, but Eric dreaded this one.

He glanced up as the door to his boss's office opened and Guy appeared, an eyebrow raised.

Lifting his chin in response, Eric shut the heavy folder quickly and pushed himself away from his assistant's desk. "I'm on my way, Pappy. Just got to grab my plane tickets so I don't get all the way to La Guardia without them."

Guy shut the door again without a word. He was seated behind his desk when Eric entered the office.

LINC's CEO wore many tags. The Guy, Chief, Pappy. All of them fit, though Eric thought The Marlboro Man would be most apt. With his lean good looks, brush dense mustache, suede Stetson, and perpetual cigarette hanging from the corner of his mouth, he looked as if he'd just stepped from one of those billboards that had disappeared with the arrival of the militant antismoking rhetoric.

As Eric took a seat in front of his boss's desk, he met his blue eyes through the swirl of smoke and hoped he was imagining the icy glints emanating from them. Guy was his superior, the man who signed his paychecks, but first and foremost, Eric thought of him as his friend. He hoped he hadn't jeopardized that friendship with his insistence on investigating the Rose Murders.

Guy eased Eric's mind at once with his casual entree into their conversation. "You and Thornton meet in the second-floor conference room before he took off?"

Eric nodded, crossing his legs in an unconscious gesture of relief. "Karen just asked me the same thing. And here we believed our covert parlays so clever. Guess we weren't as good as we thought."

Guy dragged long on his cigarette before stubbing it in the brimming ashtray in front of him. "I don't think there's a LINC employee who doesn't know about your conference room with the exception of Roni. I've promised myself to send out a memo threatening immediate termination for anyone who lets it slip to her. Hell, she won't care that it's only a fucking men's room. She'll have me kicking someone out of his office to create a conference room for her. Sharp damned investigator, sixth sense as dependable as Doplar, but royal fucking pain in the ass."

Eric laughed at his boss's scowling expression and his apt summation of his only female savant's personality. "Yeah, I once called her a prima donna to Lee, who corrected me real fast. Said she was more like belladonna . . . poisonous as hell. But neither of us'll argue that she's good."

"One of the best, and the only reason I put up with her shit."

Eric took a long deep breath. "Which brings us to me."

Guy flicked his gold lighter, raising his eyes to meet his protégé's gaze across the desk as the fire at the end of a new cigarette took hold. A mild, half smile began with his appreciation of his favorite investigator's quick grasp of the point he'd been making.

"Yup." A long stream of smoke followed the word slowly as if to punctuate it.

He picked up a newspaper clipping, taking a second to look at it before sliding it across the desk to Eric.

Eric glanced at the caption before leaning back in his chair again. "Karen just gave me a copy."

"And?" Guy asked.

"And nothing. If it's Sansom you're worried about, he isn't going to bother me. If it's the Anthony spokesperson's vehement denial that Christianne Anthony's resigned her position in Europe is related to the murders, I don't know. You're the one who's tight with the family. You tell me."

There was no mistaking the look of annoyance on Guy Jameson's face, nor did his voice offer relief. "Cut the bullshit, Keaton. You've been sniffing up one tree since the second Rose contestant was killed. The Anthony family tree. Am I wrong?" Without waiting for either confirmation or a denial, he went on. "But let me ask you again as I have for weeks now, does the name Darin Woods ring any bells for you? Doesn't the fact that authorities at every level consider him the one and only suspect carry any weight with you at all? Have you simply decided to ignore all the evidence against him? Since when does a specialist such as yourself ignore fingerprints, DNA, hair, and fiber evidence? Jesus, what else do you need?"

Eric's foot had begun to move with his agitation, but his voice remained controlled, his tone patient. "Shit, Guy. I'm not ignoring Woods. Neither am I forgetting that every piece of evidence was gathered in the general vicinity of the murders, *not* actually with the bodies. That's why the Grand Jury refused to indict and a superior court judge told the D.A. and everyone else to go away and not come back till they could provide motive, a murder weapon, *anything* that proves he's a killer and not just a fuckin' groupie. To my way of thinking, the guy's just plain pathetic.

"Look, we've been over this, what, a dozen times now? I'm well aware of your long-standing friendship with the Anthonys, Guy, but what if one of them knows something? Maybe something he or she isn't even consciously aware of. It has to have occurred to them that the killer's true goal may be to destroy them or their company. And don't we owe it to our client to find out if that's the case?"

"Of course we do, *if* that's the case, but until we know for sure, I don't want you discounting Woods. No matter what the Grand Jury said, there's a lot of evidence against the guy."

"Granted," Eric said sharply. He gave his head a quick annoyed shake, then recovered his temper. "But isn't it possible someone's trying hard to throw the authorities off the right trail and using Woods as a scapegoat?"

"Anything's possible," Guy conceded on a long stream of smoke.

"And no matter how tight you and the Anthonys are, Guy, they're not above the law or exempt from scrutiny." Guy started to protest, but Eric stopped him, a hand raised. "Now, just a sec, Pappy. I understand they've been victimized, too, but damn it, man, there are five dead women here. Lisa Marks's family hired us to get to the bottom of this. *They* employ us. Our allegiance is to them, not the Anthonys, no matter how close your ties to them. Are you forgetting that Jack and Connie Marks mortgaged their farm to pay our fees?"

Guy jabbed out his cigarette, relighting another one before the smoke had died from the butt smoldering in the ashtray. "Goddamn it, Eric, of course I haven't forgotten! I didn't want to take their money when they have local, state, and federal police agencies at their disposal at no financial risk at all. You were the one so hot to trot on this one."

Eric felt the last of his control snap. "Yes, sir, I was. You're right-on there. So, I guess I'd better get to it, huh?" He stood up, preparing to leave the office before either of them did or said something that would put a permanent rent in their relationship.

But Guy stopped him. "Just give me two minutes more . . . please."

Eric hesitated at the door, then returned to his chair.

Guy lit another cigarette. "You understand that Alex, especially, is a very dear, old friend," Guy began. "You also understand how far back that relationship goes, that he and I graduated from Harvard together thirty years ago. I'm just wondering if you realize how they're going to take me sending out one of my top investigators; one of my *Savants,* for the love of God."

"You're not sending me," Eric pointed out. "Our services were solicited, and the Marks have no personal ax to grind with the Anthonys. They simply want their daughter's murder solved. They're seeking closure, nothing else."

"I understand that, Eric, but Judas Priest, Christianne is my goddaughter! Hell, I was asked to be a pallbearer at her grandmother's funeral six months ago. You may remember, the only reason I didn't attend was because I slipped on the ice and broke my foot the day before." He stubbed out his cigarette unsmoked, the ashes barely formed, as he left his desk to walk to the window.

Eric took a couple of long deep breaths before answering the last question. When he spoke, his voice was soft yet confident. "You and I are friends, too, Guy, and I hope you trust me enough to know that I won't hurt your friends unless I find out that they are somehow implicated. Even then, I won't do anything without talking to you about it first. I've given you my word on that already. I know you believe me or you wouldn't have given the go-ahead in the first place."

Guy didn't turn around but looked at his watch. "You have a plane to catch, Keaton."

Eric pushed himself slowly to his feet, searching his memory for a time when things had been as strained between him and his boss—his mentor. Of course, there had never been such a time, and he wished he could ease the tension somehow. But there wasn't any way. "Don't smoke so much," he said at last.

Chapter Three

Eric checked into his hotel suite in Kansas City tired yet curiously restless. He always experienced an impatience to be at work, uncovering facts, ferreting out and priming potential candidates for those rare-find interviews that would lay open the heart of his probe and expose the cancer—in this case a vicious, cold-blooded killer. But tonight his enthusiasm waned, the tension and turbulence of his recent meeting with Guy having trampled on his convictions. He walked to the large window, hoping to find calm in the familiar skyline of his boyhood or a sense of déjà vu at his homecoming, but, as they had for several years now, those feelings eluded him. He was no longer the boy from Kansas City. That boy had disappeared with the years, his parents' deaths, the loss of his fiancée and brother in a single instant of insanity, and too much life witnessed and exposed at its basest level. Naïveté. He longed for it when he came home the same way a young child longs to believe in Santa Claus.

Perhaps if fate—fate and a wrong turn and a madman—hadn't intervened . . . If he had married, settled down, and started a family, he would not find himself so often looking back on a past with ties and loved ones with such hunger. Perhaps then he wouldn't have become so familiar with the dark mood that engulfed him whenever he had too much time on his hands, particularly when he returned to Kansas City.

No, that was ridiculous. He had happy memories of

a close-knit family, parents who had loved each other as well as their children, and once upon a time, the usual competition between brothers. Why, then, couldn't he let go, simply enjoy those early memories?

His career was his life; Levi, Guy, even Roni, they were his family now. It was enough. More than enough. It had to be. Since his brother's death . . . no, he wouldn't think about David. To think about him meant thinking about Brynlee, the FBI, and Michael Sansom, and he wasn't ready for that yet. He'd face that one at their upcoming reunion.

He turned his thoughts back to the place he was now, the one of his choosing.

He was exactly where he wanted to be. Had all that he needed. He led an exciting life, free of the confining shackles of marriage. He'd certainly never lacked for companionship when he had the time to devote to a relationship. So why was he brooding? He knew bloody well why—Special Agent Michael Sansom. The only man on earth who knew everything about the double tragedy that had claimed the lives of the two most important people in Eric's world—his brother and Brynlee Carroll.

He turned from the window, trying to shake the dark depression that was slowly folding around him, threatening to suffocate him as surely as the fumes that would one day snuff out the life of Feron Lee Packer when he sat in the gas chamber in Potosi and paid for his sins. *Burn, you motherfucker.*

His heart had turned cold and was layered with rime. There was nothing he could do about that, and it didn't help to dwell on a past that couldn't be changed or a future that the legal system would not allow to be rushed.

An oblique grin started across his face as he took in the opulence of his surroundings, widening with satisfaction as his eyes found the bar already stocked with his favorite Scotch, as well as bottles of vodka, bourbon, cabernet, and chablis. Precisely what he, a criminal psychiatrist, would order for a patient suffering the same symptoms.

Eric laughed aloud as he dropped a couple cubes from the ice bucket into a glass, then poured a generous amount of fiery, amber liquid over them. "Physician, heal thyself," he toasted, allowing the sting of the Scotch to mellow and warm slowly in his mouth before swallowing. As he raised the glass a second time, the jangling of the telephone interrupted him.

"Eric Keaton," he said into the mouthpiece, resting his tall frame lightly against the heavy pecan desk, his voice not sounding his surprise at the unexpected intrusion.

"Dr. Keaton, Paul Anthony here." The voice was strong, assertive.

Eric arched a brow unconsciously. So the Anthonys had been expecting him and had determined to meet him as the aggressors. He sipped slowly from his glass, ready for the game, yet prepared to wait patiently for the other man to fire the first ball, demonstrate his prowess.

"Guy Jameson telephoned earlier to tell us that you would be arriving this evening," Paul said. "My brother asked me to call and arrange a meeting."

Guy had telephoned? Of course, that's why the uncommon use of his title. Doctor. Well, fine. So be it, Eric thought, before answering. "I checked in just minutes ago. I'm impressed, Mr. Anthony. I wasn't going to call you or your brother until tomorrow, but I appreciate your attention. I'd planned to arrange my schedule tonight. When would be a good time for me to speak with you both?"

"Call me Paul, please," the man replied, his tone neither friendly nor hostile. Masterfully neutral, Eric decided, as his caller continued.

"You'll want to meet with Maryann as well, I suppose."

"And your niece." Eric smiled now, the ball returned with an effortless lob to the other man's court.

"Christianne? I . . . I'm not sure that will be possible. At least not now. She's been keeping herself rather removed since her grandmother's death . . . well, no need to belabor that. Guy's explained that to you, I'm sure. In any case, the rest of us are only too happy to accommodate you. Besides, questioning Christi at this juncture in our, ah, interviews would serve no purpose. After all, she's been in Italy for the past several years. What questions could she possibly answer?"

He hesitated again, this time almost imperceptibly, the way a man does when he is catching the last words of whispered instructions before continuing. "But as I've said already, the rest of the family—Alex, Maryann, and myself—will be happy to meet with you. You realize the pageant kicks off tomorrow night with the Rose Ball. Perhaps we could talk sometime before that. Of course, we're extending an invitation for you to attend. It's really quite something. Very glamorous, and famous for its roster of impressive guests."

Eric reached across the desktop for a pen and slip of paper. "Just tell me when and where."

The relief in Paul's voice was apparent. "We thought dinner would be nice. Say seven o'clock? Here at our home in Anthony? You're actually quite close. Only thirteen, fourteen miles. I can give you directions now or have Katy, my secretary, call with them in the morning if you'd rather."

Eric called an end to the game, his impatience taking prominence over his desire for sport. "I'll accept your invitation to the ball, but dinner would be impossible tomorrow night. Why don't we make our meeting early evening. Say five? Five-thirty?"

"My brother and I rarely arrive home before six, Mr. Keaton." Paul's tone had chilled as well.

Eric grinned. "Six-thirty, then? My preliminary questions shouldn't take up much time."

Paul hesitated again, and this time Eric could hear his agitated breathing in the phone. "Are we interrupting previous dinner plans for tomorrow, Eric? If so, we could postpone our meeting until after the ball. Say Wednesday?"

"Not at all. I just make it a rule to never break bread with folks I may be investigating. Guy did explain that LINC has been employed by the family of Lisa Marks; that my interview with you and your family will be part of a formal probe into the murders?"

"Certainly. Why else would we tolerate further invasion of our privacy? We'll expect you at half-past six, Doctor. My secretary will call with directions in the morning. Good night."

Eric opened his mouth to respond, but Paul had hung up.

Eric shrugged his shoulders and drained the last of the Scotch as he replaced the phone in its cradle. Whistling now, he refilled the tumbler as he loosened his tie and headed in the direction of the bathroom. Damn, a hot shower sounded good. His step was light again, the lonely boy he had been searching for in his thoughts earlier was forgotten. He was once more at home in a strange city being himself, a *Savant*.

Chapter Four

Eric left his hotel shortly after five o'clock the following evening for Anthony, Missouri, driving northwest as Katy Westley, Paul Anthony's secretary, had instructed in her early-morning telephone call. It was a relaxing drive, the freshly greening hills and softly budding trees filling him with spring fever as he rarely experienced in New York City.

With his elbow propped casually against the armrest, his fingers drummed an almost silent beat with the rhythm of the tune playing on the radio. All in all it had been a satisfactory start, he thought, reflecting on the morning and early-afternoon hours passed in the morgue of the *Kansas City Star*. He had gleaned very little new information, but had compiled a chart with four columns, organizing his thoughts more neatly in preparation for the meetings he had already scheduled.

In spite of Guy's implied warning to avoid concentrating his attention on the Anthonys, the Trio—as he had taken to calling them to himself—headed the first column of notes. The list of facts beneath their names was neither as long nor as interesting as those in the second and third columns, under the headings of *Murder Victims* and *Suspect—D. Woods*. But no matter what anyone else believed, the Anthonys were at the nucleus of this mystery and they would remain first on his list for questioning.

Only one Anthony stood apart on his list with a

heading all her own. Christianne Anthony had a very short and ambiguous list of facts attached to her name. At the end of the list, he had printed in bold letters the question PICTURES? He frowned as he drove, recalling the recent newspaper article about her sudden decision to remain in Missouri rather than returning to her post in Europe. He thought of the other pieces written over the past several years. Not more than five or six mentions of her name in all. And stranger still, the fact that of all the print he had pored over, he had found only two pictures of her—a grainy, poor-quality snapshot of her with her parents, grandmother, and uncle at her graduation from Harvard, and the second, a tabloid puff piece shot in profile on the arm of Anthony's European product manager and her reported lover.

Eric had probed the lives of presidents and monarchs, terrorists and underworld mobsters, but he had never come across anyone so well protected from the press. Why? Was the perfume princess truly as publicity shy as the family claimed? A stammering, easily flustered V.P.? Hard to believe.

His thoughts abruptly turned away from Christianne as he left the highway and entered the tiny town of Anthony. He slowed the car, glancing at his watch at the same time. He still had fifteen minutes before his meeting at the great family's home and he wanted to look around, get a feel for the people whose loyalty inspired them not only to work for the Anthonys, but also to live in a town owned by them. Could it be possible that the Anthonys' alibis for the nights of the murders were only as reliable as those people whose lives depended on their employer's generosity?

Guy would not be happy at that question. No, Eric's boss respected the Anthonys, held them in the utmost esteem. But why not? They were to Missouri what the Kennedys were to Massachusetts and the Grimaldis to

Monaco. Not only did they run a perfume dynasty that rivaled the oldest and best in Europe, they were renowned for their philanthropic work and generosity. Both Paul and Alex had served as advisors on presidential committees. Maryann's face was seen almost as often as the Anthony men in *Newsweek, People, Esquire,* and *Forbes.* The lady was photographed often in her jewels and designer gowns, but almost as frequently in jeans or a sweatsuit, planting saplings to replace redwood giants destroyed by a devastating forest fire in California, and working alongside handicapped children in last year's national Special Olympics. Hell, he reminded himself, they owned a town that supported several hundred families who, from all accounts, had worked happily for the power barons for decades.

Could anyone live up to the reputations these three had earned? Who knew? Somehow, though, he doubted evidence to the contrary would be found in the town of Anthony.

As he drove, the speedometer never climbing over twenty-five, he saw only a town almost identical to most others in the Midwest—the requisite general store, grocery market, a used furniture store, dress shop, feed and grain store, a gas station, of course, and a bar and grill. There was also a score of small clapboard houses along the main street, nothing distinguishing or odd. Maybe Anthony was a little better maintained than most, perhaps somewhat quieter, but otherwise not so different.

He eased his car to the curb on the left-hand side of the street, rolling down his window as he pulled to a stop to call out to a young boy on a bicycle. "Hey, kid! Can you direct me to the Anthony Estate?"

The boy stopped his bike with his Nikes scuffing the pavement, his eyes wide with incredulity and both thin eyebrows jutting up with surprise. Without a word, he pointed.

Ducking forward slightly, Eric peered beneath the sun visor to follow the boy's finger. He could just make out a long strip of rolling, manicured lawn in the distance that disappeared into a long grove of trees. He straightened, looking back at the boy who stabbed at the air a couple more times with his finger before righting his bicycle to ride off again. Eric eased the gears back into drive and pulled out onto the road again. A few people had paused in their comings and goings to give him a quick once-over before turning back to their own business. He guessed that with all the coverage on the Rose Murders, the townsfolk were getting pretty used to strangers. No big deal.

He slowed the car almost to a crawl as he approached the enormous white colonial home nestled on several hundred acres and surrounded on all sides by a large wall of trees. He was mildly curious about the absence of a fence or security station, but conceded that there was probably great advantage in living at the apex of one's own town.

He stopped his small rental car behind a silver-gray Jaguar and a sleek, cream-colored Mercedes parked at the base of the steps leading to the wide oak doors. He wanted to look around for a couple of minutes, but it was time for his appointment. He paused for an instant before raising the heavy knocker. This was certainly a beautiful place. Hog heaven, his mother would have said.

A middle-aged woman answered Eric's summons with a friendly smile, wiping her hands on a small towel before ushering him in with a diffident wave of her arm. "Dr. Keaton?" Her voice was soft and vaguely accented with a Southern drawl. Her smile widened as she shrugged, looking down at her hands apologetically. "Sorry. Been getting dinner ready. The

Anthonys are waiting for you in the library. If you'll follow me . . ."

The house was as lovely and old-world charming as its exterior had suggested it would be. Heavy columns of rich gleaming mahogany stood proudly in the corners of the expansive foyer. Eric looked around him appreciatively as the housekeeper stepped aside to allow him entrance to the library.

Two men stood across the room, their faces partially obscured by the bright light of the evening's setting sun, but Eric recognized them both immediately from the pictures he had studied often and with care.

An attractive woman sat on one of the twin classic rolled-arm sofas. Her perfectly painted lips parted in a small gracious smile of welcome as she greeted their guest. Maryann Anthony.

"Dr. Keaton," she said with a practiced smile—not wide, not eager, but neither was it thin nor tight—the smile of a woman used to her role as hostess no matter the circumstance, occasion, or guest. She raised a small hand slightly from her lap to wave in the direction of her husband and brother-in-law in introduction. "My husband Alex and, of course, Paul. I believe you spoke with him on the telephone last evening."

Eric nodded in the direction of the men as he approached the sofa, a hand extended. "Mrs. Anthony. Thank you for seeing me tonight."

Both men seemed to pull away from the wall simultaneously as if released from a magnetic force by his cordial greeting.

Paul, the shorter of the two men, came forward to shake his hand first. He was a pleasant-looking man, although he walked with a decided limp, and his graying hair had receded quite far back from his forehead. His lips were ample, and the long lines on either side of his face were proof of a quick, ready smile. Eric noticed that his face had a slightly puffy look that hinted at a penchant for drink, and his pale blue-green eyes had a tiredness about them that reminded Eric of the stories he had read about the jet-set, playboy image Paul had worked vigorously to earn. His voice when he spoke seemed overly loud, yet not unpleasant in its rich timber. "Good to meet you, Doctor."

Eric accepted the other man's hand, nodding pleasantly. "Mr. Anthony."

Paul's face broke into a web of lines as his wide, easy grin spread across it. "Please. You're to call me Paul. Remember? Besides, with so many Anthonys in one room, formality not only gets tiresome but confusing."

Alex stepped in front of his older brother, offering his hand. "Eric, is it then?"

Eric was slightly caught off guard by the younger anthony's striking good looks. Much better looking than his pictures indicated, he was also a great deal more imposing than Paul. Eric wondered if his handsome features were always so remarkable or just seemed so when contrasted with his brother's slightly worn-looking appearance. Eric wondered, too, if Paul had always been odd man out, remembering the nickname, the Trio, that he had earlier dubbed the woman and the two men. He thought further back to a conversation he had had with Guy about the fast friendship he and the two Anthony boys had enjoyed throughout their college years. He smiled, forcing his journalistic mind from its mental note-taking to respond, "A pleasure, Alex."

"We haven't dined yet, Eric," Alex said in his smooth voice. "I know you told my brother that you wouldn't be able to join us for dinner, but I hope you'll at least share a drink with us."

Eric held up a hand as if in surrender. "Why, sure. Scotch, please. On the rocks." Eric watched as the younger brother communicated his direction for his sibling to pour the drinks, his blue eyes following him with subtle patience. As Eric noted Alex's bluer eyes, slightly taller height, and his light blondish-brown hair still thick and not yet graying except for an occasional strand at the temples, he decided the differences in the two men made for profoundly separate impressions. Even Alex's soft voice had more power because of its quiet command to listen more closely.

"Please, Dr. Keaton, have a seat."

Eric walked to the large armchair that Maryann Anthony indicated, his most charming, crooked grin in place as he corrected her. "Eric, please. Your brother-in-law has insisted twice now that we be on a first-name basis."

Maryann responded to his easy friendliness with a small smile, a quick glance at her husband the only indication of her nervousness. If Alex answered with any silent communication, Eric couldn't tell, but Maryann looked down at the skirt of her navy blue silk dress for a few seconds.

Eric sat back, rubbing his chin for a moment, trying to get a feel for the people around him. All appeared to welcome him without protest, yet the air was charged with tension. Eric focused his attention on his hostess as Paul handed drinks around.

Not a beauty in any sense of the word, she was nevertheless well turned out, he thought, remembering the phrase his mother had always used for a woman who knew how to make the best of her looks. Her short, dark hair was swept back off of her small face, and her round green eyes were discreetly touched with makeup. Only her lips, which were diminutive like everything about her, were heavier colored, but the overall effect was understated and attractive.

Paul and Alex both took seats on the sofa opposite her so that Eric was left seated apart, much like a defendant on a witness stand, he thought.

"Well, Eric, Guy tells us that LINC has been re- tained to look into the Rose Murders and that you were eager for the assignment. I have to be honest and tell you how surprised we were. Please don't think this rude, but as I asked Guy, how is it you believe you can learn more than the police and FBI who've been on the case from the beginning? And how can we help you?" Paul leaned back to ease one leg across the other. It must have cost him some pain, Eric thought, recalling that Paul had suffered a badly crushed leg in an automobile accident several years before, though the pleasant, relaxed expression on his face didn't slip.

Eric took a long, thoughtful sip of his Scotch before answering. He set his glass down on the gold-leafed, crystal coaster on the table at his side. "As I said last night, Paul, our services have been requested by the family of one of the murder victims. Whether I can uncover anything the authorities haven't managed to find is something we'll soon discover. However, as a privately owned corporation, LINC is not bound by all the constraints that often restrict government offi- cials. So, who knows? Maybe I'll get lucky."

"Somehow, Keaton, I don't see you relying on luck. You seriously believe you can come in here and resolve what the best law enforcement personnel have been un- able to do. Isn't that right? And single-handedly?" Paul's voice was as even as if he had just asked Eric if he'd care for a refill of his drink, but the sarcasm of the words could not be denied by any of them.

Eric watched as Maryann and Alex exchanged a quick, unrevealing glance. "Paul, please. I'm sure Eric doesn't hope to do any such thing," Maryann reasoned.

"Well, Dr. Keaton?" Paul snapped.

A small smile tickled Eric's lips as Paul returned to the formal use of his title. He had done the same thing on the telephone the night before when he had be-

come annoyed. He looked at Alex and Maryann, but
while Alex drummed at his glass with his forefinger,
neither seemed the least upset by the sudden change
of mood in the room. Was Paul, then, the spokesman
for the family or was he merely the one whose feathers were most easily ruffled?

"Why do I get the feeling I should beg the Fifth,
Paul?" Eric said easily, retrieving his glass from the
table.

Alex raised his glass in Eric's direction taking the
question from his brother. "I propose a toast to your
success," he said. "To you, Doctor. May you catch a
killer, and at the same time, spit in the eye of government for wasting time, effort, American tax dollars,
and most of all the lives of five beautiful young women
by hiring incompetents who couldn't catch a fly much
less one lone murderer."

Somehow the subtle sarcasm of Alex's statement
riled Eric more than Paul's quick temper had. He sat
forward, his face warmed slightly with his annoyance.
"May I ask you . . . any of you"—he waved his glass
in a half circle to include the three people facing
him—"why my investigation upsets you?"

Maryann laughed, though Eric noticed that her eyes
quickly sought the others' gazes before she spoke. "To
be perfectly honest with you, Eric, we would be ec-
static. However, no matter how impressive your credentials, we have to be realistic. After all, we have
lived with this . . . this horror for years. *We* have
attended the funerals of these poor, innocent young
women, and *we* bear the burden of knowing that if
not for our pageant, they'd all still be alive. On the
other hand, we respect and understand the Marks's
desperation. And, too, there is Guy. He has asked for
our cooperation and we would never refuse him. He
is, after all, a very dear, old friend. So, while we feel
this is a grand waste of the Marks's money and our

time . . . as well as yours, we *will* cooperate. Just tell us what we can do and try to ignore our cynicism."

Eric started to answer, but she stopped him with a hand held up. "Just one more thing, Eric, please. It's obvious from what Guy told us, you don't agree with the police and FBI that Darin Woods is the Rose Murderer. Assuming you're correct and *everyone* else, us included, is wrong, what do you base your belief on? I mean, my God, even your former partner, FBI Special Agent Sansom, was incredulous when we told him you were coming to Kansas City to disprove the case against Mr. Woods."

Eric took a long slow sip of his drink before answering. When he did, his voice was as soft and quiet as Alex's had been a few minutes before. "I have not ruled Mr. Woods out, but I am a licensed criminologist as well as a seasoned investigator and I am bound not only by ethics but by contract not to discuss my instincts about a case other than with my superior and our clients." He allowed himself a brief smile. "Guy refers to me as well as two of my associates as his *Savants*. We have an unprecedented success rate: Out of more than seventy probes, we've never failed."

Maryann chuckled softly under her breath. "All right then, Eric, as you've come all this way to lend a fresh ear, we are prepared to tell you what we can. What would you like to know?"

All eyes were on him now, waiting, apparently at ease once again now that Maryann had so ably demonstrated their lack of intimidation. They had nothing to hide, no secrets to be accidentally betrayed in conversation with this *Savant*.

Eric took his time. This was another of his games. The Keaton version of Cat and Mouse. Taunt the rodent a bit, trapping it between paws, while keeping the needle-sharp claws carefully tucked. Back off. Then pounce. Now!

"I would like very much to hear about your daughter, Maryann. I'd like to hear why she has suddenly resigned her office in Italy and after you give me your version, I'd like to hear it from her."

Alex jumped to his feet, knocking his glass against the chair and spilling his drink over his slacks. Maryann and Paul were both at his side at once, acting as if he had just been doused with something vile rather than merely a half-empty glass of gin.

Eric rose to his feet, too. End of the game. He had expected to catch them off guard with his last question, but they were acting as if he had just asked one of them to confess to the murders. Was that what he was asking? he wondered. In any case, he'd had enough for one evening. He would work from a different strategy for the next few days and return to the Anthonys on a one-to-one surprise basis. "If you will excuse me . . ."

Maryann turned toward him, ready to accept his apology and show him to the door, but the words froze in her throat as she looked past him to the foyer. Paul and Alex both looked up, sensing the sudden change in her. Their eyes darted past Eric causing him to turn and follow their gazes as well.

"What's wrong?" the young woman asked from the doorway, looking down at herself as if unsure she'd put clothes on.

No one spoke.

Eric knew immediately that this was Christianne Anthony. He stepped forward, opening his mouth to introduce himself, thinking for just a second to take advantage of the others' numbed silence, but all he could do was stare with incredulity and disbelief.

She was beautiful, this mysterious daughter who had so adeptly avoided the paparazzi cameras; yet it was not her amazing beauty that held him quiet but the sudden unwanted pictures that flashed through his mind of five corn silk-blond beauty queens with crystalline blue eyes, Nordic fair skin, and slender, feline proportions. In all the hours that he had studied the victims' pictures, none of them had resembled the others so much as right this second, because Christianne Anthony, he realized, was all of them, and each of them a little of her.

Chapter Five

Maryann swept forward toward her daughter, practically throwing Alex and Paul and Eric off balance with the momentum of her flight across the room. "Darling, what are you doing home?"

Eric did not miss the tremor that had crept into her voice, but his eyes remained riveted to the beautiful newcomer.

"I'm sorry, Mother, I didn't intend to surprise you or to intrude. I arrived home a while ago. I changed, and was going for a walk before dinner. Feeling a little closed in . . . never mind. I just chanced to glance in, and when I saw you had a guest, I thought I should say hello." Her eyes moved to Eric's face, a slight blush coloring her cheeks as she offered an apologetic smile and held out a hand. "I'm Christi Anthony. Excuse the way I'm dressed. I wasn't aware we had company or I would have slunk out the back."

Eric reached inside himself for a modicum of composure as he took her hand. She had a good, firm handshake, and he liked the way she met his gaze squarely in spite of her obvious discomfort. "Eric Keaton, and the pleasure is mine."

Leaving Alex still pale with shock, Paul appeared to regain his senses sufficiently to join the others in the foyer. "Christianne, Eric works for Guy. In fact is one of his *Savants*. You remember him telling you about his trio of expert investigators?" He put an arm around her, beaming at her suddenly as if she were the long-awaited guest star instead of the well-kept mystery they had obviously intended her to remain. "I'm sorry, sweetcakes, we would have invited you to join us, except I thought you had a meeting scheduled at the plant."

She smiled in response though kept her gaze on Eric. "Terri—she's our lead chemist—went home early with a flu bug, so the meeting's postponed." The explanation out of the way, her smile widened. "Uncle Guy—honorary title since he's my godfather—has spoken of you often. In fact, you really should be embarrassed. You and your friends have practically been escalated to heroes of mythical proportions. Pretty cool, though, how proud he is of you all. Maybe you can tell me about some of the miracle crime solving you've pulled off over dinner."

"He won't be staying to dine with us. In fact we were just saying our good-byes when you joined us," Paul interjected quickly.

A brief frown of almost childish petulance creased the beautiful woman's brow, but it quickly disappeared with a sudden splendid smile and twinkle of mischief that danced in her blue eyes. "I don't believe you, Uncle Paul. I'm suddenly suspicious that the last-minute meeting with Terri was arranged as a ruse to keep me from meeting Eric." She waved a hand in Maryann's direction, laughing at the same time. "Oh, lighten up, Mother. I was joking, though I am glad for whatever bug it is that attacked the poor woman and saved me."

"Me, too," Eric said.

Christi's smile faltered for just an instant as she looked from her uncle to her parents, noting the tension none of them seemed quite able to disguise. She found it again at once as she reached forward to place a hand on Eric's arm. "Please say that you'll reconsider and join us for dinner. I would love to hear all

about your work. It must be fascinating and . . .
woops, there I go, embarrassing myself." She rolled
her eyes. "You would think being raised by a family
of sophisticates, I'd be less easily impressed, wouldn't
you? Even banishing me to Europe for four years,
where I almost overdosed on aristocracy, failed to cure
me. I'm afraid I'm hopeless. I had dinner with Monaco's Prince Andrew last year and made a complete ass
of myself."

"Christi!" Maryann shrieked in dismay.

Christianne laughed, her amusement bubbling from
her with obvious spontaneity. "Mother hates it when
I gush. I do, too! Just can't seem to help myself. I'm
afraid I'm incurably in love with the idea of princes
and heroes." She stopped suddenly, her eyes widening.
"I've probably embarrassed the hell out of you,
haven't I? My God, I need a muzzle." She laughed
again, though for the first time, it sounded forced,
strained.

Eric hadn't missed the silent exchange of disapproval between her parents and uncle. Now he realized, neither had she, for the sudden tightness in her
voice wasn't the only change. The light in her eyes
had dimmed, altering them from glittering sapphires
to murky Wedgwood.

Eric could have sworn he heard Alex curse under
his breath. He ignored him and the others as he put
a hand on top of Christianne's, which still rested on
his arm. "I'm hardly hero material, though I'm glad
to hear Guy thinks so. Maybe I'll hit him up for a
raise when I get back. As for the other, I don't know
why anyone would be embarrassed by anything you
say or do."

"Thank you," she said. "And about dinner . . ."

"You have no idea how much I'd like that, but I'm
afraid not tonight. Maybe you'll give me a rain check.
I'd like to talk to you."

"Anytime," she said.

Eric opened his mouth to suggest the next evening, but Paul cut him off. "Eric is investigating the Rose Murders, sweetheart. I doubt you want to talk about that. Besides, what could you tell him? You've been in Italy." He turned to Eric, his pale eyes at once as cold and hard as uncut diamonds. "Guy was quite specific about us not getting in the way of your investigation, Doctor. I'm sure he'd be unhappy to know you were wasting your clients' money by talking to someone who knows next to nothing about the tragic killings." He flashed a quick, gelid smile. "So, if you'll telephone my office tomorrow, Katy will arrange a meeting that is more conducive to business. Thank you for coming."

Eric hadn't missed the implied warning with the mention of his boss's name, but neither was he going to be cowed. He grinned easily, shifting his weight to assume a casual, unhurried stance. "You promised to drop the doctor business, Paul. Just Eric, please," he reminded the other man, though his eyes darted to Christianne's with the invitation. "And I will call your office in the morning. I'll be wanting to visit with each of you at some length. I'm afraid we didn't get off to a good start tonight, but the sooner I get my questions out of the way, the sooner you can all be rid of me."

Christianne's large, round eyes narrowed slightly as she looked from her mother to her uncle and then past them to her father. "My uncle's right, Eric. I know little about these horrible murders other than what my family has told me, and what I've read in the papers, of course, but I'll help any way I can." Then she directed her gaze to her father, a smile on her lips though not in her eyes. "Daddy, you'll have to remind Uncle Paul that all of this affects me as well as the rest of you. The murders did play a large part in my decision against returning to Italy, after all."

Alex nodded, once again appearing relaxed and unconcerned. "Certainly, Christi, but as we've said time and again, we don't want you involved. For the sake of the company, at least one Anthony needs to maintain a distance as you've done so far."

"Sounds reasonable to me," Eric said.

"It is that, yes," Christi said, "but hardly the whole truth, Eric. "What no one's admitting—I suppose because I'm standing here, and they're afraid I'll run shrieking with fear from the room—is that the slain women all bore a striking resemblance to me. Everyone pretends to believe it mere coincidence, but it's rather obvious that the killer could well be attacking Anthony Enterprises not only by murdering its pageant contestants, but also implying a more personal threat by selecting women of the same coloring and general physical appearance as mine. That's the real reason I've been kept away and surrounded by bodyguards whenever I'm at the plant or anywhere other than here at—" She stopped, turning to look at her parents and uncle, her face suddenly ablaze with accusation. "I was joking, but I'm right, aren't I? You did schedule the meeting with Terri so I'd be away from the house while Eric was here. You didn't want him to learn about the obvious likeness between myself and the murdered girls."

The elder Anthonys exchanged bemused glances. Eric stepped forward, his eyes locked with Christianne's. "Don't be angry with your family. You're right, I didn't know until I saw you, but I can appreciate their concern. They may very well be justified in their worries, and they should do everything they can to protect you."

Maryann and Paul both visibly sagged with appreciation, but it was Alex's soft voice that made them all turn back to the center of the library. "Thank you, Dr. Keaton. Perhaps you could spare us a few more minutes of your time so we can elaborate on that explanation. Then, of course, as you suggested, we can each meet with you later to discuss what we know in more detail."

Christianne looked around her at the others. "Does this mean you want me to leave? Because it's a little late for that. I refuse to hide any longer. I want these murders to stop. Since you won't listen to me and cancel the pageant, I fully intend to—"

"That's quite enough," Maryann said, her voice so tight with anger, her words came out in a choked whisper.

"Your mother's right, Christi," Alex said, though with a more gentle tone. "This isn't the time." He patted the cushion beside him on the sofa. "But, no, sweetheart, now that the cat is out of the bag, you're welcome to stay."

Maryann protested, "Alex, I don't think that's such a good idea. No matter how nonchalant Christianne pretends to be about the possibility of very real threat, it has to be frightening for her. And talking about those unfortunate girls is enough to upset anyone."

Alex glanced at his wife for an instant, but ignored her concern. Christianne glided past her mother before she could protest further. The others all looked to Eric.

"Thanks, Alex, but I'm inclined to agree with your wife. Besides, I think I should let you get to your dinner. You do have your party tonight."

Maryann smiled appreciatively. "Thank you. We will be seeing you at the ball later, won't we?"

"Wouldn't miss it, Maryann." He looked past her to her daughter. "Maybe you'll save me a dance."

Christi shook her head. "No. I'm afraid my imprisonment doesn't allow for many furloughs."

"Christianne!" Maryann protested.

Ignoring her mother, Christi continued. "I'm allowed to travel between the house and the plant. I don't even venture into K.C. to the executive offices."

"We'd all love for Christi to share in the pageant, Eric, but you've just heard why that's impossible," Alex said, casting his daughter an apologetic glance.

"Of course," Eric said sympathetically. He shook Paul and Anthony's hands, nodding to the ladies before leaving. They did not see him to the door, but remained clustered around Christianne as Eric pulled it shut after him.

He was halfway to his car when the door opened behind him again. He turned around to see Christianne coming down the steps.

"I just wanted to apologize, Eric. I can be such a bitch. All this confinement is getting to me. I'm starting to regret my decision to stay stateside. Still, that's no excuse for how I acted in there."

"Hey, haven't you heard? Angels are out, bitches in, and a beautiful bitch is all the better. The rage in Hollywood, I understand. Just look at today's leading ladies. Demi Moore, Sharon Stone. So you see, you're very in vogue."

The lilting tinkle of her laughter filled the night around them. "I'd better get back inside. Coming out after you is as close to anarchy as I dare with all the tension you just witnessed in there. Better not give them more than they can handle in one space. Good night, Eric." She stepped back as he climbed in behind the wheel.

"You take care, Christianne."

"Christi," she corrected, waving as he started the engine and pulled away from the curb.

Eric stopped the car, rolling down his window to call to her.

She walked around to the driver's side.

"I don't want to piss your folks off, but I'd really like to come back to talk to you again. What do you think?"

Her smile widened with her eyes. "When?"

"Thursday morning?"

"Stay for lunch?"

Eric hesitated. "I don't think your folks would approve."

"Then we won't tell them." She laughed though even in the dusk of evening he could see that her eyes had clouded to the murky gray-blue of stormy skies. "Until I went to Europe, I never so much as crossed a street without getting permission. I kind of went too far the other way in Rome." She shrugged. "Anyway, I've been working on finding a middle ground. Independence rather than anarchy. It's getting bloody boring, though. Help me out here. Come for lunch."

"You're on. Thursday, eleven-thirty?"

So much for his rule about never mixing business with pleasure. "It's a date."

Eric eased his foot from the brake only to lower it again. "I like your sweatshirt."

Christianne looked down at the words printed across her chest. A MAN'S WORLD? WHO WOULD YOU RATHER BE, KEN OR BARBIE?

She hunched her shoulders. "Yeah, me and Barbie. We both have everything. Just ask anyone."

"That bad?" he asked, referring to the bitterness that coated her words for the first time.

"Not for Barbie," she said on a weak laugh. "Empty-headed dolls don't make mistakes . . . and, well, no one wants to kill—"

The front door opened, cutting her off.

Paul stepped out. "Eric, having trouble?"

Christi ducked down hoping she hadn't been seen. "They don't know I'm out here," she whispered.

Eric's lips twitched with a small grin. "No. Thanks,

Paul. Just jotting some notes and my pen fell between the seats. I've got it, though. Good night."

Paul hesitated a second before waving his arm and shutting the door.

Christianne giggled, her brief bout with self-pity apparently overcome. "You're quick on your feet."

Eric grimaced. "Yeah, well, I've got a feeling I'm going to have to be a lot quicker if you don't get back inside before they find out you're missing." He slipped the gear into drive, and let the car roll slowly away from the house. He stopped at the mouth of the grove to watch in his rearview mirror as she darted across the drive and carefully opened the front door of the house just wide enough to slip inside. He couldn't check the crooked, wry grin that tugged at his mouth.

He was a man used to being flirted with, and he didn't doubt the enthralling Miss Anthony was as accustomed to the game as he. This time, however, they were both flirting with danger. He wondered if she understood how serious it was.

As he turned onto the freeway some five minutes later, he grinned. Yes, he thought she did, and what's more, he was pretty sure she was enjoying the hell out of it.

He'd have to rewrite his notes tonight. Christianne Anthony was a lot of things, but beautiful definitely headed the list. Few women possessed the power to take his breath as she had.

Giving himself a good mental shake, he pushed his way past his attraction to the gorgeous heiress and watched the speedometer climb as he raced the demons that were his constant companion. Letting his head fall back against the headrest, he jotted a few more mental Post-its about Christianne Anthony: Clever, intriguing, unhappy. He paused, frowning as he added a question mark behind the last:

Rose Murderer's intended victim?

Chapter Six

Paul joined Alex in the study after dinner, his face puckered with lines of worry and annoyance. He walked across the room to shut the doors that his brother had apparently opened to catch the evening breeze from the terrace. "Breeze is picking up."

Alex drew hard on his cigarette, a shrug his only answer. He stared at the television set, but Paul guessed that his mind was not on the show he watched.

"It looks like rain. I hope Christi can sleep tonight. Always had nightmares as a kid when it stormed. I don't know about now, but with everything that's gone on these past weeks . . . well, I worry."

"Stupidest damn show I've ever seen. Turn it off, will you?" Alex asked, jutting his chin in the direction of the remote control on the coffee table.

Paul scratched the back of his neck. He didn't like it when Alex became morose and sullen. He had barely spoken ten words since Eric Keaton's departure more than two hours before, responding only occasionally with forced enthusiasm to his daughter's comments about the investigator's visit. Paul scooped the remote up in his hand, hitting the switch on the set to bring the flashing images to darkness.

Alex frowned, blowing a slow stream of smoke from his nose as he watched Paul turn away to the bar. "Maryann suggested Christi take a sleeping pill tonight. I doubt she did. She's stubborn when it comes to drugs."

Paul knew that the comment was a barb directed at him, but he chose to laugh it off as he filled his glass with brandy. "She obviously doesn't inherit her aversion from me," he said lightly. "Possibly from Maryann. She won't even take an aspirin when she gets a migraine. Me, I look for relaxation in whatever form I can find it."

Alex stubbed out his cigarette, his face at once stony, his mild voice tinged with warning. "Don't start with me, Paul."

"I'm not starting anything. Just making a weak stab at levity. Apparently weaker than I thought." He looked around the room. "Where is Maryann?"

"Right here, Paul." Maryann entered the room, a cup of coffee in each hand. She handed one to her husband, placing the other on the table beside a wide, olive leather chair. "I see I was right not to bring you a cup."

Paul raised his glass to her, a devilish grin on his face. "To my keepers. 'Twould be heaven without you, but hell is so exciting, I've decided to stay." He quaffed the fiery liquid as if it were cherry soda, turning his back to refill his glass.

Maryann rewarded him with a soft chuckle as she took a seat across from her husband and picked her cup up from the table. "You're incorrigible, Paul."

"Ain't it the truth, though."

"Come sit down and join us," she commanded, the humor fading from her voice. She turned her attention to her husband. "You look tired, darling. It's been an exhausting evening. Why don't you go on up and shower? We have to leave for the ball in an hour. We can discuss Eric Keaton's visit in the morning. Christianne absolutely refused the sleeping pill, but she rarely comes down for breakfast, so we can talk then."

"I still think you should try to reach Guy tonight,"

Paul said as he seated himself at his brother's side, his deep, resonant voice at once serious again.

"Oh, hell," Alex muttered, setting his cup on the table with a sharp clink. "Look, I know you're both upset that Keaton met Christi, but I, for one, think it's for the best. I trust Guy. If he says Keaton is the best, then maybe he's exactly what we need here. Besides, do you realize tonight's the first time I've heard Christi laugh since her grandmother's funeral? Between mother's death and the disastrous affair with that goddamned Carlo Marconi, and now her upset over our refusal to cancel the pageant, I was beginning to worry." A tight smile flashed for an instant. "If nothing else, maybe the man will prove a distraction for her."

Maryann's eyes blazed with irritation. "Good God, Alex, you're not suggesting we enocurage her obvious attraction to Dr. Keaton? Why, as you just pointed out, she's hardly recovered form her affair with that damned production manager. Besides, you've heard her feelings about the pageant. She's positively obsessing about it. Good heavens, all we need is Guy's overzealous investigator stoking that fire. Sometimes, I don't understand you. Think of Christianne for a change, Alex."

Alex's blue eyes were suddenly the cold silver of aluminum foil as they met his wife's. "It is precisely Christi who I am thinking about, Maryann. I saw her smile for the first time in weeks, tonight. I heard her laugh and to tell you the truth, it was the first time I felt like laughing myself . . . in years, in fact."

Maryann sank back into her chair. "I don't think wanting to protect her from fresh hurt is the same as trying to keep her from happiness," she said quietly, her voice husky with hurt.

"Look," Paul put in, "why don't we leave the argument about Christi for another time. You're both right.

She's a grown woman, but she's still in need of protecting. Right now, the question is how we are going to handle Keaton. I mean, I think he's on our side for the time being, but when he came in here tonight, it was pretty obvious to me that the Anthonys are on his list of suspects. He could cause us a good deal of embarrassment, not to mention further damage to the company if he slants his investigation against us."

Paul reached for his brother's pack of cigarettes, causing the others to blink in surprise. He rarely smoked, in fact hadn't had a cigarette in months that they knew of. "This guy's like a terrier. He'll keep digging until he comes up with answers."

Alex rubbed a long tapered finger pensively along his temple. "And you don't want that, Paul?"

"Fuck, Alex, you can pretend all night that it doesn't bother you that Guy's turned him loose out here, but there are secrets you want to keep buried as much as I. Perhaps more than I."

Alex raised his hands, shrugging in agreement. "All right. So what do you suggest we do?"

"I suggest we charm Keaton's socks off tonight, meet with him as soon as possible, answer his questions, and avoid Guy's name. Constant reference to our relationship with Jameson only serves to aggravate. First of all, it sounds like a threat—which, of course, it is—and second, it might just make him start wondering about things that go a lot further back than these god-awful murders."

"If memory serves, it was you who brought up Guy's name tonight."

"Paul, Alex," Maryann interrupted, looking at both men with impatience, "you're both missing the point. I truly think that once Mr. Keaton has had an opportunity to talk with the authorities, he'll agree that the killer has already been named if not indicted. I know the evidence against Darin Woods is circumstantial, but I believe he is guilty, and so do most of the murdered girls' families. I'm sure it's only a matter of time before the police find the one piece of concrete evidence against him that has been eluding them and tie it all up. Right now, we have to be concerned for Christianne. At the moment she's quite impressed with Guy's criminologist. She's on the rebound and our Dr. Keaton is exceptionally attractive. And I know I'm not the only one who saw the way he was looking at her. I don't believe I'm making a quantum leap by suggesting that the two of them—"

Alex slammed his fist against the soft leather arm of his chair, his blue eyes flashing from their usual melancholy to anger. "Damn it, Maryann, so what! So what if they want to spend every night together while he's here? She sure couldn't be in a safer place than in his bed. I don't think our murderer would try and go after her with one of Guy's handpicked *Savants* holding her in his arms, do you?"

"And what about when he leaves Kansas City, Alex? Do you want to risk her having her heart broken again so soon on the heels of her affair with that . . . that gigolo?"

Alex rose to his feet, crossing the space of floor between himself and his wife to lean over her chair, his hands coming to rest on her shoulders in a way that was slightly menacing. She shrank back. "We all experience hurt, Maryann, but somehow we live through it and life goes on. She wasn't in love with Marconi. I asked her and I believe her when she says it was a case of pure lust." He grinned. "It wasn't her heart that quivered whenever he was near her, Maryann."

"Don't be crude, Alex," she snapped, though she didn't meet his gaze as she spoke.

He ignored the rebuke. "The point is, she's nearly thirty years old. She's lived on her own for four years. Longer if we include her years away at school. She's been a very successful vice president, increasing profits in Europe by nearly fifty percent. I think we can trust her to handle her own love life."

"Alex, that's so unfair. I'm the one who suggested she go to Italy in the first place," Maryann said, her tone reflecting her hurt. "I resent the implication that I am a controlling mother. But that doesn't mean Christianne can't be hurt and like it or not, I'm not going to sit by and allow him to use her."

Paul had tensed with his brother's anger as well, but he felt a spark of anger kindle in himself now. "Look, Alex, no one wants Christi to spend the rest of her life locked away out here, but I have to agree that Eric Keaton might not be the right person to help her get over her Italian friend. But even if he was, it seems to me there's a much more important reason for keeping them apart."

Alex stepped away from his wife, slipping his hands into his pockets as he faced his brother. "And what would that be, Paul?"

Paul took time to drain his glass before answering, and his words, when they came, were spoken slowly, his tone derisive and mocking. "Christi doesn't need to be interrogated about the Rose Murders. Not again. The authorities have already talked to her . . . several times. These murders don't involve her. I believe that, no matter how much she looks like the other women, someone's just using that coincidence to ruin us, our company. So you can get indignant and turn on Maryann or myself, but it won't do any good to ignore the fact that Eric Keaton is going to be questioning her about the killings whether they're in bed or out."

Maryann stood up, going to her husband, her hazel eyes more green than usual as she raised her face to his. "Please, let's not argue among ourselves. We're all a little afraid, not just for Christianne but for ourselves as well. We don't allow ourselves to admit it—not to one another, not even in our own minds—but we all know there's the chance that those women have been surrogates for the killer's real intended victim, Christianne. Maybe because at some time or other, she offended some young man, or maybe the lunatic who's killing these women knows that would be the surest way to destroy any one of us, I don't know. But neither am I willing to risk finding out by putting our daughter in jeopardy. . . . Let us get through this pageant and back to the business of living and enjoying our daughter's return home."

Paul turned his back on the other two and refilled his glass with another double shot of bourbon. "Jesus Christ, why the fuck don't we just cancel the pageant and send those girls home? Would somebody please answer me that."

"That's easy, Paul," Maryann said, her tone dripping derision. "The FBI has flatly refused to allow us to cancel anything. They're confident they're going to nail that fellow Woods when he tries to go after another contestant, and I agree with them."

"God, it's pitiful. Girls are dying because the Rose Pageant is so good for our image, and we lie and tell ourselves that we don't cancel it because the authorities are depending on us and that maybe by sticking to our guns we are actually helping them catch the killer." Paul still had his back to her, but he could feel those raisin black eyes piercing his back right between the shoulder blades. Without another word, he raised his glass over his head in salute.

Maryann sighed, then stood up and walked to her brother-in-law's side, laying a hand on his shoulder. "Please, Paul, let's not be angry. Not tonight. We have stood together through some terrible times and we have shared some wonderful moments as well. Let's not throw it away now."

Paul rubbed a weary hand over his eyes before pulling free of her grasp. "Save your energy for all your guests awaiting you at the hotel, Maryann. You have nothing to be afraid of. I've lost the energy to do more than give the same answers I've spoken so many times." He started to lift his glass to his mouth, only this time his hand trembled.

Noticing, Maryann reached around his back to give him a gentle squeeze. "I'm going to change. You'd better do the same, Paul. It's getting late." She paused on her way out of the room at her husband's side. "Coming up, Alex?"

Her husband raised his gaze to hers and in a rare display of affection, his narrow blue eyes softened, and he reached for her hand. "In a moment. But we have time yet. Why don't you rest for a half hour or so. You look tired."

As they spoke, Paul passed them by, snifter in hand, though Alex was relieved to notice it was nearly empty. Still holding onto his wife's hand, he waited until he heard his brother's steps on the stairs above him before standing and drawing Maryann into a gentle embrace. "Don't worry about Paul, sweetheart, he doesn't mean all that he said. He's a follower . . . like me." A grin that was self-deprecating spread in a thin, flat line as he rested his chin on her head. "Look at it this way. I rebelled only once in my entire life, and that was enough to last me forever. Paul's never even mustered the courage to do his rebelling in public. He'll be his charming, reticent self tonight at the ball. Eric Keaton will get nothing but a good taste of Anthony hospitality. Paul hasn't let us down yet, has he?"

Maryann's eyes were on the door as if she could still see her brother-in-law's slightly crooked frame disappearing through it. "Sometimes, I actually believe he hates us, Alex," she said softly.

"Not just us, sweetheart. Himself, too."

Alex squeezed his eyes shut. He understood all about self-hate. Once, he'd taken a step towards courage, but he'd faltered. And after that, he'd needed both Maryann and Paul, couldn't have made it without either of them. Just as they needed him, always would. If not for themselves, then for Christi.

As if following the train his thoughts were taking, Maryann said, "You're right, Alex. Paul loves Christianne. He'll come through tonight . . . for her."

Her husband nodded. "Yes, he'd stop the world for her if he had the power. Stop it and let her off and not get back on again until all this madness was ended. He can't do that, but he sent her to Italy when we couldn't think of another way to keep her away from the paparazzi. I suppose one could argue that in some ways, he's been more of a father to her than I have."

Maryann shook her head vehemently. "That's not true, Alex! You have been a wonderful father. Always. No one could ever doubt your love for her. No one!"

"Oh, yes, I love her, just not enough, Maryann. Not nearly enough. If I did, I would have found the courage to be the father I should have been. I would have trusted her with the truth. We Anthonys are incapable of the kind of love that requires courage and honesty. I'm stronger than Paul in many ways, but I'm a yellow-spined bastard, too. Even more so than him maybe, because I'm not blind. Unlike my brother, I haven't been looking at things through sherry-red booze." Walking over to the bar, he picked up the crystal decanter still half filled with Paul's favorite brand of bourbon. He raised it to his eyes, laughing hollowly at his thin joke. "Maybe he's got the right idea. The truth doesn't look nearly as ugly through here. Kind of rosy, actually. Maybe that's how he seems to get so effortlessly through each day."

Setting it down with a heavy thud, he popped the cork out and reaching for a glass, tipped the bottle. Turning just a bit, he raised the glass to his wife. "To the truth and finding the strength to face it."

Maryann raised an artfully painted eyebrow, a new

light of respect sparkling in her eyes, but all she said was, "Just don't get drunk, darling. And, please, don't try to foresee too much in your crystal glass. Remember that most of the time Paul can't even see the floor after he's been drinking much less the truth of anything." She glanced at her watch. "I'm going up. We have to leave in thirty minutes, and you, my darling husband, have to welcome our contestants to the pageant tonight. Please don't let this maudlin mood of yours persuade you to follow Paul's example to the point that he usually cuts it off. I'd hate for you to fall on your face in front of all those adoring and beautiful young women."

"My word as a gentleman, my dear, I'll be on my best behavior." His blue eyes glittered like rare sapphires with his answering wink as a devilish grin cut long slashes in his face that was as provocative and handsome as it had been when he was twenty.

Maryann felt her stomach flutter as it always had when he looked at her that way, turning on the charm that was exclusively his. She returned his smile before walking away, but it soon slipped away. Once she'd longed for that famous Alexander Anthony smile. Not anymore, for she knew too well how easily and often he gave it away, not even understanding that it, just like everything else about him, should belong to her.

At the top of the stairs, she paused to square her shoulders and pull her mask of confidence back into place. It was all coming apart, unraveling, but it wasn't her fault. She had done the best she could to hold them all together.

Chapter Seven

Eric tossed the car keys in the air as he approached the hotel lobby at a relaxed, casual gait. His thoughts sliding from the balmy weather to the tuxedo he'd sent out to be pressed that morning to the drink he intended to have before readying himself for the Rose Ball, he whistled softly under his breath.

In the dusk of late evening, he didn't notice the silhouette of the man leaning against the wall a few feet from the hotel entrance. He didn't feel his presence as he should have. In fact, he had no sense of anything until the man stepped forward. Then he felt the impact as surely as if he'd been punched squarely in the gut instead of a tentative greeting.

Eric stopped short, catching the Hertz key ring midair and depositing it in his pants pocket. "Hello, Michael," he said to the FBI agent he hadn't seen for more than six years. The normalcy of his voice both surprised and pleased him.

"Eric," Michael responded, with a smile and his right hand extended.

The last thing Eric wanted was to shake this man's hand. But since he couldn't think of a way past it, he made it tolerable by pretending it was nothing slipperier or more repugnant than an eel. His gaze passing over the man who had once been his friend and partner, he raised a brow at the natty, double-breasted tuxedo the agent wore. "What? All dressed up and no place to go?" He shook his head and clicked his tongue. "Sad, Sansom. Real fucking sad."

Michael Sansom chuckled. "Actually, I thought we might be headed for the same affair. Thought you might like a ride. Save some change on rental car miles and give us a chance to catch up."

Eric had been smiling. It fell away now. "Nothing to catch up on, Mike. I keep tabs on you always. Know just what crisis you're covering, and the exact number of casualties you leave in your wake." He reached into his inside jacket pocket, pulling out the thin, coded plastic room key. "Let's see, I had you out at the Weavers' in Ruby Ridge, then outside of Waco with the Davidians, of course. After that, you were—"

"Knock it off, Keaton." The FBI agent's voice was soft as a rabid dog's snarl and just as menacing.

Eric tensed, anticipating the attack he'd provoked. Nothing happened. Instead, Michael pulled off the familiar grin that Eric had forgotten—tired, tentative, pessimistically hopeful. He had watched it work countless times, catching the most guarded off-kilter. It worked now, surprising the hell out of the *Savant.*

"Want to come up to my room for a drink to fortify you before you take on the glitterati?"

"Maybe a glass of seltzer," Michael said, following his former comrade and friend into the elevator as soon as the doors parted.

Neither man spoke until they were seated inside Eric's suite with their drinks and Eric proposed a toast. "To our reunion," he said with a clink of his glass of Scotch against the tumbler of Perrier he'd just poured for Michael.

"How's it going for you?" the government agent asked. "Being back in K.C. and all?"

Eric let out a long, heavy breath, then shrugged his shoulders. "I don't know. Indulged myself a few minutes of self-pity last night when I first arrived. Forced myself to visit the cemetery this morning. On a scale from one to ten—one being something like taking a bullet in the gut, ten being somewhere as bad as having my nuts cut off, then shoved down my throat—I'd say it was a six."

"Jesus, man, I—"

Eric had been leaning back. He sat forward now, slamming his glass to the coffee table. "No!" It was a loud bark of complaint at the sharp sudden pain that came always in the frist mintues of discussion about the tragedy that had turned his life forever upside down, which was why he rarely allowed the subject to surface. 'Course there wasn't any getting around this one. Only way past it was directly through the heart of it, and only way to do that was calmly, carefully so that the knife didn't move any deeper. He grinned, hoping it came off sounding easier than it felt with his jaws aching and his back teeth ground together. "Sorry, didn't intend to shout. But, hey, let's leave Jesus out of this. He didn't have anything to do with what happened to Dave and Bryn even if it did go down in one of His houses as the Good Book calls churches."

"Gotten religious on me, have you, Keaton? Is that how you're dealing with things these days?"

Eric gave his head a quick, jerking shake. "Fuck this," he said under his breath as he got to his feet. "And fuck you, too, Mike."

"Hey, wait," Sansom said, setting his glass on the table alongside the glass of Scotch. "Sit down, Eric. I don't know what I thought this was going to be about. Six years is a long time. We were both hurt and angry the last time we spoke. But before that we had some good times—"

"Good times?" Eric mimicked with all the derision he could put into it. "Is that what we had? I thought it went deeper than that. Certainly more profound than some good times, don't you think? And what would you call the tragedy that ended those good times? An off day? An uncomfortable situation?"

"I'd call it a fucking tragedy perpetrated by a fucking wacko!" Samson yelled, jumping to his feet as well. His swarthy complexion was tinged almost purple now with his outrage.

"Yeah, well that's what it was all right, and the fucker who set off that bomb was loony tunes, too. I can't argue with you there. But he was also a felon with priors. We knew his history. Hell, we knew him better than his own mama, and we should've had him before he even got close to that church. But we didn't, did we, Michael?"

The two men stood face to face, only a half-dozen inches separating them and their gazes locked.

"No, we didn't."

"And when he called you, told you what he was going—"

Sansom cut him off. "Why are you doing this? We both know what went down that morning, Eric."

But once he'd started it, Eric couldn't let it go. "Yeah, we both know what went down, Mike, and we both know Feron Lee Packer wasn't the only criminal at that church that Saturday."

Taking slow, stabilizing breaths, Michael straightened his tuxedo jacket with slightly trembling fingers. "Well, at least you finally got it said. We both always knew where you laid the blame. I'd hoped some of your anger had ebbed over the years, but hey, if hanging onto it and keeping it focused on me helps you face each day, then you go right on hating me. I can handle it, brother."

"I'm not your brother, you son of a bitch. My brother was David Allen Keaton, remember? He was blasted to smithereens while he knelt in church beside Brynlee Carroll and all because a hotshot FBI agent wouldn't wait, wouldn't give his partner, whose job it was to try and talk the crazy bastard out of blowing up the cathedral."

Sansom tugged at his shirt cuffs. "Go on, Keaton, get it out of your system."

"Fuck you," Eric said, swiping his glass from the coffee table and emptying it in one long swallow.

"Well, then, if that's it, I'll show myself out. I suppose I'll be seeing you later tonight. There won't be time or opportunity for us to discuss the Rose Murders then, but I'm available anytime you want to go over the details . . . anything you need."

Eric was surprised by the Bureau agent's apparent willingness to cooperate, share evidence with a civilian. That was a courtesy rarely extended even to other law enforcement agencies. "Uh oh, why do I feel the hairs on the back of my neck suddenly standing on end like I always do when I'm about to walk into a trap?"

"Probably because you're a goddamned cynic. Must be from working in the private sector. Don't remember you being quite so paranoid."

Eric laughed. "Couldn't be those beady little eyes of yours make me think of weasels and rats?"

Mike chuckled, but his smile didn't linger. "Seriously, Eric? I wasn't happy when your boss called to tell me you were coming. Then I thought it over, had a change of heart. You were a good agent, Keaton, and word has it, you've only gotten better. We think we have our man, but I'd like to talk it over with you, see if you think the shoe fits as well as I do. But it's your call. We can work together or separately, whatever you decide." He had walked to the door while he spoke. He pulled it open, then stopped long enough to add. "One thing though, Eric."

"I'm listening."

"If you decide you can't get past your, uh, feelings

about my part in the way things ended at Saint Timothys, and you want to work it alone, I've got to ask you to stay out of the way. If we feel you're hindering our investigation in any way, we'll get you so tied up in red tape, you'll still be gift wrapped next Christmas."

Chapter Eight

After closing the door on his former FBI partner, Eric shifted his anger, redirecting it to his current employer.

Why the hell hadn't Guy told him about Christianne's remarkable likeness to the five slain women? He put in a call to the Jamesons' private number at a Manhattan penthouse apartment overlooking the Hudson, but Guy's wife informed him that he was out for the evening, attending a benefit. Could she have him return the call in the morning?

He wanted to say, "You're damn straight he can call me in the morning. He owes me an explanation. The last thing an investigator needs is a key surprise that leaves him looking like a jackass before he's even begun his probe." But of course he didn't. Instead he replied, "Just tell him that I met with the Anthonys this evening . . . also had a visit from FBI Special Agent Sansom. I'm attending the Rose Pageant Ball later, and I'll proceed from there. I'll get back to him in a day or so and bring him up to date."

He lowered the receiver, then picked it up again to call down to room service, a satisfied grin playing on his lips as he ordered Camembert and fruit as an appetizer, crab Louis, filet mignon, and a chocolate torte for dessert. There was more than one way to get even, he thought, but the satisfaction was short-lived as he thought of the five a.m. workout he would have to put in downstairs in the hotel gym in the morning.

Loosening his tie, he reminded himself not to get ahead of himself, that he still had a long night to get through.

Stripping out of his clothes, he walked naked through the suite to lay out his tux, then stepped into a steaming hot shower. He thought of Sansom . . . and started scrubbing.

As Eric entered the glittering ballroom, he paused to acknowledge the elaborate decor. Hands in his pockets, he whistled as he skipped down the three-tiered entryway. Obviously, the Anthonys knew nothing about moderation, for the expansive room—luxurious of its own accord with its twinkling chandeliers and rich tapestries—was resplendent with its lavish ornamentation. Large vases filled with long-stemmed roses sat on pedestals that filled every nook and cranny and graced every tabletop. In the middle of the room, a circular buffet was heavily laden with elegant and exotic dishes. The centerpiece was an elaborate ice carving that boasted the single word 'Anthony' and created a trickling waterfall into a pool graced by tiny ice swans.

Eric's eyes scanned the room with a raised brow as he took in the celebrity crowd, but before he had a chance to complete his mental assessment of the social register, he saw the important trio approaching from across the room.

He raised a hand in greeting, his lips sliding into his most gracious grin. As he stood in wait of them, he allowed his eyes to travel appreciatively over his hostess. Though tiny, the woman obviously knew how to accentuate the positive. Her gown emphasized her minuscule waist with its full skirt. Its hem, which tapered from tea length in the front to her ankles at the side and back, created an image of height. The pattern of gold leaves woven with threads of burnt umber and hickory were the perfect complement to her deep chestnut hair. Even the intricately woven choker of diamonds and pearls at her throat and its matching teardrop earrings had been carefully selected to enhance the perfect translucency of her skin.

As if they had rehearsed their movements, the brothers stopped a few feet from their guest, allowing Maryann to approach first and receive her due. Eric did not disappoint them.

"Maryann, may I say how exquisite you look?" He bowed slightly from the waist accepting her hand to draw it to his lips.

She laughed softly. "Of course you may, and I thank you, Eric. You look very nice as well. I think men should wear tuxedos more often, don't you?"

The others flanked her again immediately, exchanged greetings, then Paul suggested they go get a drink. Noting the man's flushed face, Eric suspected he'd already had several.

"It's Scotch, isn't it? On the rocks?" Paul asked.

"That it is," Eric agreed.

Paul snapped his finger, discreetly placed the order with a passing waiter, then turned his attention back to his guest. "So what do you think? Impressive, huh?"

"Fantastic," Eric agreed, catching a glimpse of Michael Sansom across the room speaking with a striking-looking man with shoulder-length iron gray hair and a handsome mustache. It took only a couple of seconds more for it to dawn that he was looking at the actor, Sam Elliott. "You people certainly do it up right. Lots of VIP's and celebs."

His eyes went to the red ribbon pinned to Paul's lapel. "I seem to be the only person in the room without the requisite symbol of support for the fight against AIDS."

"Well, I'm just the man who can fix that." He led him to a small table near the entrance. A crystal bowl was filled with the ribbons fixed with pins on the back. He handed one to the investigator. "It's a terrible scourge on society. AIDS, I mean. Maryann was the first to think of dedicating our pageant ball to the fight. After all, at a thousand dollars a pop—don't worry your ticket is on us—we can make a pretty hefty contribution to research."

"I'm sold, but I wouldn't dream of letting you pick up my tab. My pockets may not be as deep as most of your guests', but there's probably enough change rattling around in them to cover it. It's an important cause." He paused, letting his eyes rove the room slowly, then grinned. "Besides, I feel real fortunate to be included in such fancy company."

Paul didn't miss the sarcasm that slid smooth as Drambuie into Eric's tone. Instead of being annoyed, however, he was amused. He could like this smartass *Savant* of Guy's. Appreciate his irreverence. Obviously, not a man easily influenced, Keaton could prove to be an entertaining challenge. Following Eric's gaze around the room, he joined the game. "Well, of course, most of the Missouri folk are old friends. Alex plays golf with Senator Bond. Maryann serves on various state beautification committees with our governor's wife. I get together with Lamar Hunt over there for a game of chess whenever we get the chance. In the old days, I would have preferred tennis, but that was before my accident." He patted his injured leg for emphasis. "The rest—our mayor, the police commissioner, those two men over there—both superior court justices—support us every year, and we reciprocate back and forth with dinner invitations. Some of the others you might not recognize—CEOs of Hallmark, Western Auto, Russell Stover—our local business leaders." He looked around. "Ah, I'm sure you recognize Billy Busch of Anheuser-Busch—Saint Louis. And, let me see . . . oh, yes, you'll recognize Lee

Iacoca. And the guy practically devouring my sister-in-law with his eyes is Carl Icon. They all come out."

Eric inclined his head slightly. "Well, as I said, you've definitely blown me away. Guess I'll have to treat you all with more respect."

Paul accepted two glasses from the waiter who suddenly appeared at his side, handing the first to Eric and quickly disposing of the other. At Eric's raised brow, he grinned. "Don't worry. I've never fallen on my face yet."

"No, I'd say you're obviously a man who can hold his stuff. You know, you remind me of someone."

Paul shook his head with his laughter. "Jack Nicholson. You and everyone else. Is it the receding hairline or the devilishly handsome smile, do you think?"

"I think it's the eyebrows."

"Hmm, maybe so," Paul agreed, but then, as if to dispute this, spread his lips in a wide, Cheshire cat grin that really did rival the famous actor's. "Let's get back to our guest list, it's far more interesting than me. You've noticed the three supermodels, Claudia, Cindy, and Naomi, of course. Who wouldn't with those gorgeous bodies."

Eric raised a brow at the observation, but Paul was already moving on, not even missing a beat. "And seated over there, resplendent in all that purple and almost obscured by her entourage is Liz Taylor. Fantastic woman, but really very, very shy. Quite active in the uphill battle against AIDS, though, and very outspoken.

"The tall, statuesque blonde standing with her back to us—the one in white with the football player's shoulders, and those fantastic narrow hips—is Linda Evans. And that's Yani leaning forward and talking to Alex."

Eric nodded as he sipped his drink. "What, no royalty?"

"No, no, no. You're missing the point. Each of the ladies has a perfume named for her. That man seated to Liz's left is the top dog at Parfums International. Cher is standing beside the president of Perfume Stern. Get it? Each of the actresses is here at the command of the company who sponsors her perfume. It's our competitors' way of paying their respects while garnering maximum media attention at the same time."

"Ah, I see," Eric said, jutting his chin in the direction of a famous author. "And what about Stephen King over there? What's his connection to the perfume industry?"

Paul tossed his head back and laughed. "You're good, Keaton. I purposefully skipped him. Thought I'd save him for later. But you caught me. Actually, he does . . . sort of. Or at least, he will have. The perfume's actually been created in honor of one of his books, *Rose Madder*. It's a very heavy, seductive fragrance that King's people are quite excited about. We've coordinated a very ambitious campaign to launch the perfume in conjunction with the release of the movie based on the novel. But it's all very hush, hush. We're making the announcement just before we crown this year's pageant queen. King is one of our blue ribbon panel of judges. I wasn't supposed to say anything except that he's a judge, but I trust you. Besides, you're good. Don't miss a trick. I like your style."

"Yeah, well, what about Priscilla Presley over there? She doing a perfume for you, too?"

"Nope. She's always rejected requests to put her name on a perfume. But if you look just past her to the petite brunette standing with her back to us, you might recognize her daughter, Lisa Marie. We're hoping we may be able to persuade her to do what Mom has always said no to, but I really can't say more.

King is sewn up. Little Lisa is still merely flirting with the idea."

"Well, good luck. I'd think that would be quite a coup."

Paul grabbed a glass from a tray as a waiter passed by, again downing the drink in a single, spectacular gulp. "Mouth gets dry from all this bragging. But where was I?"

"Lisa Marie," Eric reminded him.

"Oh, yeah, right." He took Eric's arm, guiding him a few feet from the crowd. Even then, he lowered his voice confidentially. "This is strictly off the record, Keaton. King's *Rose Madder* aside—it's really just a crazy, one-time thing that'll be a giant money maker and a lot of fun—Alex and I have always shunned the celebrity thing. Women who buy Anthony fragrances like the concept of an everyday girl—an exceptionally beautiful everyday girl, I'll grant you—being named the Anthony Rose every year. We thought about approaching a celebrity as early as fifteen years ago. But we were still just talking when someone else acted. When the idea caught on, we knew we'd made a mistake by waiting. Then over dinner one night, Maryann and Mother were talking about the young woman who'd won the Miss America title the night before. The next thing you know we'd hatched the idea of the Rose Pageant. It was a huge success, as you know. But in the past couple of years, Alex and I have been seriously considering discontinuing the pageant. Because of the murders, obviously. You may be witnessing history in the making, Keaton. This could well be the last year of the Rose competition. If we do make that decision, we will jump on the bandwagon and put our money behind a famous face." He looked at Stephen King and chuckled. "A famous beautiful face à la Presley, or if not her, someone else."

"Well, I can think of a hundred questions, but since

they have zip to do with my investigation, I'll butt out. But, hey, thanks for filling me in."

"No problem, Eric. Come on, let's really get the show on the road. Let me introduce you to the gorgeous Presley women."

"I appreciate the offer, Paul, but I think I'll just stand on the sidelines and observe."

Paul shrugged his shoulders. "Suit yourself, but if you'll excuse me, I think I'll go over and see how they are. Unofficially, they are our guests of honor."

"Hey, go do your thing. Knock yourself out, man. Just one thing before you go?"

"Shoot."

"Where are all the contestants? Don't they make their debut tonight?"

"Of course, but the show doesn't start until midnight. Stick around. I think we'll impress your ass then. It's not anything hokey like the Miss America Pageant. The girls will be presented by Alex, and then Maryann will welcome them. Bette Midler will close the show with a pretty powerful rendition of *The Rose.* By the way, speaking of roses, what do you think of them all? Ten thousand perfect blooms, sacrificed for tonight."

"They're fantastic. As a matter of fact, I was wondering how you can have so many in one room without overpowering everyone with the scent, but I can't smell them at all."

"Neat trick, huh? They're unscented. Bred by a European. We order from him every year. Couldn't have it smelling like a funeral parlor in here, or competing with all the perfume." He reached for another glass of bourbon, paused long enough to raise it in Eric's direction and gulped it down. "Enjoy, Keaton."

Eric nodded in return and went off to find Cindy Crawford. He'd met her a couple of times in New York and even attended her wedding to Gere. After

he spoke to her, he'd slip on out. He'd seen enough.
He could call Guy and tell him truthfully how his old
friends had blown his socks off.

As he passed a large urn brimming with blood-red
roses, he paused to touch one of the velvety buds.
They were pretty, but without their scent they seemed
lifeless. The thought provoked a memory of the contestants who had been killed. At the scene of each
murder, roses had been left behind as calling cards.
The thought provoked a shudder.

"Know how you feel," a voice said just behind him
on his left. "Hardly makes a guy think of the blooms
that have inspired poetry and been the gift of lovers
for centuries, huh?"

Eric didn't turn. He didn't need to track the voice
with his gaze to identify it. The raspy quality of Michael Sansom's voice was as distinctive as a finger-
print. Besides, it irked Eric that his former partner
hadn't lost his knack for reading his thoughts and it
damn sure galled him to admit it. "Yeah," he said,
"made me think of those young women, and that
makes me sick." He turned then to look at his once
best friend. "And it makes me wonder what in the
fuck you were thinking when you insisted the pageant
be held. Is winning still the be all of everything with
you, Mike? Even worth the life of another beautiful
young woman whose only sin is the desire to break
into show biz via a few lousy perfume commercials?"

The agent's face darkened with anger he didn't try
to disguise. "Look, Keaton, you don't know shit about
what I think. You've read what? A few newspaper
clippings? Watched an episode of *Unsolved Mysteries*
or *Inside Edition*? Talked to one of the victim's grieving parents? Well, let me tell you, bud, the Bureau's
been on this one for six years. In the past three
months since I was brought in, I've studied every scrap
of evidence we've got. Read and reread the compos-

ites of scientific data on the computer printouts till my
eyes burned and I couldn't sort the words any longer.
I've gone over every aspect of the profile we've put
together until I was so crazy I couldn't even look the
President of the United States in the eye last week
when he was here without seeing him as a potential
suspect. And you know what, Keaton? I still have
questions. So, damn straight, pal, we're gonna go
through with another pageant just like nothing ever
happened, 'cause it's the only way we can be a hundred percent sure we nail the right boy. But this time
we're going to catch the sick son of a bitch who's
butchered five girls. I guarantee it. I hope to God it's
Woods, but it don't matter much if it is or it isn't,
'cause this time we're not going to miss a trick. This
time, we're bringing the bastard down."

"From your lips to God's ears," Eric said, the insult
clear in his bland tone. He turned away, starting for
the exit.

Sansom stopped him with a hand on his arm. "I'm
not the enemy, Eric. Work with us on this one."

Eric started to answer, started to tell him where he
could put his offer, but at that moment Christi appeared at the top of the stairs and Michael Sansom,
along with everyone and everything else, disappeared
from Eric's thoughts.

Chapter Nine

Call it corny, ridiculous, the stuff of romance novels and old movies, Eric Keaton fell in love in those few seconds it took him to cross the ballroom and reach her side.

Every gaze in the room followed his progress before moving past him to settle on the exquisite newcomer. He imagined their reactions: Curiosity. Admiration surely. Perhaps jealousy and resentment. And from the men seeing her for the first time, certainly keen, ferocious hunger. What else when she looked so damned delicious? Like French vanilla ice cream.

Every inch of her from the fair tint of her skin that the gently curled ends of her blond hair brushed at her shoulders to the neutral tones of subtly applied makeup and the pale lemon satin of her form-fitting gown and even to the single long-stemmed white rose she carried in her hand.

Taking her arms and cupping her elbows so that her hands were brought up to rest against his chest, he leaned forward to kiss her cheek and whisper in her ear, "You look good enough to eat."

Her responding laughter was husky, appreciative. "Then I accomplished what I was striving for."

His hand clasping her fingers, he led her down the steps. "Ah, so it was premeditated. There are laws against that in Missouri, you know."

"Really?" she asked, not looking at him, instead letting her gaze glide over the faces turned toward them and keeping a radiant smile in place as she spoke. "Well, yes, it was planned, but illegal? I didn't know. Are you positive?"

"Absolutely. My dad was a cop for twenty-five years, and my brother, a lawyer. Between the two of them, I was kept pretty well apprised of the statutes and I definitely remember the law being quite specific about driving a man to thoughts of cannibalism."

This time her laughter was fuller, reflecting her utter delight. "Dare I ask what the punishment is for such a heinous crime?"

"Why, you get devoured, of course. It's only fair."

She stopped then, turning to face him, her blue eyes—the only jewels she wore—glittering every bit as brightly as the chandelier overhead. "Please tell me ignorance isn't a viable defense, because I do want to accept my punishment."

The playful grin slipped as he let his gaze move over her exquisite features. "We'd better dance," he said, his tone reflecting every measure of his desire.

"But there isn't any music."

Eric didn't answer. He only squeezed her fingers tighter and led her onto the dance floor. He took her into his arms. "The orchestra will just have to catch up. Trust me. We either dance this second or everyone in this room will discover how badly I want you."

She didn't argue. Instead, she pressed herself against him, responding to the hard swell against her lower abdomen with a soft moan of pleasure.

Eric ground his teeth against his need, and motioned with a jut of his chin to the startled gray-haired man standing with the baton in his hand in front of the musicians just settling into their seats.

Almost at once, a man rose from his seat and began to play the first strains of a familiar song from his saxophone. Seconds later, the rest of the orchestra joined in. Even when performed as an instrumental tune, "When a Man Loves a Woman" was sultry and provocative. Hardly the best choice to speed a man's recovery from his current discomfort, Eric observed silently. And when he felt Christi's nipples swell against his chest, he gave up the fight and pulled her even closer. It looked like they were going to be dancing for quite some time.

Maryann didn't allow her smile to slip, though she was quick to notice her husband's fierce scowl even from a distance of several dozen yards. Uttering an apology to the mayor's wife, she hurried to Alex's side. "You look as if you've got murder on your mind, darling. Hardly the most appropriate expression considering that half the men and even a few of the women standing around the room are law enforcement officials of some sort."

Paul joined them, speaking up in his brother's defense before Alex had a chance to reply. "Kind of difficult to stand here beaming like her fucking fairy godmother, sister, dear."

"Don't be crass, Paul. Your voice carries like a tomtom. And please, both of you, if you can't manage to smile, at least quit glowering. She went against our wishes. The cat's out of the bag, so to speak. There's nothing we can do about it now except make the best of it."

"This is Keaton's doing, Maryann," Alex bit out. "You saw the way he got to her the second she appeared in the doorway. This was no last-minute decision on her part. He knew she was coming. Somehow, they planned it."

"And so what?" she asked quietly, anger just beneath her tone. "As I've already said, there's nothing to do about it now except make it look like the grand surprise we were all awaiting. The moment the music ends, I want you to dance with her, Alex. Only for a few minutes. Then Paul, you interrupt. Explain in that marvelous resonant voice of yours that it's almost time for the contestants to make their first appearance. I'll escort her around the room. Introduce her to some of our guests."

"And what about Keaton?" Alex demanded.

"Get rid of him, my darling," she said. "Or if you can't manage that, keep him away from Christianne. Enlist the aid of Mr. Sansom. Guy said there's bad blood between them. Use it to keep him occupied. Paul and I will involve her with the pageant, introduce her to the contestants. Make very sure she doesn't have any more opportunity to make a spectacle out of herself with LINC's *Savant*."

"She's a grown woman, Maryann. I hardly think she's going to tolerate you treating her like an errant schoolgirl who's just been caught necking in the backseat of a car."

"I hardly intend to make her feel any such way. But neither will I allow her to embarrass us by acting like a common slut." She felt her husband stiffen beside her and quickly placed a hand on his arm, an apology already in the offing before he could open his mouth. "Forgive me, Alex. I didn't mean that. She's my daughter, too, and I've never been anything but proud of her. It's just . . . well this affair she had with that production manager and all the tension tonight. I'm sorry. Just please, let's regain a modicum of control."

Alex didn't answer, but as the music ended, he strode away to claim the next dance with his daughter.

Paul watched him go, then leaned down to whisper in his sister-in-law's ear. "Careful, honey, your claws were showing for a moment there. Wouldn't do for Papa Bear to realize that Mama Bear is just a wee bit jealous of her own little Baby Bear, now would it?"

Eric's frustration revealed itself in the ticking muscle in his jaw as the trio of senior Anthonys conspired to separate him from Christi. Screw it, he thought, stopping long enough to pluck a long-stemmed red rose from a nearby vase, then heading for the exit. His other hand was already in his pants pocket after his parking stub.

Mike Sansom stepped in front of him before he could start up the stairs. "Well, bud, I gotta hand it to you. Zoned right in on the sweet stuff. I mean, twenty-four hours in town and you're already mixing it up with the big man's daughter. The private sector undeniably more liberal about its hands-off policies, it's no wonder you don't miss government work. Shit, if I wasn't so happily married, that just might be lure enough to convince me to give up my badge and join the ranks of the well-paid and unrestricted." He scratched his neck. "On the other hand, I never did have your way with the ladies, so don't guess it much matters where I work, huh?"

"Stick it in your ear, Sansom."

"Well, I could do that, Eric, but I gotta admit that doesn't appeal nearly as much as thinking about where you're sticking it."

Eric knew his former associate—hell, his former best friend—was purposefully goading him. He knew it in his head, but he wasn't reacting with his head and that wasn't where he was feeling it either. It was in that place just above his gut, and damn it, Sansom knew not to push those buttons. Eric doubled his right hand into a fist as the thumb of his left hand fidgeted with the ring he wore on his third finger. It was identical to the ring the agent wore on the opposite hand.

Michael's gaze was drawn to the ring. He immediately covered his own with his other hand. His expression said he'd forgotten for a few minutes. Remembered now.

Their bond had once transcended obligation, even friendship. Once upon a time, they'd stood side by side in an elite class of graduating students. Sworn an oath. Once upon a time, each had promised to lay down his life for the other if it ever came down to that.

Neither man spoke, but after a long heavy silence, Eric started around his ex-partner.

Michael laid a hand on his shoulder.

Eric stopped, waited.

"I don't like this, Eric. Don't want it to be this way. Maybe we can't work through what happened to Dave and Bryn, but damn, bud, maybe we could try going around it?"

Eric didn't answer.

Michael sighed. "Okay, well, then just use your head. Nothing matters to them as much as their girl. She's their heart, man. All these years, they've kept her out of the mix. Don't mess it up by putting her in the middle where she might be in danger."

"I think you've got this confused, Mike. This is your territory, your game—" He stopped as the contestants appeared above them on the landing and began to file past, one at a time.

Neither man spoke until the last beautiful young woman had descended into the room and they stood alone again. Then Eric raised a brow. "Any of them remind you of anyone else? How about the third girl? Or number six? Either of them look like five other contestants who are all dead now? And while we're seeing those faces with our mind's eye, any of them remind you of Christianne Anthony? Yeah? Well, good. Now ask yourself who's putting who in danger?"

"Fuck you, Keaton."

"Yeah, gee thanks, but maybe some other time, huh?"

He left the agent standing there and climbed the stairs, but at the top, he turned for one more look at the goings-on and found Christi's eyes on him. Even from across the room, he caught the apology she offered and shook his head. *No apology necessary* he told her with a crooked grin. She smiled in return and wiggled her fingers.

"Yeah, babe, till next time," he said as he turned away.

In his car, Eric loosened the knot in his bow tie and freed a studded button at his throat. Turning the key in the ignition, he spied the rose he'd dropped on the seat beside him. He picked it up, twirling it back and forth. Somehow, they all fit together—Christi, the roses, the dead girls—and he was damned sure going to find out how.

Chapter Ten

It was approaching three a.m. when the Anthonys arrived home. Christi preceded them by four or five minutes and went straight upstairs to change into a T-shirt, jeans, and tennis shoes. She was already coming down the stairs again, pulling on a nylon windbreaker, when her parents and uncle entered the house.

"And just where do you think you're going, young lady?" her mother demanded.

Christi froze in mock horror. "Oh, my God, have we entered some kind of time warp? That's exactly the tone you used with me when I was, what? Fifteen? Sixteen?"

"Which is exactly how mature you acted tonight," her mother snapped. "What in the hell were you trying to prove, showing up like that and then making a spectacle out of yourself with that . . . that—"

"Man?" Christi finished for her with an impatient roll of her eyes.

"Don't be rude, Christianne. I don't care how old you are. I won't tolerate disrespect."

"And I won't tolerate you trying to control my life. If that's the way it's going to be, just tell me and I'll pack my bags and move into a place of my own."

"Don't be ridiculous," Maryann said.

"Don't talk to me like I'm a witless two-year-old," Christi countered. "I'm not a child and I won't be treated like one. Especially when it comes to where I go or who I see."

Maryann took a step toward the stairs where her daughter still stood on the landing.

Alex grabbed his wife's arm, stopping her. "That's enough, both of you," he said, his tone quiet yet commanding obedience.

"Fine," Christi said, zipping her jacket and circling the newel post, headed for the back of the house. "I'm going out to check on Mustard."

Mustard was her eight-year-old golden retriever, but he was much more than her pet. Other than her grandmother, he was the single most important thing she'd missed in her years away in Europe.

"He has a doghouse, and I'm sure he's curled up inside out of the rain, dry and safe," Maryann snapped.

Christi stopped, ran her hands through her hair and blew out a long frustrated breath before turning slowly back to face her mother. "I'll only be a few minutes, okay? What's the big deal? And why are you so bent out of shape over me showing up at the ball tonight? Jesus Christ, Mother—"

"Don't profane, Christianne!"

"Damn it," Christi murmured, then louder, "Will you please listen to me? I am a vice president at Anthony Enterprises. Translated, that is I have a title, responsibilities, some pretty good ideas. What I don't have is a single friend here outside of work to share anything with. I am bored out of my mind as I have been since I returned home from Italy. All I do is work at the plant and hang out around the house. And last but far from least, I am a red-blooded woman who has met and is attracted to a gorgeous red-blooded male."

"You're also choosing to ignore the most important issue at hand. The Rose Murders," her uncle put in. "You know why we've gone to such lengths to keep you distanced from the pageant."

"Yes, I know, Uncle Paul. But I'm not going to stay

in hiding any longer," Christi said. Her father opened his mouth to speak, but she held up her hand. "Hold on. Hear me out. I'm not stupid. I understand that those women may have been murdered because they were unfortunate enough to resemble me. Someone very likely has a real problem either with me personally or with one of you or even our company, and there's the very good likelihood that I am the killer's ultimate target. The police have been over all of that with me. Hell, we've discussed it ad nauseam. So, let me ask you something. Did any of you take a good look at Jillie Peters tonight?"

Jillie Peters was the third woman to enter the ballroom as the contestants were paraded in. She was tall, thin, and fair. Most of all, anyone not knowing better would swear she and Christi were sisters, maybe even twins. The three senior Anthonys all exchanged glances.

"Of course you noticed," Christi said, her satisfaction clear. "Everyone in that room did. The point is, I wanted you to cancel the pageant. I *begged* you. So did Grandmother. She wrote to me about it. She was sick, but even from her bed, she was worried enough to write a long letter about how badly she wanted you to end the pageants."

"Oh, Alex, please do something. Say something. The FBI insisted that the pageant be held according to tradition. Tell her! We had no choice but to comply and just getting through another year of looking at those beautiful young—" Maryann shook her head. "Well, it's simply more than any of us should have been asked to endure. Now, I'm to stand here and be blamed by my own daughter. No. That I won't do."

Christi was amazed at her mother's uncharacteristic display of emotion. She could count the times on one hand when she'd witnessed Maryann lose her cool. Now, her mother's hands trembled as she reached down to slip her pumps from her feet, and Christi felt a twinge of remorse. Her gaze moved from her mother to her father to her uncle. They all stared back, but she couldn't read their thoughts any more than she had anticipated her mother's outburst.

Perhaps she should apologize. But for what? For reacting to being treated like a ten-year-old kid who hadn't come straight home from school? For refusing to remain closeted away like someone's dirty secret? Or for stumbling across their meeting with Eric and feeling excitement stir in her veins for the first time since her return from Europe? No, she had nothing to apologize for. "I'm going to check on Mustard," she said.

"Christi, wait," her father said, his reasonable tone working much more successfully on her conscience than her mother's tantrum.

She turned to him, granting him a smile.

"Be annoyed with us, sweetheart; for the way we recognize your contributions to our business, then tend to treat you like our little girl. But don't blame us for wanting to protect you and keep you safe. As much as we grieve for every one of those poor women, we also are just as grateful to God that you haven't become one of the victims. None of us could survive that, Christi."

Uncharacteristic tears shimmered in his blue eyes, bringing them to burn behind Christi's as well. "You certainly know the way to a girl's heart," she said as she stepped up to him and hugged him tightly.

"Then you'll demonstrate more good sense and prudence in the next few days than you did tonight?" her mother asked.

Christi felt her father stiffen in her embrace and gave him one last squeeze before stepping away to look at her mother. "I'll be careful, but I won't step back inside the cage."

"Oh, my Lord, how unkind you are!" Maryann

gasped, covering her mouth with her hand and looking at the men for support.

"I don't mean to be," Christi said, her tone gentler as she saw Maryann's brown eyes darken with hurt. "I'm just trying to make you see, Mother. If those women are as safe as everyone keeps insisting, then I shouldn't have anything to worry about."

"Christianne, the authorities are watching them around the clock. I've no doubt the contestants have trouble showering without an officer looking on," Maryann objected.

"If the police and FBI can keep tabs on them, they should be able to keep me safe as well, and if I'm the killer's true intended victim, then let's smoke the son of a bitch out."

"I'm sorry, sweetheart," Alex said, "I'm with your mother on this one. I'll sell Anthony Enterprises, lock, stock, and barrel before I'll put you out there for some maniac to get a shot at."

Running the back of her hand over her eyes, Christi shook her head. "I'm sorry. I know how much you all love me. I . . . I don't know what's the matter with me—"

"Hey, brat," her Uncle Paul said, catching her elbows, and surprising her with the use of his childhood name for her. He was smiling that wide, wicked grin of his that had delighted her since the first time she'd seen it as a tiny infant. "It's okay. You've got a right. You're a member of this family and an honest-to-God grown-up same as the rest of us."

"Thanks, Uncle Paul."

His grin disappeared though not the devilish gleam in his eyes. "Well, enough said. I'm going up to bed."

"And I'm going out to check on my dog like I started to do fifteen minutes ago," Christi said. "Besides, I think I figured out a thing or two I might not have done otherwise."

"And what exactly does that mean?" her mother asked.

"That if you're this worried about me, those contestants are not as safe as everyone would have me believe." She gazed at each of them, her long, straight hair a golden veil around her face. "And if one more woman dies, I hope you can all live with yourselves for having gone ahead with the pageant."

None of them responded and nor did she wait. She hurried from the room and out of the house. She started off toward her dog's pen at a hard run through the wind and slashing rain. If she'd inherited anything from her mother, it was a slowness to anger, but once she was there, it was an even slower burn.

Chapter Eleven

Eric had passed a long, restless night, the few minutes of sleep he managed, disturbed by dreams of a beautiful young woman wrestling with a shadowed attacker for a knife that gleamed in the darkness.

By the time he showered and dressed the next morning, he was ready for some straight talk with someone he trusted. Thirty minutes later, he walked into Chief Dan Small's office at the Kansas City P.D.

It had been six years since he had seen the police chief who had started on the bottom rung in the police academy alongside Eric's father, Oran Keaton. The chief had eulogized him at his funeral the same year Eric graduated from the university. It was ironic that the last time they had come together again had been on the occasion of another funeral—the double service for David and Brynlee. Then, Dan's full, heavily jowled face had been creased with sadness as they stood side by side at the grave site of the victims of a mad bomber's. Still, the man had looked vital, alive, his puffy eyes alert and sparkling.

Today, Eric was not prepared for the toll time had taken on his old friend. His skin had a sickly yellow tinge, and he had dropped more than fifty pounds, but the most distressing change that struck Eric was the flat, defeated look in the man's eyes.

Dan was sitting behind his desk, flipping a pencil against a stack of papers when Eric knocked. He jumped to his feet, a wide, eager grin flashing across his face. "Eric Keaton, you rabble-rousin' s.o.b., I've been expectin' you!"

Eric stretched out a hand, his earlier sour mood disappearing like a bad taste sweetened by mint. For the first time, he realized, he loved this man, had since his childhood. But it wasn't just Dan Small's influence that charged his spirits. It was the comfort and security he found in the familiarity of his boyhood surroundings.

He had passed many hours sitting in these offices with his brother waiting for their dad to wrap up a day's work for 'guys' night out. Too often, both boys had ended up going alone or catching up with school pals at the last minute when another phone call forced a change of plans, keeping their father on the job for most of the night. Eric had been resentful more often than not. But he hadn't known then that Officer Keaton's promotion from uniformed beat cop to suited detective would last only three short years. Maybe if he had . . . but, hell, no point in dwelling on it.

Shaking off the sudden surge of depression, Eric grinned and offered his hand.

Dan refused the handshake, pushing his arm aside to grab him in a tight bear hug. "Been too long, boy," Dan said, his voice curiously tight as he released his captive to give the handsome face a thorough once-over. The chief's eyes were suspiciously bright, though he quickly brought his emotions under control as he pressed his lips together, nodding his head slowly and crossing his arms over his chest. "You being a hotshot and all, I guess you're too busy to stop around and see an old friend, huh?"

Eric laughed. "I live sixteen hundred miles from here, Dan."

Dan waved the excuse away as he returned to his seat behind his disorderly desk. "Yeah, well, much as you get around, can't see that a visit would take you much out of your way. Kansas City's home, Keaton. Always will be, even after all that went down. The bad and the good, Eric, you can turn you back on 'em, but it won't change anything. Both molded the man you are."

Eric took the chair in front of the desk. "Yeah, I know and I haven't been avoiding it. Really," he added at the chief's dubious frown. "Used to be easy to get here, Dan, but ever since TWA made Saint Louis its hub, I pass through there and never see more of K.C. than a dwarfed view from thirty-five thousand feet up through a tiny oval window."

"What about vacations? Or don't you people do them in the Big Apple?"

Eric laughed, but his eyes studied Dan carefully. He had never known him to be effusive by nature. Even at Dave and Bryn's funeral, though angry, certainly, at the senseless killing of two innocent young people, he had been reserved, quiet. So why the desperation Eric was picking up? It was out of character and disturbing. Something was bad wrong.

Remembering his earlier comments about having expected him, Eric wondered if Mike Sansom, or Guy, or even the Anthonys, had called the police chief. He changed the subject from his errant neglect of his home city. "You said that you had been expecting me, Dan. Did someone tell you I was coming?"

Dan retrieved his pencil from his desk, thumping it again as he considered his answer. "Better question might be who hasn't called to discuss your involvement. Answer to that would be easier. No one. You're hot stuff. Folks take notice when the biggest private investigative firm sends in its top man. 'Sides, I keep tabs on you. Haven't you been specializing in serial killers ever since you got that fancy certificate entitling you to put 'doctor' in front of your name? Truth is, I looked for you to be back snooping around long before now. Pity you had to wait for one of the dead women's families to send you. If I'd thought of it, I'd've pressured the city council to come up with the money to buy your services."

Eric nodded, looking down at his hands folded in his lap, a small smile playing on his lips. High praise coming from a man normally territorial as a pit bull when it came to crime in his city.

He looked up. "Well, I'm home now. So what's the count? One man glad I'm here, everyone else pissed off?"

The chief's pencil thudded heavily on the thick stack of reports in front of him once more before he laid it aside to retrieve a partially smoked cigar from the ashtray. He worked to relight the old stogie, his cheeks puffing in and out, creating an eerie flashing image of the more robust man of Eric's memory. When Dan exhaled at last, his face giving into its thinner, ravaged lines, Eric felt his spirits flag as he wondered again what was wrong.

His brows furrowed together as he thought for a second of taking advantage of their long-term friendship to ask him straight out, but Dan was already moving them along, getting on to talk of the unsolved murder case, and the chance to ask was lost.

"I used to sit and watch CNN and every now and then I'd get a mention of you, or actually catch a glimpse of your pretty mug, and I'd say to Jo, 'We could sure use that boy's help on this one. He's a lot like his daddy. Got a knack for ferritin' out the truth.'" He leaned forward, his eyes catching a spark for just an instant. "I'll tell you, son, the feds never admitted they were as stymied as the rest of us, but I knew and there was a time there when I didn't think we were going to solve this one. Arrogant bastards those federal boys. Never had much use for the way they do things, but truth is, there was that time I wished real hard you were still one of 'em. Strikes me as kinda ironic that you show up now when we think we've finally solved the case. I woulda thought . . ."

Eric held up a hand. "Whoa, Dan. Let's back up. I know you made an arrest last year, but I was under the impression you hadn't closed the file. The Grand Jury refused to indict, am I right?"

Dan laughed, choking on his amusement for a few seconds before answering. "You're as full of crap as your daddy was, Eric. Going all around this like you're afraid of stepping on my feelings. Hell, stomp away, boy. Don't pussyfoot. You know damned well the Grand Jury said our prima facie evidence was too circumstantial and refused to hand down an indictment. Fact is, though—" His face reddened as he began to cough and sputter again. He stubbed the thick, short stogie out in the ashtray, reaching for his cup of coffee to help stifle the spasm. "Offer you a cup?" he asked when he was able.

Eric shook his head.

The chief gulped down another swallow, then cleared his throat. "Okay, let's get one thing clear between us. We can both shoot straight here. You don't have to soft pedal around me, and I damn sure ain't gonna do any sidesteppin' with you.

"We never found the murder weapons, and we don't have a single eyewitness who can put Darin Woods at the murder scenes, but he was there. He admitted that much. And even if he hadn't, we knew 'cause we have good, solid evidence.

"We're 99.9 percent positive we got our man, but we're still digging for something that'll tie it all up in a fancy little package. Then we can hand it over to the feebs since they get the tag on this one, and we can wash our hands."

He hunched his shoulders. "It's a done deal, Eric. Someone's going to come up with that missing piece of the pie—who knows, maybe it'll be you—but when it's found, it'll have Woods all over it, and the poor slob'll have earned himself a place in the history books as K.C.'s most notorious serial murderer."

Something in the way Dan had phrased the last nudged a question to the surface, but before Eric could voice it, the chief started up again, catching him neatly off guard with an artfully executed segue.

"And speaking of crimes recorded in the annals of our fair city, how you doing with the fact that the feebies replaced the case agent assigned to the Rose Murders with Mike Sansom? You live with that?"

Eric responded with an easy sliding grin that didn't jibe with the immediate tight coil in his gut, but then wasn't that typical of every facet of his association with his former partner? They'd been friends. Once. But even then they'd been at odds, never in sync. As disparate as fiery recklessness and icy cool reserve.

"Well?" Dan pressed.

Eric laid an ankle across his knee, clasped it with his hand when his foot would have rocked. "Matter of fact, he came to see me last night. We did the requisite sniffing, growling, circling."

Dan chuckled, then made a looping motion with his hands, encouraging his young friend to get the rest said. "And?"

"And I think we figured out we can each let the other do his own prowling long as we don't raise too many back hairs."

Dan sat back, entwining the tips of his fingers over his paunch. "Well, probably won't be as hard now as it might have been even just a couple of days ago. Like I said, we've 'bout got this one wrapped. Soon as we're sure of that, we can say a few words over this whole sad mess and be done with it. Might even find a benign sentiment or two for that crazy son of a bitch, Woods."

Eric let his foot drop to the floor as he sat forward eagerly. "Hey, am I hearing something more than you're saying or are you talking about the guy as if he's dead, Dan?"

The chief looked past his guest through the glass doors, then leaned forward and lowered his voice as if afraid the others in the large room outside his office might hear. "Off the record till Sansom's people take it public?"

Eric shrugged. "I think you know you can trust me not to do anything that would hinder a murder investigation."

Chief Small nodded. "Four a.m. this morning, we got a call from State Patrol. Seems Mr. Woods was out strolling along Interstate Twenty-nine when he was struck and killed by a hit-and-run driver. His car was parked along the side, jacked up, flat not yet removed.

"The patrol officer who filed the report observed that there wasn't a spare in the trunk. Looks like he was going to hitch a ride to the nearest station. We can't know that, of course. Just guesswork on our part. He was dead when the officer arrived on the scene."

"Any witnesses?"

"Two, but neither one actually sure what they saw. Both said it happened so fast everything was a blur. They did agree it was a pickup—gray, light blue, maybe—that hit him. Driver didn't hang around, of course, and neither of our witnesses got more'n a glimpse. Both think there was only one person in the cab, but they're not even sure about that. One of 'em—a retired postal clerk—got the first two letters on the tags. FourJ. Not much to go on, but we have an APB out."

"But I-29 is a major highway. Hell, the airport's right off it. You mean to tell me there were only two cars on it? Where did it happen?"

"Matter of fact, about four miles south of the airport, just after Barry Road. Well-traveled between seven a.m. and oh, ten, eleven at night. But this happened just after four a.m., don't forget. Not much traffic anywhere that time of morning."

"Did Woods live up that way?"

"No. Just the opposite. Raytown. But one of the Rose contestants was from those parts. Saint Joe. She wasn't there. We already had all the girls tucked away at the Ritz-Carlton, but he didn't know that, and her folks called in to tell us they'd received one of Woods's calling cards that morning: a single rose."

Eric could feel the tension beginning to burn in his shoulder blades. He had a hundred questions, but he took a long, deep breath to slow himself down. "Okay, Dan. Let's back up again. Woods is the only guy ever arrested, right?"

Dan nodded. "Uh-huh, but that's not to say we didn't have our share of nut cases wantin' to confess. We did. Twenty-eight in all, if memory serves."

Eric couldn't resist a small, rueful smile. He didn't suppose there had ever been a time when memory hadn't served the police veteran. His father had once said the man had a memory like a steel trap. Eric went on down his list. "Woods sent a rose or delivered one himself to a contestant, and sometimes to as many as three or four women every year that the pageant ran. And five times in these half-dozen years, one of those women was killed. Why did you wait four years before picking him up?"

"Hell, Eric, almost every contestant in those pageants receives gifts, and you just said it yourself, he was clever enough not to target only one of them. He sent roses to several of them. Also, as you have pointed out, there was one year when no one was killed or even threatened so much as we can tell. We never knew when he was going to strike, and we spent countless hours just trying to keep track of the contestants' whereabouts for the month encompassing the big event."

Eric was well read on the details of each woman's murder. He knew that the first one had been killed the night before the pageant in the hotel while sitting alone in the sauna. After that the women had been hit as soon as two weeks before the contest actually began and as late as two days after the Rose Spokeswoman was selected. One of the contestants was killed in her home in Chicago. Another was slain as she climbed into her car outside her apartment building in Omaha on her way off to Kansas City for her weeklong competition. He recalled that the last young woman, his clients' daughter, in fact, had been killed in a particularly daring assault while her boyfriend showered in the next room. He wasn't going to waste time discussing the futility of trying to predict either the time or place of the next killing. He waved his hand, conceding that he understood how hard the enforcement agencies had worked.

"Look, Dan, I've got all that down. I know you did everything you could to protect those women. This butcher was damned clever, no doubt about it." He scratched his ear. "In fact, that's what bothers me. I don't have much on Woods, just what the papers have reported, but correct me if I'm wrong, his nickname wasn't Einstein."

The chief scowled. Much as he wanted to, he couldn't argue with the private investigator. Truth be told, the man was an effing genius with an effing 'doctor' in front of his name to boot. Still, Dan couldn't just sit there like some backwoods Barney Fife. He had to suggest doubt, no matter how lame. "Way we read it, he wasn't a rocket scientist, no. But plenty of wackos out there don't have a dozen brain cells rubbin' together upstairs, but still wily enough to get away with murder."

Chapter Twelve

Eric thought he could be right and told him so. "I can't argue with you. So let me ask some more questions."

"Go for it."

"Okay, first, why would Woods send a rose that even an imbecile could figure out would be traced back to him sooner or later? Why not just sneak up on the girl, vow his love or whatever, and then kill her? No clues. No fingers pointing back in his direction."

Dan hunched his shoulders. "What's your guess, Eric? Ego? A need to be found out? How can we know for sure? When we first brought him in, he confessed. Then twelve hours later after he meets with the attorney his mama got for him, he changes his mind, recants his statement. Says he just wanted the girls in the pageant to notice him, so he took the credit. *The credit.* That's what he called it! Can you believe it?" His ire set off another bout of coughing, this one briefer though harsh and racking. After a moment of concern on Eric's part, Dan took up where he left off though on a milder note. "Anyway, the next morning, he claims he's thought it over, doesn't want anyone else getting hurt so he's gonna tell the truth: He didn't do it. Even says he saw someone come out of Lisa Marks's house just before he placed the rose there."

"But no one believed him." Eric cupped his chin in

his hands, his expression serious and reflective. "Why him, Dan? I mean, what made you look at him different?"

"The kid was a fruitcake, okay? And not such a kid either. Thirty-three years old last year when we brought him in. He still lived with his mother. Maybe not so strange until you meet her. She's as wacky as he was, and you're forgetting that he always got a rose to them sometimes within minutes of their deaths. But he complicated matters by leaving one for two or three contestants. See? Crazy, but not stupid."

"So what specifically turned us onto him? He made a mistake—they always do, don't you know? And his was the flowers just like you thought. He always bought 'em from the same store. Not a florist, a grocery store. And not even a supermarket, mind you. Just a little Piggly Wiggly. A simple mom and pop operation in Raytown."

"The gal who finally called us said she knew him, assumed he had a special girl he was too shy to talk about. So she brought it up, kind of asked him who the lucky lady was. Said he got all upset and nervous. You know, like a whore in church. Turned all red. Got to shaking and broke out in a sweat. Even started stuttering. Then he spouted something about his gal being real special, the kind of woman who'd win a beauty contest. The clerk jokingly suggested she might oughtta try out for the Rose Queen title. Seems our Mr. Woods paled white as these walls once was before the nicotine from my cigars tainted 'em yellow. Anyways, started our clerk thinking and adding. When she totaled two and two and got four, she called us.

"That was his first mistake, just like I said. The second and most important was what he gave us that no one but the killer could have known." He paused, turning his chair around, giving it a slight jump-start with the heel of one foot to roll over to the table behind him and refill his cup with fresh coffee. "Sure you won't join me?"

Eric laughed. Dan always was a ham, big on drama and holding his audience till the drumroll. And everyone played along, gave him his moment. Keaton wasn't about to be the first to disappoint. "And?"

Dan wheeled his chair back to his desk. "The Marks woman was asleep when her killer entered the house. Apparently—though this is just what the guys in forensics have put together—he wanted her to know she was going to die because he woke her up: turned her over. Her nightgown was pulled up at the side while the other side was still tucked down below her knee. Didn't keep the lady waiting after that. She didn't have time to sit up or back away from him, otherwise her gown would have been bunched up under her behind. But the point is, Eric, he told us about the nightgown, even about how one side of it had slipped down off her shoulder and been torn with the knife. Poor kid. She was stabbed eighteen times."

Eric rubbed his brow. "Couldn't he have been telling the truth when he said he saw the killer just before he went to the door to deliver the rose?"

"I don't think so. He was too vague about that. Wouldn't even give us a description. Besides, if he saw someone leave the house and then sneaked over to leave a rose, why not just drop it on the doorstep? Why go into the house to the woman's bedroom?"

Eric shook his head. He was inclined to agree with the Grand Jury. These details didn't add up as conclusively as the chief would like him to think. He decided to move the talk in a different direction. "Tell me about the Anthonys," he said, winning a faint, surprised look from the police chief.

"What's to tell? You've already got it all. Don't try to tell me you don't. I already know you were at the pageant's kickoff last night." At Eric's surprised look, he chuckled. "My boys reported in. Told me all about you and the girl. Created quite a spectacle, not to mention quite a lot of complaints that went straight to the commissioner who brought 'em straight to me and dropped them in my lap first thing this morning.

"But that's neither here nor there, I know you do your homework, and even if you didn't, all you have to do is pick up a newspaper. They're renowned not only for their perfumes and cosmetics but also for their activities with charities and the powerful political connections they enjoy. Alex and the governor play golf. Shit, the Anthonys have had dinner in the White House with three Presidents."

"Is that why they've never been seriously considered as suspects?"

Dan's friendly expression slipped for a second, so quickly brought back into place again as to be almost imperceptible, but Eric knew he had touched a nerve. "Of course we checked them out. Especially in the beginning. No one is above the law, son. I ain't gonna pretend there might be exceptions to that rule in some quarters of the country—especially in our nation's capitol—but you know me well enough to know that it's the truth here. There just wasn't motive or anything else to tie them directly to the murders. We investigated a whole slew of people connected to the Anthonys—highfalutin business rivals, disgruntled ex-employees, a few of Paul's ex-girlfriends, as well as the people who still work for Anthony Enterprises including the two hundred or so who live in their town. We uncovered a couple of surprises, but nothing to implicate anyone in these murders."

Eric didn't answer immediately. He hated to bring Christianne's name into the same conversation with the dirty topic they were discussing, but there was no way around it. Somehow, she was smack dab in the middle of it.

"What about Christi, Dan? The minute I saw her, I knew these murders were more personal than anything I'd read in the papers. I don't know why or how. Have these women been surrogates? Have these murders all been a blatant form of extortion? You know, pay attention to who we're killing and why or we get the prize? Did she piss some guy off at one time or other? And what about Darin Woods, Chief? Did he know her? Because, I'm sorry, without making some association there, I not only think you've got reasonable doubt he's your man, I think you can be damned sure his only sin is being the unluckiest bastard around."

It was Dan Small's turn to hesitate. Then he shrugged his sloped shoulders. "Nope, you've got us there, son. And I admit we all share the same conviction that Christianne Anthony is at the center of this . . . one way or other. Shitfire, we'd have to be a bunch of effing morons not to have linked her amazing similarity to the murdered women. But we haven't made the hookup between them and her any more than we've tied your heiress to the suspect. And you know what really galls me? I don't think we're gonna."

Somewhat placated by the honesty of the admission, Eric backed off enough to give the man some wiggling room. "Why's that?"

Chief Small threw his hands up in the air. "Why's that? Because we've gone after it from every angle, son. And I've come to a conclusion that's pretty hard to chew on."

Eric waited, not offering any help this time.

"I think we got about as much chance of tying the Anthony girl to the victims as an elephant has of shittin' in a Dixie cup." He leaned back, brought a leg up to rest it on his knee and folded his arms over his chest. "Now that's what I think."

Eric grinned. "Well then, it's not hopeless. I've seen some pretty talented elephants in the circus."

"Smartass," Dan growled, some of the old spark returning to his eyes for the moment. The light went out as quickly as it had come. "Some of the boys on the task force have decided to chalk up the resemblance to coincidence. And the Anthonys have taken every measure to protect that girl. Packed her off to Europe just weeks after the first murder. Hired bodyguards while she was in Italy to make sure no one bothered her including the paparazzi. Some folks knew, of course. Hell, she wasn't locked away in an ivory tower or anything, but all in all I'd say they did a good job of keeping the media from transposing her face over those of the murdered women.

"Can you imagine, Eric, what would have happened if word got out that she looked so much like the victims? God only knows how many copycat crazos would have come crawling out of the woodwork."

The chief picked up the pencil he'd been thumping earlier, and tapped it quickly to a rhythm that was lost to Eric. The corners of his lips twitched with his repressed smile. He may not have known the tune, but the *Savant* recognized the stall.

"You want to say something, Dan. Go on. Get it out."

The chief gnawed on the inside of his jaw for another second or two, then spit out the vile-tasting words. "I don't know how right they are, but the Anthonys are saying their daughter showed up at the ball last night 'cause you encouraged her. I don't know if you did or you didn't, but if they're right, you were wrong."

Eric had already come to the same conclusion himself, but he wasn't quite ready to fall to his knees in contrition. "Why?" he challenged. "If you had a righteous bust and Woods was your man as everyone keeps insisting, Christi never was in danger. It was all just a colossal coincidence. And even if she was his target from the start, the man's in the morgue, so he can't hurt anyone again."

This time there was no hesitation from Chief Small. "Knock the chip off your shoulder, fella. We may not be on the same team, but we all have the same goal here. We don't want any more victims. Not beauty contestants and not the beautiful Miss Anthony. And, yes, we're confident we had the right suspect, which will end this case once and for all. One more thing, though . . . about that chip?"

"Let's have it."

"Don't be so hard on her family. They're just trying to protect her, and they haven't had an easy time of it. She's had a tough life . . . There was a kidnapping attempt on her when she was a baby." He held up a hand, warding off the questions he saw coming. "No, no. Totally unrelated. Some bum working as their gardener got it in his head he could snatch the kid and make some fast change. He broke into the house one night during a storm. The electricity was out, and I guess he thought he could grab the baby and get away in the dark without anyone seeing. Anyway, to make a long story short, the nanny was reading by candlelight in the next room. She literally set his ass on fire with the candle. He died in prison three years later.

"Naturally, they've been very protective ever since. Hell, until Christianne went away to college, she was a virtual prisoner out there on that estate. And it wasn't easy for her, staying in Italy when everyone she loved and worried about was here dealing with a murder investigation and nose-diving stock shares from all the associated negative publicity. If that wasn't enough, she was under a lot of stress last year because her grandmother was so ill and her family refused to let her come home. Ultimately, she defied them and returned home anyway, but the old lady died the night before she got there. Paul Anthony says she took it real hard. Apparently, the girl believed the woman hung the moon and his mother was just as crazy about her only grandchild. Maryann says her mother-in-law was Christianne's only confidante when she was a child."

Great, Eric thought, feeling like a first-class jerk. In a defensive tactic, he changed direction. "Let's go back to Darin Woods. I can't understand why I didn't hear about his death on the news this morning. I mean, the one man ever seriously considered a suspect in Kansas City's most heinous crime spree dies, and Guy didn't even get it off the wires in time to call me?"

Dan sat forward, putting his hands on his desk in a symbolic gesture of laying all the cards on the table. "We John Doed him, Eric. We don't want some lunatic jumping on the bandwagon just to try and prove us wrong. We've notified his mother, of course, but she agreed to keep her mouth shut after we hit her with some pretty heavy-duty threats—accessory after the fact, aiding and abetting—you get the idea. The coroner won't release the body until after the pageant's concluded, and we think she'll keep cooperating at least until then even though she's about as loony tunes as her son. But outside of that, no one's been told. There's also that one-tenth of a percent chance I mentioned that we're wrong. By keeping news of Woods's death from the press and the public, we'll soon know. If someone else makes a try for one of the contestants, we'll either catch him or start this ball game up again. Otherwise, we'll be satisfied that it's a closed case."

Eric rubbed his chin thoughtfully. He didn't remind the police chief that one of the murders had gone down a couple of days after the Rose Queen was selected. "The pageant's Saturday. I'm going to keep digging until then, Dan. If I don't turn up anything new, I'll call my clients and tell them the case is solved. Just don't be too quick to close your files. I don't know, but I'm beginning to get an itchy feeling at the back of my neck when there are too many coincidences."

Dan laughed, throwing his head back to let himself go with it. "Goddamn if you didn't sound exactly like your old man just then, Eric. He'd be real proud of you, son."

"Thank you sir."

Dan looked at his watch. "I've got a meeting upstairs, Eric. Don't mean to rush you off, but can't keep the brass waiting either."

Both men stood up.

"Thanks for your time, Chief. I'll be in touch if I uncover anything, and I'd appreciate you letting me know anything new you turn up. In fact, I'd appreciate a look at the autopsy report on Woods if it wouldn't ruffle too many feathers." He looked down at his shoes as a grin spread. "Maybe you wouldn't mind asking the FBI to filter anything they might want to slip my way through your department. Fewer channels, less likelihood of anyone getting their wires crossed."

Dan laughed. "Yeah. I hear ya." His expression sobered. He walked around his desk to put a hand on his young friend's shoulder. "Doctor tells me it's time to hang it up, Eric. Seems my health's not holding up too good. This case has weighed heavily on me. It's important that I get it tied up. I'm going upstairs right now to turn in my resignation. It won't become official until we put the file on this one to bed after the pageant, but once that's done, it's over for me. I'm going to spend some time with the family. Of course that's all to stay between you and me for right now, okay?"

"Sure," Eric said.

The two men walked to the door together. Chief Small reached for the doorknob, pausing to add, "Want to hear something funny? I just told the wife last night that if my resignation goes through all right, and I pack up things here on the day I plan, it will be exactly forty years to the day since your daddy and I entered the academy. Now that's a coincidence you can believe in!"

Eric agreed, but as he walked away, he thought there might just be a couple too many coincidences to suit him.

Chapter Thirteen

Christianne awakened to a bright midmorning sun, its rays needle sharp and piercing. Snapping her eyes shut once again, a muted groan of protest escaped her lips. She blinked several times, testing the pain until it slowly settled to a dull ache as she accustomed her eyes to the light. Sweeping her long hair from her face with the back of her arm, she rolled over, squinting and bringing the clock on the nightstand into focus. Ten-thirty! The alarm had been turned off, and she growled her annoyance.

Damn it! She'd scheduled an important meeting with the director of research and development for eight a.m. Snatching the cordless phone from its cradle, she jabbed the familiar seven-digit number.

No more than a dozen sentences were exchanged before Christi broke the connection. Just as she had suspected, her mother had taken it upon herself to reschedule her calendar for her.

Damn it!

From the back of a chair, she grabbed the pair of jeans she'd worn to go check on Mustard. Soaked. Her tennis shoes were grass-stained and soppy as well.

Irritable and impatient, she raked her fingers through her hair as she crossed the room to the closet. She yanked a chenille bathrobe from its hanger and was already knotting the sash by the time she padded barefoot from the room.

As much as she loved her mother, she was not going to tolerate her continual interference.

And not just her mother's. All of them were guilty. As a child she'd enjoyed it; expected and even exploited it. But that was then. This was now, a distinction her parents and uncle seemed unable to make especially since her return from Italy and her grandmother's death.

No, she amended as she skipped down the stairs, they'd been every bit as bad before she graduated from high school. Control freaks! That was why she'd selected a college out of state. That was why she'd jumped at the offer for the job in the multinational corporation's European central office. She'd been shocked when her father proposed it; positively blown away when he announced that a tag of vice president was attached to the position. Outwardly, she'd exuded eagerness, excitement, and pride. Inwardly, though, she'd recognized the ploy for the creative vehicle it was, designed to deliver her out of harm's way.

But she'd vowed to change all that, to learn everything she could about the company's European operation, and influence its growth and success.

She'd arrived in Rome with her proverbial shirtsleeves rolled up, her pencils sharpened, and her intuition fine-tuned. She'd ignored the whispers and smirks of the female employees, the patronizing tolerance, and sexual harassment she soon learned were as much a part of the Italian men she worked with as their religion.

Secretly, she'd been terrified, and she'd screwed up more than once . . . especially when she'd allowed herself to be seduced by Carlo Marconi. She flinched. That one still smarted.

She squared her shoulders. Ultimately, though, no matter what it had cost her, no matter how painful the lesson, she'd proven herself, shown them all the merit of her 4.0 average she'd maintained throughout her four years of college and her graduation with magna cum laude honors. She'd demonstrated a core of metal no one in her family—except her grandmother—had credited her with.

But once again, their coddling was driving her bonkers. She had earned their respect, damn it.

At the top of the spiraled staircase, she rounded the corner, just about to start down, when her mother appeared just a step or two below.

Surprised, Christi jerked back, stepping on the hem of her robe and barely catching hold of the balustrade before losing her balance. The sash she'd knotted loosely fell away revealing her nudity. She saw her mother's eyes widen with shock before immediately narrowing with disapproval. Well, too bad.

Lifting her chin, Christi casually looped the sash. She was embarrassed, which heightened her anger. How did they do it? No matter what the circumstance, somehow her family always managed to put her on the defensive.

Unaware of the sensual picture she posed, she shifted her weight to one leg, creating an opening in the floor-length robe and revealing a long shapely leg. Her full, pink bottom lip formed a soft pout, but her big blue eyes were glaring as they met her mother's.

Maryann seemed to falter for a moment in her mission, her daughter's sullen, accusatory demeanor surprising her. "Sweetheart, I was just checking to see that you were awake. Your father and uncle left for the office hours ago and I'm going out to the greenhouse to work with the roses." Maryann smiled. "I take it you found Mustard snuggled up in his doghouse safe and sound?"

With the question, a rush of fear, primal and ardent, coursed through Christi's body like an electrical shock.

For the first time since she'd awakened, she recalled the terrifying episode at the dog pen.

The retriever had been asleep in his house, content to snooze away in the tempest. Christi'd called his name several times before unlatching the gate and slipping into the large pen to make sure he was indeed burrowed deep inside.

There was no moonlight, not with the heavy storm clouds, but the rays from a dusk-to-dawn light illuminated the entrance to the doghouse. Christi crouched low and whistled into the doorway and in a fraction of a heartbeat she heard Mustard's toenails clickedy click against the wood flooring as he bounded toward her.

The tale actually wagging the dog, Mustard woofed sharply. He leaped in the air, his front legs crashing into Christi's chest. Reaching behind her, she grabbed the fence post and saved herself from being knocked down on her backside. She was laughing as she wrapped her arms around the retriever's neck and tolerated the bath he gave her face with his wet, slobbery kisses. She scratched his ears and roughhoused with him for a few minutes, before crouching down to stare him in the eye. "I was worried about you, you big old oaf. And here you were sound asleep and not the least bit worried about any silly storm."

A jagged lightning bolt cut through the night, startling a yelp from her and a frightened yip from her pet. The crash of thunder followed a split second later. Too close for comfort.

"Go on, boy. Get back inside your house. We don't want to get fried out here tonight. It'd give Mother too much satisfaction to be able to say I told you so." She smacked his shoulder soundly and pushed herself to her feet. The rain that had been pattering gently when she left the house was picking up. There was a bite to it now as it struck the exposed skin on her face and hands. "We'll go for a run tomorrow as soon as I get home from work."

Normally, Mustard responded to the promise he picked up in her tone with a decisive woof. Not this time. Suddenly, he wasn't listening. His raisin black eyes were directed past her toward the wooded boundary on the west end of the estate. His rain-soused golden coat bristled and he let out a low rumbling growl.

Ignoring the sting of the slashing rain, Christi tracked his gaze trying to find the source of the threat only his keen canine senses had detected.

Nothing. Only the dancing shadows of trees in the swatch of light that cut across the yard.

She listened. Nothing. Only the rustle of leaves and the groan of tree branches.

Still, she sensed the danger, felt fear curl in the pit of her stomach.

Hunkering down beside the doghouse, she turned her head slowly back and forth, her gaze narrowed and oscillating over the grounds.

Mustard's body went suddenly rigid, his ears laid flat against his head.

And then Christi saw it, the shadow that materialized under the narrow strip of light. Rain dribbled from her hair into her eyes forcing her to squint as she tried to distinguish features that were distorted to a ten-foot bogeyman before shrinking and disappearing in the next instant. In the aftermath, Christi thought she heard the quick staccato of running footsteps, but she couldn't be sure. It could just as well have been the skittering thrum of her own heart as panic sent it racing. One thing she was sure of, someone had been out there. And in a moment of terrifying clarity, she knew it was the Rose Murderer and understood he'd come to spy on his next intended victim.

Chapter Fourteen

"Christianne? Darling, are you all right?" Maryann asked. She placed a hand on her daughter's arm, and her dark eyes widened. "Good Lord, you're trembling. What's wrong?"

Christi shook her head and a shudder rocked her as she recalled the eerie certainty she'd experienced that the darting shadow belonged to the Rose Murderer. And that it wasn't Darin Woods. Of that she was positive. She pressed a trembling hand to her brow and the perspiration that had surfaced with the terrifying memory. As horrible as it had been, though, she couldn't tell Maryann. Already her mother was overprotective. She could only imagine the restraints that would be applied if she told her about the frightening episode. Or even of her harmless confrontation with Woods in the hotel garage. So she lied. "It's . . . it's nothing, Mother. I just flashed on a lurid nightmare I had last night. I'd forgotten all about it." She managed a thin, tight smile and even a laugh though it sounded tinny and unnatural to her own ears.

"Are you sure? You're as pale as your bathrobe."

This time when she smiled, it came easier and she was feeling steadier. After all, what had she actually seen? A fleeting shadow that could have belonged to a deer or even a dog from the nearby town. "It really was just a nasty dream. Come on, let's talk about something else."

Her mother smiled and Christi noticed the relieved

sigh and was glad for the lie she'd managed. Her
mother was making a special effort at friendliness in
spite of her displeasure at Christi's unexpected arrival
at the ball. The least she could do was return the favor
and try to ease tensions between them.

Her own smile widening, she motioned toward her
room with a thumb hooked over her shoulder. "I'm
going to go dress."

"Christi wait" Maryann said. "I want to apologize
for last night. I'm sorry. Really. I know you're not a
child. Hard as that is for me to accept, I really do
recognize that you are all grown up now." She paused
to gaze up at her daughter's face. "As a matter of
fact, since you've been home, I have to pinch myself
to keep from staring. Sometimes I can scarcely believe
you're mine. You're so beautiful and such an intelligent woman. I think it's obvious the Anthonys get
credit for the first, but I like to think you inherited
some of your quick mind from me."

"Mother! Begging for compliments? I can't believe
it." At her mother's blush, she giggled. "Oh, don't be
embarrassed. I was teasing. Good Lord, if there's one
thing I know about you, it's that you're much too
refined to beg for anything."

Tears actually glistened in Maryann's eyes and Christi
was blown away. In all her years, she'd never seen her
mother so much as sniffle at a sad movie. "Mom?"

It was Maryann's turn at surprise. She made a small
hiccuping sound that was mostly laughter. "Mom?"
she repeated. "I don't think you've called me that
since you were five years old."

Christi's eyes twinkled with mischief. She asked jokingly, "You didn't make me eat a bar of soap for such
a serious lapse, did you?"

Maryann chuckled, but suddenly her tone and expression were all seriousness once again. "I'm so glad
you're home, darling. I've missed you so much these

past years. And I want us to become friends. Real friends. This . . . this terrible ordeal has prevented us from bonding as we should have, but I don't think we should allow it to do so for even one more minute. Life is too short. Just look at how brief our time with your grandmother turned out to be."

Christi didn't want to talk about her grandmother. That wound was still too sensitive. She covered the hurt with soft laughter. "Okay, Mother, I hear you. Just don't oversell it."

Maryann laughed as well, and Christi's heart swelled with love for her as it hadn't in many years. Usually, Maryann was so remote, so contained, and it touched Christi that she was trying so hard. "Well, I'd really better go shower."

"Your father and I of course weren't happy about your decision to attend the ball, but since the cat's out of the bag, he thinks we should do our best to cooperate with Dr. Keaton; help him resolve this . . . this horrible ordeal. I suggested that you contact him and get your interview over with." She'd kept her gaze focused somewhere outside the bedroom window, but she looked at Christi once again, this time her smile tinged with sadness. "I didn't want you involved at all, but maybe there is some connection between you and those five women."

Christi was taken aback by this turn of events. "I don't get it," she admitted. "What do you think I could tell him?"

"I don't know. Maybe nothing. But Guy tells your father that this young man is the best in his field. God knows his credentials are impressive. And Guy says he's so good it's scary. Got a way of ferreting out details most people don't even realize they know. So, why not let him see what he can help you remember. Who knows? Maybe there's a boy in your past who became obsessed with you. I don't know." She held up her hands for a second as if the answers might be right there in her palms, then finding them empty, let them drop. "Anyway, I suppose it can't hurt."

Christianne leaned forward with sudden suspicions. "You're sure Daddy and Uncle Paul agreed, no argument?"

Maryann laughed. "There was some discussion, yes, but in the end, they acquiesced." Her voice trailed away for a moment before she sighed and added, "Well, I think I'll get on with my day. I need to pinch some old blooms off my roses. I've neglected them because of all the rain. But today is bright and glorious."

Christi studied her mother's face, which had only moments before been as radiant as the weather outside. Now, all at once weariness dulled her eyes and sounded in her voice. "Is there something wrong?" she asked.

Maryann looked down at the gardening gloves she'd carried tucked in her waistband and now clutched in her hands. The fingertips were soiled with grass and mud. She rubbed absently at the permanent stains as she answered. "No, darling. I was just remembering the way you looked at Dr. Keaton last night while the two of you danced. I suppose, if I'm entirely honest, I'm hoping you aren't about to let yourself be hurt as you were with that Marconi fellow." She raised her gaze, and a smile trembled on her lips. "There, see, I've made you angry. Never mind. I'll see you at dinner, darling."

"No, Mom, wait."

Maryann paused. "Really, Christianne, it's your business. I shouldn't have spoken. It's just . . . it's hard being a mother, wanting only the best for you . . ."

Christi resisted the urge to roll her eyes. Sometimes her mother could be absolutely pedantic. "Oh, don't get your panties all in a bunch. Yes, I am very attracted to Eric. I think he's gorgeous, and he definitely turns me on." She laughed at her mother's prim expression of disapproval. "—but two meetings do not a relationship make and I'm hardly ready to rush out to choose a wedding dress." Then, on a deliciously wicked whim, added, "As a matter of fact, I haven't even taken my diaphragm from my nightstand drawer and dusted it off, so let's not start hyperventilating yet."

Maryann frowned reprovingly as she stood up and straightened her neatly creased jeans and starched cotton shirt. "Well, perhaps you can reach inside yourself and somewhere amid the raging hormones, find a modicum of decorum as you remember that he is here for the purpose of investigating several savage murders."

"Whoa," Christi said, shaking her wrists. "That one stung. Guess I'd forgotten how well you aim, Mother."

Maryann ignored the sarcasm, though her eyes reflected her indignation. "He's staying at the Airport Marriott. The telephone number is in my address book in the desk in the study." She turned away and started down the stairs without waiting for a reply.

Behind her back, Christi made a face, but as she reentered her room, she picked up the sadly wilted rosebud from the corner of her dresser.

She dropped it into the wicker trash basket with a twinge of regret. It was the only souvenir she'd brought home to remind her of those few perfect moments in Eric's arms and somehow, even it had been blemished by her mother's visit.

Chapter Fifteen

Ten minutes later, her good mood recovered, Christi was dressed in a silk pantsuit and skipping down the stairs. She met the housekeeper on the landing as she slipped by in the opposite direction, fresh linens folded and stacked high in her arms. "Good morning, Jeannie," she said, without missing a beat on her way to her father's office.

She found her mother's address book in a nook in the desk. Setting it on her lap, she took the chair in front of the large antique roll-top and picked up the phone.

The hotel clerk informed her that Dr. Keaton was not in his room. "Oh," she muttered, feeling both foolish and disappointed. Of course he wasn't in. He'd come to Kansas City to work. It was practically the middle of the day.

"Are you still there, miss?" the hotel clerk asked.

"Yes, um, sorry. I'd like to leave a message for Dr. Keaton. Please tell him that Christianne Anthony called to confirm our appointment for tomorrow morning. Eleven-thirty."

"And your telephone number, Ms. Anthony?"

Christi chuckled. "Oh, he has my number. Thank you." She hung up, pausing for a few seconds as satisfaction like the warmth of hot chocolate filled her up with its sweet, mellow flavor.

She had work to get to, but still she lingered for a few minutes, reluctant to let go of the heady sensation of contentment that she'd forgotten could feel so good.

She closed the address book, then stroked the smooth, soft grain of its leather cover for a moment. It had been a difficult few months since her return home. Although she loved her parents and uncle, she'd suffered greatly over her grandmother's death . . . and of course there had been all that self-flagellation for her stupid affair with Carlo. Even now just thinking about it, she flinched. No. No more. Today she was going to concentrate on the future even if that was only as far as tomorrow.

Pushing the chair back, she stood up to bend over the desk and replace her mother's address book. The sleeve of her dressing gown caught on a stack of manila folders, pulling them to the floor.

"Oh, hell," she murmured as she stooped to gather them up. Several papers had fallen from the folders, and it took her some time to right them all, her thoughts not really on the task until she came to the contents of the last folder. Her eyes widened as she stared at the face in a glossy black-and-white 8 x 10 photo. Her hands trembling, she reached for the next and the next, falling to her knees as she spread them out across the floor in front of her.

Five pictures in all. Publicity photos of the murdered Rose contestants. She had seen most of them before, but not like this, so lifelike and real in their smiling closeups. She had glimpsed their pictures in the newspapers, but they had not seemed so real to her then, the photographs small and their features obscured by the grainy reprint quality of the paper.

One by one, she picked them up, studying each beautiful face, tears stinging her eyes as they found each woman's wide smile.

She wondered what each contestant was thinking as the cameramen snapped the picture that could well influence her future as a Rose contestant. Only when her eyes met theirs—some looking confident, others merely hopeful—did she turn the pictures over, unable to cope with the pity that knotted in her throat. She wiped at her eyes and nose, feeling such compassion and pain she thought she would suffocate with the power of it.

As she laid them all out on the floor, lined up like miniature coffins, she read the names penned in ink on the upper left-hand corner in her father's florid scrawl. There were dates written there as well, though she ignored those, concentrating on the names.

Rianne Swanson
Jessica Dale Bartlett
Debbie Yates
Mia Lindstrom
Lisa Marks

She repeated each one aloud, as if by doing so she could somehow know the girls and bring them to life, at least for herself. But the tears continued to flow. Christi hugged her knees, rocking back and forth for a while, grieving for them and feeling so incredibly selfish for allowing her parents to shuttle her off to Europe, then making only halfhearted attempts to convince her family to cancel the pageant. No wonder everyone had been so willing to keep her at a distance.

She stopped rocking. Pushing her grief aside, she gathered up the pictures, slipping them back into the folder, one at a time, pausing to study them again, forcing herself to acknowledge the resemblance that was uncanny and chilling.

She felt drained as she pulled herself to her feet, but also strangely glad for the accident that had forced her to confront the photos. If the murders were tied to her in any way, or even if they were merely victims of some deranged madman, they were all still contestants in a pageant her family sponsored and she had an obligation to each one of them.

As she tucked the folder into place among other documents pertaining to the murders, she wished as she did so often that her grandmother was there to talk to. She sighed. At least Gran would be proud of her, she thought. She had always faced life head-on and had encouraged Christi to do the same; to learn to face her fears and to stop running away from reality. She sat in her father's chair once more and ran her fingertips over the thickly padded arm. She pictured him sitting there, studying the photos as she just had, mourning the deaths. She felt the familiar pang of hurt in her chest, but this time it was for him; for all of her family. How many nights had they passed in this room, trying to find answers to stop the killer? she wondered.

Her gaze stopped on a porcelain-framed photograph. Reaching for it, she picked it up, letting her index finger trail the delicate pattern of roses that had been painted around the border and focused on the faces of her parents and uncle taken at the White House two years before. She'd missed a lot in the four years that she'd been gone, and she was just beginning to understand how great the lengths her family had gone to for her protection.

Bodyguards were hired to accompany her every time she stepped from the offices of Anthony Europa Enterprises. Countless excuses made as to why she shouldn't return home even for the holidays. And virtually every photograph snapped of her by the paparazzi was paid for and destroyed. All because they loved her, and until now she'd never fully understood.

Chapter Sixteen

Eric sat in his rental car jotting notes on his conversation with Chief Small. Checking his watch, he decided to use the few remaining minutes before noon to set up the appointments he had been unable to arrange before leaving the hotel earlier that morning.

Turning out into traffic, he drove through the streets as if he had traveled them only yesterday, marveling at how quickly familiarity settled back into place. He was unconsciously heading toward the Plaza though his ultimate destination was Raytown and the home of Ellie Woods, mother of the deceased. Poor bastard. He searched for a pay phone despite the cellular phone that lay on the passenger seat beside him. Couldn't use that without risk of picking up an escort. Not only did cellular calls go out over the airwaves, the feds had operators tuned in twenty-four hours a day on the chance of picking up a conversation between parties of particular interest. If there was one thing Eric intended to avoid, it was interference into his probe by his old buddy, Mike Sansom.

He spotted a public telephone at a service station and hung a sharp right into the parking lot. He called the Marriott first to retrieve any messages. The list was predictable until the last one. The message from Christi was definitely a pleasant surprise. He replaced the receiver, digging in his pocket at the same time for two more quarters.

He looked up Ellie Woods's number in the phone

book, loosening his tie as he punched in her number. She answered on the fourth ring, sounding breathless and astonished that the phone had rung at all. Her faint "hello" was questioning and tentative.

Eric turned on the charm. "Mrs. Woods, my name's Eric Keaton. I'm calling from—" he glanced around him and found a reference point on the street sign— "a service station at the corner of Thirty-fourth and Broadway. Now, don't hang up. I'm not with the media and I'm not police or FBI. I'm a private investigator. I work for a company called LINC." He paused a couple of seconds, not expecting a reply, but waiting for the information to settle in, relying on the prestigious firm's name to guide her past the suspicion.

"Yeah? So, what do you want with me?" she asked, wary though not entirely disinterested.

Good enough. He pressed on, speaking quickly and keeping his sentences short and to the point. "Mrs. Woods, I want to talk to you about your son. I know the police have instructed you not to discuss him with anyone. I'm putting you in a tight spot, I realize. The thing is, I'm not inclined to agree that Darin's guilty."

He heard a gasp punctuated by a long silence.

"This is difficult for you. I respect that, but believe me when I tell you I want to help."

"How you gonna do that?"

"Well, I'm not sure yet," he answered candidly. "First of all, I'd like to come over and talk to you. Get your side of the story."

"I'm going to bingo with a friend at three," she answered carefully.

Eric scratched the back of his neck. So much for the grieving mama he'd expected to have to tiptoe around. So, maybe this was better. He'd never liked dancing on eggshells. "Look, the police are going to close the case any day now and Darin's going to go down unless I can prove my theory that he's just a wrong guy in the wrong place." He turned down the volume, modifying his tone. "I can't do it alone, Mrs. Woods. What do you say? Will you help me?"

"I don't want to talk about Darin no more, Mr.— what did you say your name was?"

"Keaton. Eric Keaton." He tossed the remaining quarter in the air as he gave her a few seconds to decide. "It's nearly noon now. Why don't we make an appointment for, uh, one-thirty? I can be out of there by two."

"You private investigators don't come for free. Someone's gotta be paying you, so that's who you're looking out for, ain't it?"

Eric was impressed. He'd misjudged Ellie Woods. She might not be well-educated, but she wasn't stupid. "I'm investigating the Rose murders on behalf of one of the slain girl's family, yes, ma'am, but that's not necessarily in conflict with what you want for your boy. We're all after the same thing, I think. We want the truth about who committed these murders. I've talked to the police and heard their side. I'd like to hear yours as well. Does that sound fair?"

"Why didn't you ask for Darin?" she asked warily.

Eric didn't hesitate. "Originally, I had planned to do just that, but I think Darin has been through enough, don't you?"

She didn't answer for a few seconds, and Eric felt a jab of shame, though it was quickly dispelled with her next words. "Do you people pay for good, solid information . . . if it pans out, I mean?"

Eric caught the quarter as it flipped through the air one last time, slamming it angrily against the narrow ledge beneath the phone. His voice was tight with his reply. "No, ma'am, we don't. As I said before, we're interested in getting to the truth. If you'd prefer not to help me do that, you just say the word, and I'll let you get back to your plans for this afternoon."

There was an almost imperceptible pause before she agreed to meet with him, and Eric concluded their conversation promptly after getting directions to her house. So much for grief and motherly love, he thought.

Shoving the next quarter into the coin slot, he looked up the Piggly Wiggly store where Woods had purchased the flowers and jabbed out the numbers. His temper had started cooling by the time he was connected to the clerk who had given the suspect's name to the police. "This is Connie Felter," the woman told him as she came on the line. "How can I help you?"

Eric spoke to her for less than five minutes, but it was enough for a clear impression: She didn't believe Woods any more guilty than the man in the moon. She gave him a little more: She'd been an employee at the store for eleven years, and yes, she'd known Darin for almost that long. When asked to describe him, she'd used three adjectives—polite, shy, and sweet. Okay, okay, he knew what they said about Ted Bundy. Handsome, charming, brilliant. So what? Eric still wasn't buying Woods as a killer. It was possible, but his gut just wasn't digesting that one.

Next, he phoned the Samuel Clemens Boys Home, a state-funded institution for troubled youth just on the outskirts of St. Joseph, Missouri. Dr. Henry Looper was on the other end within seconds, his voice exuberant and earnest. Another refreshing surprise. The day was getting brighter.

"Dr. Keaton, I got your message earlier this morning. I apologize for not getting back to you before now. It's been rather hectic around here. Had a couple of runaways."

"Find them?"

"Oh, sure. No one ever gets too far, especially this time of year. We're smack in the middle of farm country. Open fields and crops just going in. No six-foot cornstalks to hide between, and well, the folks in these parts keep an eye out for boys dressed in the school uniform.

"But I understand from my assistant that you'd like to talk with me about one of our former residents, Darin Woods. Have I got that right?"

"Yes, sir. Of course, I realize he was a minor at the time he was, ah, with you, so there may be some confidentiality issues to deal with. I'm on my way over to see his mother now. What if I could get her to sign a waiver allowing you to answer my questions? Would that make matters easier?"

Henry Looper chuckled. "I can see you've been around this obstacle course before, and, yes, it absolutely would. However, I'm afraid today's not the best, though I might be able to manage an hour or so around six if all hell doesn't break loose." His gusty laughter filled the telephone.

"Sounds like my kind of place," Eric responded with a chuckle of his own. "I appreciate this, Doctor. Mind if I ask if you remember Darin?"

"I remember Darin well, and of course, his name has been tossed around by the media with some frequency these past couple of years."

"True enough. Well, I won't keep you. I'm eager to get your insight."

Dr. Looper hesitated, but his voice lost none of its eagerness. "Insight, possibly, but most assuredly my very decided opinion and impressions. More than that I'll have to leave to the *Savants*." He was clearly delighted at his small joke.

Eric chuckled, too, covering his mild surprise. So the doctor knew about LINC and the title Guy had given his three specialists. The question was, how?

As he hung up and climbed into his rental car, he realized he was looking forward to the evening appointment. Something in the doctor's tone had promised a rewarding payoff.

Climbing out of his car in the driveway of Ellie Woods's home, Eric detoured slightly to admire an aging blue Impala, amazed at its fine condition. His father had driven one like it when Eric was a small boy, but even then, the almost-new car had not gleamed with such care. Eric wondered if it belonged to the accused man. Rubbing the shiny blue fender in appreciation, he turned toward the house. The screen door opened as he crossed the lawn.

A short, robust woman came out onto the porch to meet him. At least fifty pounds overweight, she wore a loose-fitting, brightly flowered shirt, and although it was neither well made nor flattering to her coloring, great care had obviously been taken to coordinate the large purple hyacinths with her neatly creased slacks. Her practical, rubber-soled black shoes were well tended, also, Eric noticed. Everything about her, the neat and tidy house, the perfectly maintained old car, and her inexpensive, yet carefully chosen clothing were all evidence of graceful acceptance of her circumstances and aging.

Only her hair and face lent incongruity to the picture. Her face was as round and puffy as her thick figure, but every feature was defined with exaggerated color. Her lips were painted bright crimson, and a deeper shade of red liner made the thin lips appear fuller. Her cheeks were heavily rouged, and her heavy-lidded pale blue eyes seemed almost to sink into her head beneath their thick fringe of long false lashes and lavender shadow. Her brows, which may once have been naturally dark, were grotesquely penciled in a high black arch. She looked like a carnival caricature, Eric thought as his eyes traveled surreptitiously over the meticulously painted mask, but it was the long, bleached hair that caused a small involuntary shudder to quake up his back. Giving himself a good mental shake, he offered a wide smile, raising his hand in greeting. "I'm Eric Keaton."

Folding her arms beneath her ample bosom, she offered a tentative smile. "Thought you must be. Wasn't expectin' nobody else. Besides, none of my friends drives a new car like that one."

"It's a rental car, Mrs. Woods. I was admiring your Impala. It's a beauty."

Her eyes seemed to spark with pride for an instant, but her voice was gruff as she answered, turning her back on him at the same time to pull the screen door open again and usher him inside. "Darin fixed it up. He was a fine mechanic." Her eyes darted to Eric's as she clasped her hands suddenly, a small almost inaudible gasp hiccuping from her throat.

Eric understood at once. He wondered how many times she had slipped in the last several hours, referring to Darin in the past tense. Looking around him, he admired the neatness of the small living room. "You have a lovely home, Mrs. Woods. It's easy to see where your son gets his thoroughness from."

She smiled with his praise, her confidence back in place as she fluffed her long coarse hair with her hand. "Yes, well, we're humble folk, Mr. Keaton, but that don't mean we don't have pride."

"Of course not," Eric said sincerely, his gaze moving past her to the hood of the long Chevy that he could barely make out through the venetian blinds. "Doesn't look like he drives it much. What's the mileage, do you know?"

"Oh, no, I wouldn't have any idea. Pretty low, I'd guess. Only takes it out on special occasions. Mostly he drives his Nova. Now that one don't look like anything fancy, but it got . . . gets him where he needs to be." Her face reddening with her second slip in as many minutes, she wrung her hands nervously. "Can I get you a cup of coffee or some soda?"

Eric shook his head. "May we sit here while we visit?"

As she sank into the big oversized chair across from the sofa, she turned her face away from his, concentrating on the dainty points of a lace doily on the table beside her chair as her fingers worked to straighten each one.

Eric experienced an uncommon flash of sympathy for the woman, his mind flinching away from the questions he was going to have to ask and the pain they would surely cause. For all her clownish makeup and tough act on the phone with him earlier, she was just an ordinary middle-aged woman who took pride in her home and her son.

"There's no room in this job for sentimentality," Guy had once said, *"and there'll be times when you have to go right in aiming for the jugular. Usually, finesse is the key. Woo them, stroke them, cajole and flatter if you have to, but never forget that there are no tricks in that bag of yours too dirty to bring out if that's the only way to get to the truth."* Eric hadn't much liked his boss in those few minutes of conversation. Besides, he knew all about the end justifying the means. Nobody taught that lesson better than the FBI, and he'd employed every trick in the book at one time or the other. And hadn't he lost a brother and the woman he'd loved because of that very philosophy?

Still, he had a job to do. He sat forward, getting to work.

"Mrs. Woods, I know this has been hard on you, having your son accused of these heinous murders, and the press and police hounding both of you day and night for the past year since Darin's arraignment. But if we could go over everything one more time, I think LINC might be able to put together a report that will force the police to admit their mistake."

She sniffed, raising her chin slightly, her pale eyes watery but accusing. "Yeah, you'll tie it up, all right, but the noose'll be around Darin's neck, won't it?"

Eric hesitated, choosing his words carefully before answering. "You and I both know that the local police and the FBI are convinced your son is the killer. We also know that the evidence, while circumstantial, is pretty damning. I've listened to their side, and I've pored over more documents and newspaper accounts than you can imagine, but I'm not convinced. At least, not yet. All I want to do here is talk." He sat on the edge of the sofa, his expression earnest. "You see, Mrs. Woods, I believe there's something—something important—that the police have missed. It may be something you know, or I might have to talk to several dozen more people before I find it, but one way or the other, I'm not stopping until I find it. And you could be right. It might well turn out to be the one the thing that'll cinch Darin's guilt, but as God is my witness, I don't think so." He shrugged. "Don't ask me why. It's a gut thing, but I've got a hunch that if you'll help me, we might just be able to vindicate your son."

Ellie hung on every word and he could almost recite her thoughts as she nodded.

What could it hurt to go over it one more time? Darin was dead, wasn't he? Nobody could hurt him anymore. There wasn't anyone else left to live with the shame and she might be able to stand it, but why suffer if there was a way to prove him innocent?

"What do ya want to know?" she asked.

Eric offered her a grateful smile, settling back on the sofa to cross a leg over his knee. "Why don't you just tell me about Darin. Anything that comes to mind. You're his mother, after all, and you knew him better than anyone."

"Darin was a good boy." Her fingers nervously plucking at a button on her blouse, she continued. "Even as a child he never caused no trouble. His grades wasn't real good, you know, but he could work with his hands, and that's mostly what he done. I'd go looking for him after dark, and he'd be out in the garage working on a broken toaster or takin' apart one of his daddy's radios. He got a lot of lickin's from his dad, but I knew he was just curious, you see, so I'd wait till Lonnie—that was Darin's daddy—left for the tavern and I'd get Darin out of bed and let him come into the kitchen for some cookies and a soda. We'd talk till all hours, just my boy and me, and then I'd feel bad the next day, 'cause he was so tired and couldn't hardly get his lessons at school." She reached for a tissue in the blue crocheted box on the coffee table, dabbing at the corners of her eyes. Eric didn't rush her.

"When Darin was thirteen, his daddy came home real drunk one night, and I got mad—I was always gettin' mad when he was out carousin'—but this time he comes in the door and I start yellin' and hollerin' 'cause he was such a mess and smellin' like a French whore. Anyways, he didn't deny that he was with a woman. Called me a . . . well, lots of real mean names and then he hauls off and belts me across the face. We didn't know that Darin was awake, but there he was, out of nowhere holding a butcher knife and threatenin' to kill Lonnie if he hit me again." She stopped to blow her nose, shaking her head at the same time. "I know what you're thinkin'. Same as the police done, but he wouldn't've hurt him. He just wanted him to leave me alone, and it worked 'cause Lonnie, he went in the bedroom and packed a bag.

Fifteen minutes later, he walked out that door, and we never heard from him again."

"I'm sorry." Eric said quietly.

"I was, too, for a while, but Darin said he never did miss his dad after he'd gone. And, anyways, we got by, you know? Darin got a job deliverin' papers, and I worked at the supermarket that used to be around the corner till they tore it down. It wasn't easy, but we made it, and Darin and I, we got real close. Even later he never cared much for kids his age and he'd take me to the movies or out to dinner. He was always saving his money to buy me presents. Usually, they was somethin' old that he had to fix up, but he always made 'em work like new." She stopped talking. Brushing her long hair back from her face, she tilted her head to the side, her eyes squinting defiantly at him suddenly. "Suppose you want to hear about the prom," she said.

Eric nodded agreeably. "Whatever you want to tell me, Mrs. Woods."

"Well, that's what the police kept askin' about at first 'cause they think that's when Darin went nuts. 'Course that's pure silliness. He was just hurt, you know, and I didn't understand how sensitive he was."

"What happened?" Eric interjected, bringing her back on track.

"Darin started staying after school more and more. I didn't really mind, but I was lonely so I started going out with my girlfriends. We'd go over to a little dance place downtown or sometimes over to the church to play bingo. Darin didn't seem to care none. I don't know exactly how it happened, but we just kinda stopped talkin'. Anyways, he never told me what was goin' on and I thought it was his business. He was seventeen, almost eighteen, after all, so I didn't think it was my place to pry. Then one day, he comes home real excited. Takes my hands and pulls me right in here and makes me sit down. He's met a girl, he says real proudlike. He's been staying after school to watch her practicin' her cheerleadin'. He's finally worked up the nerve to ask her to the prom." Ellie's round face lit up with the brief, happy memory, and her hands fluttered about her as she showed Eric how Darin had kept moving around the room, unable to sit down in his excitement.

Eric turned his wrist, glancing surreptitiously at his watch. He opened his mouth to move her along, but she started up her story again.

"I was excited for him, too, and I thought it would be a good time to tell him that I had a boyfriend, but he never stopped talkin' long enough. Anyways, the night of the prom he looked real nice and had a pretty yellow rose corsage for her dress. He was so jittery he couldn't sit still." She giggled with the recollection of it all. "He said for me not to wait up. All the kids at school stayed out almost all night goin' to parties after the prom. I promised him I wouldn't. I wasn't worried about him. He was real responsible and I had plans of my own for the evenin'."

"My boyfriend—Fred was his name—and me went dancin' after Darin left. We stayed out real late."

"Fred showed me in the house when he got home, but it was all torn up. Looked like a tornado'd ripped through here. Lamps was knocked over and the curtains and furniture was all ripped up."

"Well Fred took off out of there like a bat out of hell. I went lookin' for Darin. Found him in the garage all curled up and cryin'. Seems the girl and her friends thought it'd be a real funny joke to pull on him, her agreein' to go out with him when she'd already promised a boy on the football team. But it wasn't funny! It was mean and spiteful, and Darin was hurt all the way to his soul."

"I sat on the edge of his bed that night, hatin' that

girl and hatin' his daddy for not bein' here when he needed him. Darin stopped crying long enough to tell me about her. He even had a picture of her except it was mostly crumpled up by the time I saw it. She had long blond hair and big, pretty blue eyes. He said she looked just like me." She smiled self-consciously. "He wasn't right after that. Kept gettin' mad out of the blue and breaking things. Didn't matter if he was at school or the store. He'd just kind of go crazy and start breaking stuff. And then one day, he went over to that girl's house and broke all the windows out of her parents' car with a baseball bat. The police picked him up and then a judge decided he should go to a place up in Saint Joe."

"I was real torn up about that, but it was the right decision, 'cause when he came home, he was just fine again." She looked at Eric and managed a tremulous smile. "He was a minor and the records was supposed to be gotten rid of after he turned eighteen, but they wasn't. So, when all these beauty contestants started getting killed, the police came looking for Darin straightaway. And 'course, soon as they found out about him leaving a rose for some of 'em, they had him good as convicted."

"They must've asked me a hundred times what kind of knife he used to cut up the curtains and I kept tellin' them it was just an ordinary little pocket knife his dad had gave him. 'Sides, I told 'em, all he cut was *stuff*. Curtains and cushions and the like. He never hurt no girl." She leaned forward as far as her ample middle would allow. "He never threatened nobody with that knife and he never hurt nobody with it. I told 'em over and over and over, but they never heard me."

"Anyways, Darin didn't want to talk about it after he came home, so we just didn't. He never went back to school. He was embarrassed and I understood, so

I let him get a job instead. He started working at a fix-it place and by the time he was twenty-two, he was assistant manager. Making good money, too. He bought all this furniture and these curtains a little at a time and I knew he was making up for what he done. But neither of us never said nothing again about it."

"What about the roses he started sending to the girls in the pageant?"

She shook her head. "He didn't tell me why, leastwise, not for a long time. Then one day, it just sort of came out. Guess he had the need to talk about it. I still remember how pitiful he looked sittin' in that chair over there in the kitchen. He said he always thought about Carrie—that was the girl that tricked him about going to the prom—and every time he saw them pretty blond girls' pictures he thought that one of them might be pretty on the inside, too, like me. He wanted to ask one of 'em out just to see, but he never could work up the nerve. He said he wanted them to have the roses so they'd know how pretty he thought they was, but he was happy just comin' home to his mama."

Eric was sickened by the terrible twist of fate that one mean, spiteful trick had provoked. Abruptly, he changed the subject. "Could I see a picture of Darin, Mrs. Woods?"

The woman pushed herself to her feet, offering him a grateful smile. "Right in here, Mr. Keaton. I keep all his pictures on the buffet in the dining room."

There were over twenty pictures of the dead murder suspect, but as Eric studied them, he couldn't think of him that way. The man had been a victim, too. Eric's eyes passed over Darin as a small boy, moving on to his high school picture—the image of a nice-looking young man, his thick, dark hair slicked back, the sideburns left long, the thin lips barely parted in a tight, self-conscious smile, and his deep-set, hazel eyes shy and unsure. Most of the later pictures were snapshots taken while working on his car or playing with a large, black husky.

"That's Baby, Darin's dog," Ellie Woods explained.

Eric was struck by the uncanny sameness of the pictures. Except for the natural maturing that occurred through the years, the man had changed little. Even the hair and sideburns had remained the same. Peter Pan, Eric thought.

"It's after two, Mrs. Woods. I know you have plans, but I have one more question for you, if you don't mind." He led the way to the front door as he spoke. "Chief Small, of the Kansas City Police Department, tells me that Darin claimed to have seen someone leaving the house of the girl who was murdered last year. Did he ever tell you about that?"

Ellie Woods stepped back, fear clouding her eyes. She nodded, looking down at her hands.

"But he couldn't give the police a description?"

Ellie's chest rose with her sharp intake of air, but she met Eric's dark eyes. He was touched by the trust he found in them as she answered. "Not at first. He knowed more than he'd say, I think, but he was innocent, and he surely wasn't going to point the finger at someone else who might be innocent, too. Anyways, he really didn't know who it was." She clamped her lips together in a grimace, searching the floor with her eyes as she worked to decide something. She raised her head abruptly and asked, "You know, don't ya . . . about Darin, I mean?"

Eric met her eyes squarely. There were times when a man made a choice and lived with the consequences if he was wrong. He decided to take the chance. "That he's dead, Mrs. Woods? Yes. I know. I'm very sorry."

Her eyes filled with tears that slipped down her face in great black streaks. Her voice faltered, but she wanted someone to know. "He found out who that person was that he saw coming out of the Marks girl's house. In the courtroom. He saw the person there, but he wouldn't tell no one. Said a person had a right to explain before he started slinging arrows. Now we'll never know."

"He didn't tell you anything? Not even what this person looked like?" Eric asked earnestly and took one of her hands in his.

The grieving woman shook her head. "Nothing. He wouldn't tell me nothing."

"Well, you're wrong about one thing, Mrs. Woods. It's not over. I'll find out who your son saw."

Ellie Woods pressed his hand to her cheek, her face puckered in fierce gratitude. "I'm sorry about askin' you for the money. My friends told me I should if reporters and such kept houndin' me, but I wouldn't've taken it. I don't want nothing except my son's name cleared."

Eric smiled to ease her shame. "I'm sorry, but I just thought of one more thing I'd like to ask." He looked at the houses around them to make sure that no one was around to overhear. "Did Darin say where he was going last night when he was struck by the car?"

She shook her head. "No. I didn't even know he'd gone out till the police showed up to tell me about him being dead. I take medicine to help me sleep. But they're probably right—the police, that is. They think he was on his way to give a rose to another girl. They found one in the front seat of his Nova."

"Huh," Eric said, gazing at the gleaming Impala. He tugged at his earlobe thoughtfully for a few seconds, then looked at Mrs. Woods again. "You said he only took this car out on special occasions. Did that include times when he was delivering a rose to one of those women?"

Her eyes widened and a huge grin spread across her

face. "Why, yes, sir, Mr. Keaton, that's exactly the times he liked to drive his fancy car. Just in case any of them girls looked out and saw him. Wanted to make a good impression, don't you know?"

Chapter Seventeen

Paul rapped firmly on his brother's office door, not bothering to wait for a response before entering.

Alex waved him in, holding up a finger to indicate the impending end to his telephone conversation. "Yes. Yes, that's right. Eight o'clock then." He paused, his weary expression belying the enthusiasm in his voice. "Right, Senator. We're grateful." He flagged Paul to one of the twin chairs in front of his desk as he replaced the receiver.

"I had hoped that was Guy," Paul said, before pushing himself from the comfortable gray suede chair to walk to the bar. "Fix you something to soothe the old nerves?"

Alex shook his head. "It's only three o'clock, Paul. I still have at least two more hours here before I go over to the Ritz for the cocktail hour with the girls, and then we have the party for the judges. You're going to be there, I hope."

Paul filled his glass, taking his time. He enjoyed a long, slow sip and smacked his lips.

"You come in here to talk or get drunk, brother?" Alex asked, his quiet voice heavy with irritation.

Paul laughed as he lowered himself into one of the chairs in front of Alex's desk once again. "You gotta learn how to relax, kiddo. You're too uptight. To quote my beautiful niece, chill out. And in case you've forgotten, I'm a certified grown-up. Got a driver's license, voter registration card, the whole shebang. I can have a drink whenever the fuck I choose. Hey, I wanna tie one on at eight a.m., I'm allowed."

"And often do." Alex tossed the papers he'd been holding onto the desk, disgust written in the lines across his face.

Paul asked, "So how's our favorite senator?"

"Enjoying his role as a contest judge," Alex replied, slipping his reading glasses from his face and rubbing closed eyes with his thumb and forefinger. Why did he and Paul always seem to be sparring lately? Was he really too critical, or was Paul baiting him by throwing his intemperance in his face every chance he got? He formed a steeple with his long fingers, resting his chin on its tip as he looked across the desk at Paul. Probably both, he decided, but for now, they needed to ally themselves . . . if only for the next several days. After that, well, he intended to talk to Paul about that before they left the office today. But one thing at a time. "You didn't answer my question. Do you plan to attend the party tonight?"

Paul raised a brow at his brother's suddenly friendlier tone. "Sure. Wouldn't miss it."

"Good. Maryann would be disappointed if you pulled one of your no-shows."

Paul guffawed. "Yeah, right! Maryann wouldn't notice if I fell off the face of the earth, as long as you were standing at her side."

Alex's hands slammed down on the desk with a loud bang. "Damn it, Paul! We've got important things to discuss. Does everything I say have to be inhaled as fuel for whatever fire is burning you up lately?"

Paul held up his glass, his shoulders hunched in apology. "Sorry. You're right. We do have some important things to talk about, but not the pageant. I'm about pageanted-out . . ."

Alex's blue eyes glittered with icy anger. "I'll decide what we discuss unless you're finally willing to take over as chairman of the board. Don't forget that you dumped this on me when you elected to go running off around the world playing the jet-setting ass, Paul."

The two men's eyes locked in challenge, but Paul gave it up quickly. "If I remember correctly, that's not exactly the way it happened, but we'll let it pass for now. Okay, you want to discuss the pageant. Discuss."

Alex sighed. "Jesus Christ, you make this hard. The pageant's running smoothly, as you well know. I want to talk about our visitor, Eric Keaton, and how we're going to handle his investigation."

"I take it he still hasn't returned your call."

"He hasn't, and I haven't been able to get through to Guy. I've called him three times, but his secretary insists he's unavailable." He glanced over at the clock on the wall behind his brother. "It's four o'clock in New York. I get the feeling my old friend is avoiding me." He sighed. "But maybe I'm getting paranoid."

Paul's laugh was nasty, mocking. "Keep talking. You'll convince yourself yet." He set his glass on the table at his side, leaning forward to add momentum to his next words. "When are you going to get it, Alex? Men in our position don't have friends. Hangers-on, groupies, kiss-ups, even important connections, and a panoply of gorgeous, willing women, but no friends."

Alex waved a hand, dismissing the volatile subject. Paul had always been jealous of his friendship with Guy Jameson. Like so many things in their lives, it stood between them like barbed wire in the night, recondite and disguised, but always there, potentially dangerous. He shouldn't have spoken his thoughts aloud. There was, however, one important matter he couldn't sidestep any longer. He had avoided it for too long, allowing it to fester. Now was as good a time as any to tell him about the decision he'd come to.

Pushing his chair away from the desk, he stood up, walking away to stare out the window.

Paul rubbed a finger over his bottom lip. Alex was worrying him. He'd been behaving differently ever since Guy's phone call on Monday. He asked cautiously, "Something wrong?"

Alex turned around to look at his brother, his blue eyes clouded and melancholy now. He leaned against the low windowsill, his hands braced behind him. He smiled ruefully. "Wrong? Yes, Paul. Our whole damn lives are wrong. You're wrong. I'm wrong. We should have stopped the pageants four years ago when the second girl was murdered, but we didn't. That's wrong."

Paul jumped to his feet, taking a couple of quick steps toward his brother before rethinking to stop midway. "Hey, whoa, partner. We discussed that with the police, remember? They didn't want us to cancel the pageants then, and they've never wanted us to stop it since. You've read most of the mail we've received over the years. No one wants us to discontinue it. Hell, the Anthony Rose title has become more prestigious than Miss America, and whether you want to admit it or not, whoever the sicko is that killed those girls, we owe a great deal of our profits to him. Nothing like a good murder spree to keep the public focused."

"Well, leave it to you to find a flowering lily in this scum pond."

"Hey, am I wrong?" Paul held out his hands, palms up.

Alex shook his head. "No, you're absolutely right as much as it shames me to admit it, and honestly, I'm glad you brought it up because it makes it easier for me to tell you about my decision."

"Uh-oh, sounds heavy. My knees are knocking and I might just piss my pants."

Alex's hands balled into fists, but he kept his voice even. "This is it, Paul. End of the ride. After Saturday night, it's over. I'm calling a press conference to announce my decision Monday morning." Paul opened his mouth to protest, but Alex held up a hand to stop him, hurrying on with the rest of his revelation before Paul started with all the objections. "And I'm going to talk to Christi. Tell her the truth."

"Okay, Alex, now hang on here. What are you—"

"All of it, Paul. I want you and Maryann there when I talk to her."

"Have you lost your mind?" Paul demanded angrily. "You've sat in this room separating yourself from everyone and everything, all high and mighty with your quiet directives, always quick to ask for advice yet right up there in front to take the credit and in the end, always, always doing as you damned well pleased, regardless of who got stomped on! And now you want to throw everything away, destroy your daughter and wife in the process with no more care than you'd give a cat you're booting out of the way? Well, no way, Alex. No damned way!"

The buzzer sounded on Alex's desk, interrupting Paul's furious protest. Alex's brow was deeply furrowed as he stepped past his brother to push a button on the intercom. "Please hold my calls, Katy."

His secretary's words came back in a flutter of embarrassment and confusion. "I'm . . . sorry, Mr. Anthony. You . . . uh . . . you said that you wanted to be told as soon as Dr. Keaton called."

"Take a number, Katy," he said firmly.

"He's here," came the hushed reply.

The two men standing in the large office looked at each other. Paul's eyes still gleamed with anger, while Alex's reflected uncertainty. He paused a long moment, then inhaled sharply. "Well, then, Katy, show the good doctor in."

Chapter Eighteen

The good doctor pulled on a grin and sauntered into the chief executive's office, thinking he deserved a Tony for his performance.

"Eric," Alex greeted him quietly, not moving from behind his desk.

Eric nodded, rocking on his heels slightly, his hands in his pockets. "Hey, guys, sorry to come in on you like this without an appointment. Hope I'm not interrupting anything."

Paul cast him an ill-humored glance, his blue-green eyes stormy as roiling ocean waters as he headed for a refill from the bar.

Alex searched for words to ease the strain, and finding them, offered a smile. "Not at all. Paul and I were having a pretty lively discussion, as you may have heard. But, hey, we're family." He shrugged his shoulders. "And families argue. What can I say? Besides, we've left several messages. Obviously we were anxious to talk with you and I think your timing might have just been perfect." He chuckled. "As kids, Paul and I could really duke it out. We're both getting up there in years, so it's a good thing we just throw verbal blows now."

"Glad I could help," Eric said, impressed at the CEO's able recovery.

"We've both had a harried day, I'm afraid," Alex went on. "And there are still several long hours ahead of us. As a matter of fact, Paul just came in a few minutes ago. He's having a drink or two to unwind. Could he get you one?"

The smile Eric returned was every bit as smooth and practiced, though he cut a wary sidelong glance at the other man standing with his back to them at the bar. Relaxation didn't appear the goal he was after. He looked back at Alex as he replied. "Not for me, thanks."

Alex waved a hand to a chair. "Please, sit down." He turned toward his brother. "Paul?"

Paul shook his head, not bothering to turn around. "You two go ahead. When I become sufficiently provoked I'll jump in."

Alex cleared his throat, ignoring his brother's humorless remark. "How's your investigation going, Eric?"

"Well, it's going," he said slowly, considering his words with care. "I met with Chief Small at KCPD this morning. Not many surprises there, but my appointment this afternoon proved interesting." Alex raised his brows and Eric could have sworn that Paul's back stiffened slightly. "I met with Ellie Woods."

"Ah, Darin's mother. I met her once, I believe."

Eric sat up slightly. "At his hearing before the Grand Jury?"

Alex shook his head. "No, no. I was there, of course, but I don't remember seeing her then. No, she was at police headquarters with her son when they brought him in last year, the morning after the . . . uh . . . last girl—your client's daughter, Lisa—was killed."

"Uh-huh." Eric turned his attention to the other man. "And what about you, Paul? Have you met her?"

Paul popped the cork back into the decanter before coming across the room to join them.

Eric couldn't help but notice how pronounced his

limp was today, much worse than it had appeared the night before. A light sprinkling of rain had started up again in the past hour and Eric knew about arthritic bones, having a bum shoulder that acted up from time to time from an old football injury.

"Ellie Woods? Sure, I remember her. How could I not? She was crying the entire time her son was being booked; begging the cops not to do it. Her heart was broken. It was pathetic."

Eric was surprised by the compassion. He had expected some unkind remark about the woman's bizarre appearance. "Did you see her at the hearing as well?"

Paul canted his head at an angle and tapped his brow with his glass as if to jog a memory. "The hearing? I don't know. I'm sure she would have been there, so I suppose I did. Why? Is it important?"

Eric offered his lopsided grin. "Probably not. Just curious."

"And who are you going to talk to next?" Alex interjected.

"Dr. Henry Looper, the director of a home for troubled youth. Darin Woods was an inmate there for a time."

Both men reacted as if he'd just delivered a mild electric shock.

"Am I missing something here?" Eric asked.

Alex recovered his equilibrium first. "We—Paul, Maryann, and I—are all extensively involved in charities. Clemens Boys Home is one of our pet projects, if you will. Every summer we open our home to four or five boys. They stay a week. Go fishing with Paul and myself. We usually have a cookout or two, and Maryann supervises a sing-along. That type of thing. When Christi was home, even she participated." He slanted a glance at his brother, then focused on the

Savant once again. "I'm telling you, the coincidences in this . . . ordeal are pretty damned astounding."

"Yeah, well it gets better. The reason Darin was sent to the home in the first place was because of a violent episode where he cut up his mother's house with a knife after a popular girl promised to go to the high school prom with him, then stood him up as she'd intended all along. Made a fool of him, you might say." Eric tugged at his earlobe before adding almost as an aside. "Mrs. Woods described her as blond, blue-eyed, exceptionally pretty."

"Son of a bitch," Paul muttered before tossing back the last ounce of bourbon in his glass. He set the empty tumbler on the table at his side with a loud clunk and shook his head. "I guess that about ties it up for me. Gotta admit, though, I'm blown away. I mean, I always hoped the police had the right guy, but I never really believed it. Just seemed too easy, too pat, you know?"

"I wouldn't be popping any champagne corks just yet, Paul. This may be news to you, but the grand jury had all this and refused to hand down an indictment." His ankle that he'd laid over his knee, rocked as he thought. "Neither one of you remember him as one of the boys who spent a week in Anthony?"

The brothers exchanged questioning glances and shook their heads. "No," Paul said. "But he could've been, I guess. I don't remember the name or face of every boy we've fostered for a week. Hell, we've been doing it for almost twenty years."

"Have you ever told the police or the FBI about your connection to the home?" Eric asked.

Paul didn't hesitate. "Why would we? They didn't ask and we didn't know that Darin Woods had ever been a resident there."

Alex rubbed his chin thoughtfully. "It's crazy, but I still don't get what one thing has to do with the other.

So Darin was at Clemens. So what? And even if he stayed with us, what does that have to do with anything? I mean, we're good to the kids. So, it can't be some kind of revenge thing."

"And that's not what I'm suggesting, but you said your daughter was involved, interacted with the boys before she went away to school."

"Understand one thing, Keaton. Christi was a good kid with a heart of gold. Hell, if she'd had her way, those boys would have stayed year-round. She wouldn't have done anything to hurt them."

"I hear you, and I'm not implying otherwise," Eric said. "Look, we don't even know that Woods was ever at your place, but if he was, just seeing her might have triggered the feelings that cheerleader created. Don't forget the description I got from his mother. Uncommonly pretty, blond, and blue-eyed."

Alex reached for the phone. "That's enough for me. I'm going to call Agent Sansom. Fill him in."

Eric held up a hand. "Hey, hold it. We might be onto something here and we might not. I'm all for keeping the authorities informed, but why not wait until I meet with Dr. Looper. If Darin Woods was ever a guest at your place, he can confirm it in a few minutes." He shrugged. "If he wasn't, then we don't have anything except another weird coincidence linking you and Woods and those dead girls."

"Okay, but what happens in the meantime if he manages to get by the police and hurt another of our contestants? Doesn't that worry you?" Alex asked.

Eric started to answer, but Paul jumped in.

"And tell me this, Keaton. Why don't the police or the feds have men on Woods twenty-four hours a day? Sweet Jesus, if they're so certain he's the lunatic who's been cutting up these girls, why are they watching the contestants and not him? And don't tell me they are, 'cause they're not. I asked."

Knowing as he did that the point was moot, Eric didn't look Paul in the eye as he answered. Instead, he found a spot on the wall to focus on. "I'm sure he explained about Mr. Woods's constitutional rights."

"Yeah," Paul said, biting the words out in angry chopped pieces. "And I'll tell you just what I told him. Fuck his rights. He can shove them straight up his ass, far as I'm concerned. There are five dead women who're never going to be able to speak for their rights again."

"Paul's right," Alex said, "but this isn't getting us anywhere. If Woods is protected by some legal mumbo jumbo, that just means we have to do every- thing in our power—just as we are—to ensure he doesn't get anywhere near our contestants this year."

Eric looked from one man to the other, then back to his neutral spot on the wall. "Well, let's just hope Woods is the right guy. Then we won't have to worry about anyone else being killed."

Paul's eyebrows shot up. "You're so sure he won't get past the police?"

Eric met his gaze straight on. When it came to lying, he was a trained pro, but in this case he could look the man in the eye and tell him the absolute truth. "I can guarantee it, Paul. If Darin Woods is our killer, there won't be another victim."

Paul grinned as he swiped his glass from the table and got to his feet. "I think that kind of reassurance deserves a drink. Sure you won't join me, Eric? Alex?"

Both men ignored the question as Alex picked up the ball Eric had dropped and Paul hadn't noticed. "But you're not convinced Woods is the killer. Isn't that what you're really saying?"

"I'm not saying anything."

"But you are implying," Alex said softly. "Why not spit it out?" He laughed abruptly and leaned back in his chair, folding his hands over his taut stomach. "I heard a very big 'if' when you were talking about Woods being the Rose Murderer. And then there's the part about the guarantees you want to make us. How can you give us assurances even the police and FBI can't?"

Eric perked up. There was challenge in Alex Anthony's tone. Why? Was it possible he knew about the hit-and-run death of Darin Woods? No way . . . unless he was the driver of that unidentified truck that had mowed the guy down. Eric's heart quickened. Then slowed in disappointment at Alex's next words.

"It's been a long day, Keaton, and I can't see an end in sight, so why don't we just stop all this Mickey Mouse bullshit. Tell us where you're coming from or leave me to talk to my source inside the KCPD."

Eric smiled congenially. "I'm just trying to earn my bread and butter and keep another young woman from getting butchered. So, instead of fighting me, why don't you"—he drew a circle in the air with his finger—"all you Anthonys—come over to my side and help me wrap this six-year murder case up, huh?"

"We'd be glad to help, Doctor, only we—" He paused, retracing the imaginary circle Eric had just drawn in the air. "—All of us Anthonys can't help but feel you don't care which jackass you pin the tail to as long as he has 'Anthony' written all over him."

Eric considered that for a moment. "You know, Alex, I haven't focused on you as suspects. Really. At least not above anyone else. But now that you bring it up, I haven't been able to exclude you either. Can you help me exclude you?"

The brothers exchanged enigmatic glances, but neither spoke.

Eric tapped his chin with his forefinger, his dark eyes glowing with appreciative respect. It was always more fun when the mice understood the game as well as the cat. He waited them out, allowing the silence to stretch taut.

Alex glared at him, an angry tic working in his jaw, and Paul stood swilling his drink, his expression as murky as the amber liquid in his glass.

"Where does Christianne fit into all of this, do you suppose?" Eric asked suddenly.

Alex's face paled perceptibly, and Eric noticed that his hands trembled as he gripped the arms of his chair. When he finally found his voice, he managed little more than a whisper. "We're not fools, Keaton, and we're not blind, but I can assure you the police pursued this same line of questioning from the beginning. And know what they learned? Not a damned thing, because there isn't anything . . . except some demented killer's desire to hurt this family."

Paul slammed his glass on the bar, sloshing the drink over the rim and onto his hand. Reaching into his pocket for a handkerchief, he wiped at it unsteadily. "Look, do us a favor, hotshot, and go find someone else to bug, while you take those people's money. The police and FBI have worked this from every angle, and we've done our best to accommodate you because of our long-standing friendship with your boss, but we don't have time to oblige this kind of crap any longer."

Eric smiled, not a bit disappointed with the rise he had gotten from both men. "I guess there's no question I've overstayed my welcome. Sorry I upset you."

He stood up, then took his time straightening the crease in his trousers. "I just don't want anyone forgetting that Christi could be in danger. I have barely begun to dig into the rubble here, and I've no doubt there'll be a few skeletons uncovered. But I'm only concerned with investigating the facts I come across as they pertain to the murders and, of course, with keeping Christi and the current contestants in the pageant alive." He'd kept his tone grave, but offered a friendly smile now, directed at both men. "I'll confess I haven't learned much more at this point than I knew last night, but just between us? I think the police and feebies, ah, FBI, are wrong about Darin Woods. I don't believe he's our man."

Alex's brows rose with that. "Yeah? And where in the hell is that coming from?"

Eric pursed his lips as he considered his answer. He jabbed his stomach just above his belt. "Right here, Alex. Instinct born in the gut. Hardly scientific, but I've been listening to it for a lot of years." He stepped forward to shake Alex's hand, then Paul's. "I'd like to talk to each of you alone, as I said last night. I might have some personal questions that you'd feel more comfortable answering if we keep it one on one."

"Call for an appointment," Alex said, his tone cordial though his message was clear and pointed. He didn't like being intruded upon unexpectedly and wouldn't tolerate it a second time. "Tonight's out, of course. Perhaps we can set something up for tomorrow."

"I'm booked in the morning, but talk to your secretary about something later in the day. Or you can leave a message at the hotel. Anytime after two." He hesitated. "And Maryann? Should I phone the house to schedule an interview with her?"

"I'm sure that would be fine," Alex said, hardly managing a civil smile any longer. "She's very anxious to help, so—"

"What kind of personal questions?" Paul asked.

Eric resisted the urge to grin. He'd laid out the cheese and the mouse had come sniffing. So now the cat would have a little fun. He shrugged easily. "Nothing specific. You know, anything that might help me know each of you better or help me understand why someone would want to destroy Anthony Enterprises and use your daughter as a kind of hostage."

"Hey, we've bent over backward here on account of Guy, but you don't have any authority to go prying into our private lives," Paul said tersely, his quick temper surfacing again.

Eric crossed the room to the door and pulled it open a few inches before stopping. "No, you're right there, Paul. I'm not a cop. I have to rely on your desire to help and I just thought . . . well, you seemed so eager to cooperate last night."

Ignoring the implication, Alex jumped in with one of his own. "I understand you were with the FBI a few years back. Why'd you decide to trade it in for work in the private sector?"

Eric smiled, though he was caught off guard. He pushed back his shirtsleeve cuff to reveal a handsome Rolex watch and felt both men's gazes follow him there. "Pay's better."

"Huh, and here we thought it had to do with that psycho, who bombed the cathedral and killed your brother and fiancée," Paul said.

This time the grin was stiffer. "That, too," Eric said as he stepped from the office and pulled the door closed behind him. He took a deep stabilizing breath. He'd been sucker punched and it was going to take him a moment to recover from the residual sting.

Chapter Nineteen

Eric returned to his hotel, satisfied as he glanced at his watch that he still had time to make a few phone calls and grab a shower before leaving for his appointment at the Samuel Clemens Boys Home. He stopped at the front desk to pick up his messages, then detoured to the bar to order a sandwich and beer to be delivered to his room. He nodded to the other people on the elevator before turning his attention to his messages. Guy had called again, and he was reminded to return Christi Anthony's phone call. He was digging into his pocket for his room key when he came to the last message taken just ten minutes before. It was from Dr. Looper.

Regret emergency. Must postpone appointment.
Please call to reschedule.

Eric muttered a curse as he entered his room and tossed the small slips of paper onto the desk as he shrugged from his jacket. Well, it appeared that he had the entire evening to himself. Maybe he should cancel the sandwich and go out for a relaxing dinner.

First things first, he decided as he pulled the phone from the desk, flopping down across the bed to return his calls.

He dialed Guy's private number at the office. His boss answered on the second ring, sounding harried.

"Hey, Pappy," Eric said.

"Keaton. I've been waiting for your call."

Eric frowned, sitting up slightly, his boss's impatient greeting alerting him. "What's wrong, Guy?"

"Well, for starters, the Anthonys have phoned me three times today. I didn't take their calls—couldn't actually, but it's just as well since I thought I'd better find out what you've stirred up before talking with them."

Eric relaxed, tucking an arm behind his head as he lowered himself to his pillow and nudged his loafers from his feet. "Far as I know, everything's about as copacetic as expected. Initially they were cordial, friendly even. Things are a bit more tense now, but that's only normal." He could hear the flick of Guy's lighter as he lit a cigarette.

"Then why the hell has Alex been trying so hard to reach me?" he demanded, his voice angrier than the situation warranted.

Eric could feel his good humor fading. "Probably because of their little secret I stumbled across last night," he answered testily.

"What secret?"

"Your friend's daughter, Guy. That's why I was calling you last night. Why the hell didn't you warn me, give me a clue, something?"

"Christianne? Why would I warn you about her? What the hell are you talking about, Eric?"

Eric didn't answer right away. Swinging his legs over the side of the bed, he sat up. "Judas Priest, Guy, didn't you think that maybe you should've clued me in about what to expect when I saw her?"

"Goddamn it, what are you talking about!"

"White-blond hair. Blue, blue eyes. Beautiful. Tall. Classically Nordic. Anything sound familiar, Pappy?"

There was a long pause from the other end. Eric could hear the faint sound of knocking and then Guy's muffled voice as he spoke to someone else in the room with him. "Okay, I'm back. Sorry. Now what did you just say?"

Eric shook his head. Where was the man's mind tonight? "Hey, what's up? Something wrong?"

Guy's voice was softer when he answered this time, weary and more strained than Eric could ever remember. "Yeah, Keaton, something's very wrong, but let's get through this first. What about Alex's daughter?"

Eric's reply was mechanical, his thoughts on Guy's mysterious and troubling admission. "She's practically a dead ringer for the five murder victims, Pappy. Same coloring, gorgeous. So much like those women it's spooky. Why didn't you tell me?"

"This is news to me. Christ, last time I saw her she was, I don't know, four, maybe five. She was fair, yeah, but I wouldn't have made any connection."

"Well, I swear she could be the sister of any one of those dead women. When you see her, you don't think about her parentage. You see Rose Murder victims, Guy." He paused, his teeth clicking softly as he wondered about his boss's admission. "I thought you and Alex Anthony were close friends, Pappy."

"We are. Very good friends." Guy's tone was almost cold. Eric flinched with the inexperience of meriting his boss's ire. "I wasn't aware that frequent visits with the whole family were a prerequisite for friendship, Keaton."

Guy fell silent, and Eric could imagine him sitting behind his big desk, lighting another cigarette and taking his time to let the soothing smoke stream from his mouth. "Okay, so go on. What have you found out?"

"Not a hell of a lot," Eric admitted, "but the two things I have learned are important. First, Christianne Anthony. The police and FBI agree that her likeness to the murder victims is probably a key factor here. Second, there are a lot of coincidences that bother me, but we can get into all that when I've separated the wheat from the chaff."

"You've met with Mike Sansom?"

"Sort of. He paid me a visit here at my hotel last night. Went fine. Don't worry."

"Yeah, I can hear how fine it went by the way you're clipping your words. What about your old friend, Chief Small? You see him yet?"

"Yep. First thing this morning. Same old Dan. Warm but stubborn. Thinks the case is sewn up. Doesn't want me stirring any hornet's nest just as he's retiring."

Guy was silent for a few seconds, chewing the morsels his *Savant* was tossing his way, getting a taste for how well the probe was progressing. "Anything else?"

"Yeah, one thing, and this one is major. Of course the police have decided the case is wrapped up. But the feebs agree. They're convinced Darin Woods—the suspect arrested last year—is guilty."

"But you're not certain."

"Well, this Woods character had opportunity, motive—an apparent obsession with blond, blue-eyed babes—maybe even a connection to the Anthony girl. Also confessed when they brought him in."

"So where's the problem? Why not call our clients, fill them in, and let them decide if they want to keep paying for something the authorities have resolved?"

Eric rubbed a hand through his hair, frustration stirring a restlessness he wasn't accustomed to these days. Hell, he wasn't even close to wrapping this up. "I met the poor jerk's mother today, and I'm convinced that he was a fruitcake, all right? Abused by his dad as a kid, and lonely and pathetic as a man, but not a killer. He retracted the statement he made to the police the next day, even said he had seen someone leaving our client's daughter's house, but the police didn't buy it."

"Did he ID anyone?"

"No. Said he didn't know who it was, but a few weeks ago, he told his mother that he had found out who the person was."

"So who was it?" Guy asked impatiently.

"He wouldn't say, but he did tell her he was going to confront the person on his own."

"Wait a minute. You're saying you think he found out who the killer was and decided to blackmail him? Jesus Christ, Eric, have you talked to Woods and asked him about it?"

"No can do," Eric said, building to his surprise. "The guy's dead, Pappy. Struck down by a hit-and-run driver in the wee hours this morning."

Another long silence followed the bullet Eric had just fired. Finally Guy asked, "So you think he went out to meet with the Rose Murderer, and was mowed down. Makes sense. With him dead, the police wrap the case and the perp can't be blackmailed."

"I don't think he intended to blackmail the guy. From what I get, Darin Woods was a loser, but he wasn't a criminal. But the other part—him being killed to keep him quiet—yeah, I buy that. And the best part—or the worst depending on which side of the line you're standing on here—I think I can prove Darin Woods was innocent."

"How?"

"I haven't got it all together yet, but I don't think you're going to be very happy with the way I'm leaning here," Eric admitted cautiously.

"This your way of pussyfooting around the fact that you believe the Anthonys are involved somehow? Shit, Eric, you aren't telling me you think one of them is the killer, are you?"

"No," Eric said slowly, carefully. "I'm just saying that whoever murdered those women is connected to the Anthonys, and either your friend's daughter is the real target or whoever this son of a bitch is, wants them to think she is."

Guy heaved a weary sigh.

"And I'll tell you," Eric went on, "they're all nervous about me being here. At first I thought it was just the look-alike thing with Christi and the murdered contestants. More and more, though, I'm thinking there's something else. I don't know what it is, but I'm convinced they're hiding something. Maybe they're just frightened or could be they're covering for someone. Whatever, I'm getting under their skin."

Guy's voice was tired when he spoke, though lacking its earlier anger. "Has it occurred to you that they may be simply trying to work past a lot of pain? This can't have been easy for them."

"Of course. In fact, I'm certain that's part of it, but there's more. How about I call you in a day or two? I'm meeting with all of them tomorrow, one at a time. If I don't call you tomorrow night, you'll know I'm still running on hunches. But if I land on anything concrete, I'll let you know."

"All right, but tread softly, Eric. You may be snooping in the wrong alley."

"Will do," Eric agreed amicably, his tone light. "Okay, Pappy, your turn. You're upset, so what's up?"

Guy hesitated. "We're not sure what's going down yet, Eric, but it looks like we might have big problems in Tingo Maria."

Eric could feel the spread of icy fear through his veins. "You've talked to Lee?" he asked cautiously, hopefully.

"Not a word," Guy admitted quietly. "You remember that Torres was going down there with him?" It was a rhetorical question. Guy went on. "We got a call last night from the informant Thornton's been working through. He said everything was all set,

Servetus had bought their cover and they were going in early this morning. Said he'd call us back as soon as he had Thornton and Torres out of there. The way we figure it, he's six hours late."

Eric quickly computed the facts. He and Lee had discussed the assignment in Tingo Maria. Servetus—the drug lord Lee had gone to investigate—was one bad dude, but Lee was good—no, make that the best. And, too, he had Andy Torres with him. The junior investigator had pulled two tours in Nam and thought like a fox. No, Eric thought, he wouldn't count them out. Guy had known what he was doing when he teamed Lee and Andy against Servetus. "Maybe they're just running behind schedule," Eric offered.

"Yeah, well, we hope so, but we just got news over the wires of a big bust down there. If our boys were in the middle when it went down, we're in trouble."

"Oh, shit," Eric muttered. "Look, my appointment for tonight fell through. I'll stay in my room all night. You call as soon as you hear anything."

Guy tried for a laugh. "Get back to work, Keaton. We've been in tight spots before. No sense you sitting around on your ass. If you're not in the room, I'll reach you on the cellular, so keep it turned on."

Eric was pacing the room. He stopped, putting the phone to his chest as he reached inside himself for a modicum of calm. He'd been on enough undercover assignments to understand the real potential for danger. He hoped to God that Lee hadn't gotten himself in a mess he couldn't dig out of. He brought the phone back to his ear, trying to match Guy's brusque, business-as-normal attitude. "Stay in touch, Guy. You know how much Lee—" His voice caught, and he choked off the rest of his sentence.

"You got it," Guy promised before hanging up.

Eric dropped the phone back on the bed, not bothering to hang it up as he flopped down beside it to cover his face with his hands. "Oh, Jesus, don't let anything happen to Lee," he prayed.

A sudden knock on his door jarred him from his painful suppositions. Crossing the room with heavy steps, he opened the door and motioned a room service boy to the table in front of the window.

Moments later, Eric drained the bottled beer into a glass, then poured himself a hefty shot of Scotch from the minibar in a second tumbler. Sandwich and chips were forgotten as he downed the Scotch, then chased it with the beer. He pulled his lips back in a satisfied grimace, as the boilermaker spread its warmth. Refilling his glass with a second shot, he thought of Paul and reluctantly noted the parallel between Paul's heavy drinking and the relief he was pursuing with a vengeance. Staring through the wide picture window at the horizon that blazed red under the setting sun, his thoughts darkened further.

Maybe it was the city.

Maybe it was just unlucky for some people. Like him.

Maybe for the Anthonys, too.

Sure hadn't been too fucking lucky for those five murdered women.

Or that poor slob, Darin Woods.

Or Brylee and David. Never forget about them.

Huh. Could be he was just on a real downer and spiraling lower and lower with every sip of booze.

So maybe he should stop drinking and get back to work. Get this probe behind him and get out of Dodge.

Chapter Twenty

Get out of Dodge.

The phrase reminded Eric of his friend and their parting words at the top of the escalators. He rolled the icy glass of beer across his forehead. Oh, Jesus, he hoped Lee hadn't gotten caught in the cross fire.

No, damn it, he wasn't going to do this. Nobody was as good as Thornton. The former CIA agent knew every trick in the book. If he was in trouble, he'd get himself out. *Finito.*

"And you've got to get your ass back to work," he told his reflection in the window.

Retracing his steps to the nightstand, he snatched up the telephone.

A moment later, Christi's voice, breathless and hurried, came over the line. "Eric, hi. I just came in from the plant. Glad I didn't miss your call."

"Yeah, me, too," he said. Then, "Man, you just don't know."

There was the slightest hesitation on the other end before she laughed. "Wow, you're really good for a girl's ego."

Eric laid back, folding an arm under his head, and closed his eyes. "I could just lie here and listen to the sound of your voice. Let it work its magic."

Again that full, sexy laughter. "Mmm, I like that, but what's wrong? Bad day?"

"Pisser," he admitted.

"Sorry. Can I help?"

The question inspired an idea; a flash of brilliance. He raised up and swung his legs over the side of the bed. "As a matter of fact, I think you can. What are you doing tonight?"

"Well, my family's hosting a party for the pageant judges. I thought I might put in an appearance, though I don't know what they'll say about that. They weren't too happy about my unexpected arrival at the ball last night. Probably prefer that I stay upstairs in my room. Why? Are you coming 'cause if you are, all the frowns in the world couldn't intimidate me out of being down there, too."

"No, actually, I was hoping we could cut out of there for a while. I know a great little out-of-the-way place in Platte City. Great food, good music. Real laid back. What do you say?"

"I don't know, Eric," she said slowly.

"Okay, never mind. Just mark it up to a crazy notion from a crazy guy who's had a real crazy day. I'll see you in the morning. We're still on for eleven-thirty?"

"Yes, but wait. Does this out-of-the-way place have charbroiled hamburgers?"

Eric grinned. "The juiciest damned burgers I ever tasted."

"Well, then, how long will it take you to get here?"

"You mean it?"

"Sure," she said, though he heard a caveat in the single syllable.

"Sure, but what?" he pressed.

"Uh . . . you're not going to believe this."

"Hey, I've heard it all. There's nothing I wouldn't believe, trust me. So, go ahead. Lay it on me."

"Okay, what the hell," she said, then quickly: "Would you mind if we sort of did this on the sly? I mean, could I sneak out and meet you?"

"Ah, ha, it's like that, is it?"

"Well, I don't know. I just don't want to complicate matters." She laughed, and he could hear the embarrassment in her voice.

"That's cool," he told her. "So, tell me how you want to handle it."

"Well, I'd meet you in Platte City, but they've got guys out front to valet park their guests. One of them might slip and say something. Could you come get me? I don't mean pick me up at the front door. There's a different way onto the grounds." She lowered her voice. "You can drive within a few hundred feet of the back door, and no one will ever know you're there."

Eric raised a brow with the portent of her information. "Christi, do very many people know about this way onto your property?"

"I suppose they might, but no one ever uses it except Mother and Daddy and Uncle Paul when they want to come home without passing through town. Why?"

"Never mind. We can talk about it later. Just tell me how to get there."

He listened closely as she described the three narrow lanes he would pass before coming to the turnoff. He didn't think he'd have any trouble. "Okay, got it. What time?"

"I don't think I'd better try to slip out until eight-thirty. Is that too late?" she asked, sounding worried that he might change his mind.

Not a chance, babe, he thought. Okay, so it was weird; a grown man sneaking out with a card-carrying adult woman. But sometimes that's just the way life was and tonight that suited him fine. He was stressed. He flinched at the thought of his best friend, maybe burned, maybe dead even. No, he wasn't going to go there. Not now.

"Eric? Are you still—"

"I'm here. Sorry. I'll see you at eight-thirty . . . and Christi?"

"Uh-huh?"

"Thanks."

"For what?" she asked.

He laughed. "For everything. Coming with me tonight, making me feel good, et cetera, et cetera, et cetera. Tell you what, I'll make a list and give it to you when I get there."

"Ooh," she said, "I think I'm going to enjoy this."

Chapter Twenty-one

The doorbell chimed below as Christi tied the laces on her tennis shoes. Another guest arriving. She smiled, choking back little hiccups of laughter. She was excited. Giddy, like a teenager sneaking out on a first date!

She pulled a hooded plaid jacket from the closet, peeking around the corner of the wall dividing her dressing room from her bedroom to peer at the clock on her nightstand. Eight-twenty! She had to hurry.

Cracking her bedroom door a few inches, she listened to the laughter and music drifting up from the living room. She slipped quietly from her room to sneak down the stairs and crouch a few feet above the last flight. She chewed nervously on her bottom lip and listened again. The party was in full swing. She could hear her mother's tinkling laughter and Uncle Pauls's deep, booming voice as it rose above those of their guests. She waited a few seconds more, listening for her father. There! His soft chuckle in response to a woman's flirtatious comment.

All three accounted for, she tiptoed up the stairs once again, hurrying to the rear staircase. Jeannie would be in the kitchen with the caterers, but Christi could slip out unnoticed if she could get past the doorway and to the dining room to make her escape.

She peered through the archway seeking out the housekeeper among all of the additional temporary staff working around her. When she spotted Jeannie busily directing two men supporting heavy trays into the living room, Christi dashed past the room and out the door to the terrace. She almost gave a victory shout as the brisk night air kissed her cheeks, but she rushed on, satisfied simply to hug herself with congratulations as she ran through the yard.

Rain splattered the earth around her, but she sprinted on, concentrating on the garden and the long row of trees beyond, looking for the place where they parted, separating the land into a narrow lane. Eric would be waiting for her at the other end. She wouldn't worry about the rain. Not tonight. Her feet flying, she kept her eyes straight ahead as she passed the dog pen, her mother's garden and greenhouse, and finally the huge oak where she and Mustard often picnicked. The night got much darker as she entered the mouth of the forest, forcing her to slow to a cautious walk as her feet met the uneven terrain.

A hand snaked out of the dark to grab her arm, bringing a sharp shriek of surprise to her lips.

"Shh. It's me, Eric. I didn't mean to frighten you. I was waiting for you. I didn't want you to have to walk down the drive alone."

Christi collapsed against him, the rich sound of her relieved laughter filling the night.

"Shh," Eric whispered again. "They'll hear us."

Christi laughed harder, burying her face in his coat. "Sorry, I think I'm hysterical."

Eric wrapped his arms around her, pressing his mouth against the back of her head to muffle the sounds of his own laughter, which he suddenly couldn't contain. "It's catching," he said, then, "Come on." Taking her hand, he encouraged her to an easy jog along the drive to his car.

Christi was breathless by the time she climbed into the car beside him. She inhaled great gulps of air, still trying to stifle the laughter that bubbled from her as

Eric backed the car out to the gravel road. She rubbed her cold hands together briskly. "Oh, Eric, this is so much fun."

Eric smiled but kept his eyes fastened to the rear-view mirror, alert for any sign that someone had seen them. The night was still and quiet. They were more than a mile from the house before he let out his breath. "Okay! I think we've lost the Indians, Kemosabi."

Christi pulled the hood of her coat back, her appreciative laughter spilling out again along with her long, silky hair.

Eric looked over at her, his eyes bright with appreciation. "I like your hair like that," he said.

Pulled back in a loose, casual plait that began at the bottom of her neck, long, pale tendrils framed the delicate features of her face.

"You're beautiful, Christianne Anthony," he said softly, reaching for her hand to offer a quick sincere squeeze.

"Thank you," she replied simply.

Eric chuckled.

"What? Why are you laughing?" she asked, turning to the side slightly so that she was leaning against the car door.

Eric shrugged. "Oh, I don't know," he began. But he did know, and he suddenly wanted to tell her. "Because you make me feel good. You're different. You're wealthy, intelligent, gorgeous. Yet you seem so utterly unaffected. Like the way you accepted my compliment."

"You were expecting coy? Well, that's Mother. She has it down to a science. I'm no good at it. My grandmother used to say I had too much of her in me."

"If that's true, I probably would have liked her a lot."

"Mmm, yes, I'm sure of it. She was special."

"Like her granddaughter," he said.

She smiled, letting her head fall back. "So tell me about you. Your work is fascinating. Which reminds me, Uncle Paul said you're one of a trio of handpicked elite investigators who get the big-time assignments and always nab the bad guys. So, are you all like the Mission Impossible guys? Never run out of tricks or get in corners too tight to wriggle out of?" Her tone was light, teasing, but a frown quickly knotted between her brows when she noticed the expression on Eric's face. "Hey, I was joking."

Eric's throat constricted with pain, the sudden picture of his friend's laughing dark face flashing before his mind's eye. "It's nothing. Forget it."

"Eric," she said, laying a hand on his arm, "something I said upset you. I can see that. Please tell me. Otherwise I'll worry about it all night."

Eric reached for her hand and drew it to his lap to squeeze her fingers gently. "Not tonight. Tonight is yours."

"Well, I won't enjoy myself unless I feel like you can confide in me, too. Won't you trust me . . ." She stopped in midsentence, embarrassment flooding her face with high color. "Oh, my gosh, this has something to do with another woman, doesn't it? One of the other *Savants* is a girl, right? And the two of you . . . oh, wow, am I an idiot or what? Sorry. Really! I wasn't prying, I swear."

Eric did laugh at this. He laughed hard. "Roni? The two of us involved? Now that's rich, but no. No way."

More confused than ever, Christi could only shake her head. "I'm lost."

Eric got his amusement under control once more and explained. "Yes, one of the *Savants* is a woman. Veronica La Marc. Roni. But the two of us are not involved in any sense of the word except as members of Guy's Dream Team as he sometimes calls us.

"Don't get me wrong, she's an ace investigator, one of the best, and we're friends in the same sort of crazy way that guys become buddies when they're sharing a canteen in a trench or crossing a mine field side by side. But that's as far as it goes." He laughed again, the release feeling good.

Christi smiled, liking the sound, yet still curious about what it was she'd said to hurt him before. Better to leave it alone for now, she decided. He'd said he wanted to relax, so relax they would. "Okay, so what's wrong with this Roni person? Too much competition?" she teased.

"Ah! She'd love that one! She's very much the feminist. Can do anything a man does but better. Seriously, though, she's okay. Just not my type. Everything's over the top with Roni. Could make a guy old before his time."

Christi giggled at his admission. "Kind of like my mother?"

Eric grinned. "Uh-uh. I wouldn't touch that one. Lee would—" His words came to a sudden halt as he drew in breath over a sharp, ragged edge in his throat.

"Sure it wouldn't help to talk about it?" she prodded gently.

Eric took a moment for the worst of his pain to pass, but this time he didn't back away from the subject. It was easy to talk to Christi, and he needed to talk about his friend. "Maybe, yeah."

She took his hand that had been laying on his thigh and held it between both of her own, but she didn't push.

After a few seconds with only the drone of the car engine filling the quiet of the night, he spoke. "I don't know if there's anything to tell yet. Lee—Levi Thornton—is the third specialist. One of LINC's so called *Savants.*" He chuckled, then explained. "He hates being called that. I used to be uncomfortable with it, too. It's so damned pretentious sounding, but after a while it became just another tag like investigator, detective, specialist. Anyway, Lee and I are tight. Like brothers. In fact, I used to have a brother. David. He was killed a few years back, but that's a whole other story. The thing is, we were pretty close, though never like Lee and I. I don't know how to explain it. I don't even know how we got to this place, but it's like our souls are linked, you know?"

She didn't. How could she? She'd never had a friendship like that. Still, she nodded, encouraging him to tell her.

"We liked each other straight off, but it was more than that. Right from the beginning, he'd think something, and I'd say it out loud or the other way around. There was never any professional jealousy, and neither of us has ever needed to prove anything to the other. I'm his youngest son's godfather."

"But something's wrong," Christi nudged gently.

"That's the thing. I don't know for sure. He's working in Tingo Maria. Left for there the same day I flew out here. Monday, was it? And today's only Wednesday. Jesus, it seems like weeks instead of only days."

"I've read about that place. There are some big-time drug dealers trafficking out of there, right? Is that what your friend is doing? Working a sting?"

Eric glanced over at his beautiful passenger, his eyes wide with apprecation. "Exactly."

"And you're worried something's gone wrong?"

Eric rubbed a hand over his face, sighing deeply. "This wasn't supposed to go this way, you know? I wanted to take you out for some fun, and here I am unloading on you."

Christi looked straight ahead, her hands folded in her lap. "Well," she said at last, "it wouldn't really be much fun for either of us if we had to pretend to be having a good time. Besides, I don't have to have fun to enjoy being with you."

"You're something else, Christianne Anthony." He reached for her hand again, clasping it tightly and resting it against his thigh as they drove. "Okay. Levi. He's missing or in trouble or maybe just keeping low, but we've lost contact with him for the time being. He's probably all right. He's not just good, he's the best, and he's gotten out of tight spots before. I know. I've been with him. But I can't help worrying that he may be in too deep this time."

"I hope you hear from him soon," she said quietly.

"Me, too," he said. Then as a whispered plea to the universe, *Oh, yeah, please, me, too.*

Chapter Twenty-two

They didn't speak for the next several miles. Their conversation had touched Eric deeply. His thoughts stayed with his friend for a few mintues, but he found them turning back to the woman riding beside him.

Privileged, pampered, and protected.

An only child and the sole heiress to a dynasty.

An intelligent young woman who had actually put her credentials and smarts to work to prove herself more than a beautiful corporate figurehead.

And very possibly the polestar of a sinister murder scheme.

Yet so little of that was reflected in the woman she'd revealed. She was poised, certainly. Confident and clever, sure. But where was the pigheaded arrogance he'd encountered in her parents and uncle?

Out of nowhere, a memory flashed through his mind. A memory of another woman from another time. As if she were seated beside him, he heard Brynlee's voice:

"I don't know why it went so wrong, Eric; why *I* went so wrong. Some people are just inherently good. It's something, I believe, that radiates from the core of their souls. They're not subject to the temptations and sins as are the rest of us. I wish I were one of them. Then I wouldn't be hurting you like this. I wouldn't—"

Eric squeezed his eyes shut for a heartbeat as he pushed away the painful memory. He felt Christi's fingers tighten around his hand, heard her ask, "Are you okay?"

He looked at her and smiled. "Yeah," he said, and it was true. Bryn had been right. Sometimes people were just plain good and all the ugliness in the world couldn't influence that one way or the other. "I was just remembering something a friend once said to me. I didn't understand it until I met you."

Christi tilted her head, her brows raised though the corners of her lips were quirked in the beginning of a smile. "Well, I don't get it, but I'm not suppose to, huh?"

"Nope."

"Okay. Once when I was twelve, Mom took me to a child psychologist." She tucked a long tendril of hair behind her ear and cast him a playful, sidelong glance. "Don't worry, I wasn't crazy or anything. I just got up one morning and decided I didn't want to go to school anymore and no one was going to make me. All the cajoling, threats, and bribery failed to change my mind. I simply decided I was smart enough, and besides, I had a new puppy—"

"Mustard?"

She giggled at that. "Oh, gosh, no. That was sixteen years ago. No, this was a little black lab named Licorice. Anyway, I wanted to teach her tricks, then try out for the *Tonight Show*. Remember how Johnny Carson always had animal tricks on there? I just knew I'd get a shot at show business, then I could get work as an animal trainer for the movies. You know, work with dogs like Lassie and Benji. But Mother was convinced I was having some sort of nervous breakdown. So she took me to see this lady shrink, and she did all these tests. Rorschach, word association, fit the different shapes in the right slots, blah, blah, blah."

"Uh-huh, and what happened? You become a famous animal trainer or did the psychologist convince you to go back to school?"

She wrinkled her nose at him. "Smart-ass."

"Sorry."

"Apology accepted, and to answer your question, neither one. She told my parents I was a perfectly normal preadolescent. So if you're trying to analyze me, Doctor, you're wasting your time."

"Actually, that's exactly what I was thinking," he confessed. "You are the most amazingly down-to-earth woman I've ever met, and you've had every opportunity to be spoiled rotten."

"Oh, great, now I'm blushing, and I don't blush well. Instead of looking all pink and pretty like most girls, my skin's so fair it gets all blotchy. So, let's talk about something else."

"Okay," he agreed, nudging her arm with his elbow. "Tell me how the animal training went."

"It didn't. Never even got started. Someone killed my puppy, Licorice . . ." Her voice caught, but she quickly recovered. "Cut her to ribbons. The sheriff said it was probably kids from town. I just couldn't understand it. She was a beautiful black lab. Playful, smart. Who would hurt her? I was devastated, so my parents refused to let me have another one until I graduated from high school. That's when I got Mustard. I took him through a six-week obedience course, but that's as far as my career as an animal trainer went. Just as well, anyway. I have a hard time even being stern with him. Especially after someone, maybe the same kids tried to kill him, too." She shuddered.

"Want to tell me about it?"

She shrugged. "Not much to tell, really. It was just like the other time—storming like crazy. Except this time I woke up. I was eighteen, too old to be fanciful, but the wind was whipping the trees and I swear it sounded like they were crying. Anyway, for some reason I started worrying about Mustard, so I went out to check on him, and he was laying under a big oak, bleeding and badly cut up. This time we were lucky. We got him to the vet and of course, as you know, he pulled through. After that, Daddy had our grounds-keeper build a pen for him so he couldn't roam and get into trouble, and he's been safe ever since. But now that I'm home, I still get nervous when it storms and I have to go out and check on him. We're buddies."

"I didn't see him in the pen."

"No. He's curled up fast asleep inside his doghouse, I guarantee you. He doesn't like the rain, but also, he's getting older. Prefers sleep to guard duty."

"Okay, so I've learned you're a sucker for dogs. What else do you like?"

"Going to football and baseball games, though I had to substitute soccer while I was in Italy. I like music. Doesn't matter what kind. Classic, country, rock. Almost everything except maybe heavy metal."

"Yeah, me, too. Okay, go on. What else?"

"Umm, the typical girlie stuff like shopping for to-die-for clothes and shoes—I'm an absolute shoe freak, which suited me perfectly to Rome! And I love old movies that make me cry, and sitcoms that make me laugh and . . . jabbering," she added, her eyes suddenly huge. "Good grief, why didn't you stop me?"

Eric was laughing. "Because I like listening to you."

"Lucky for you," she said.

They'd turned off the highway at the Platte City exit, and though Christi had grown up in the area, she looked around as if he was taking her into a whole new world, and Eric thought that in a way he might just be.

He pulled up in front of a small restaurant called Rowdy's. The owner, Wally Barnes, an old school friend of Eric's, greeted them with typical downhome friendliness. "Why, speak of the devil, and up he jumps!"

Eric hunched his shoulders in reply to Christi's questioning look. "I have no idea what he's talking about."

Wally slapped him on the back, pointing at the television set positioned in a corner above the bar. "You were on the six o'clock news, son. We was jest talkin' about how you made it to the big time, just like it was predicted in our senior class yearbook. They're saying as how you quit the FBI after that bombing that took Dave and—"

"Yeah," Eric said, cutting him off. "That's old news, buddy. Now I'm just a private citizen like anyone else."

"Oh, sure, ya are. That's why it's your mug I just seen up there on the television with all them fancy folk at the Rose Ball last night." His eyes were doing a quick two-step, shuffling back and forth from Eric to Christi. It was obvious he was itching for an introduction, but was trying hard not to overstep the boundaries that folks in their parts defined as good manners.

"Hey," he finally said. "Now that you're here, you can tell us what a *Savant* is. See the fella at the end of the bar? The one with the handlebar mustache? That's Jeff Franklin and he says it's like one of them people you see on *Geraldo*. You know, ain't smart enough to tie their shoes, but can paint a picture good as Michael Angelo or figure out a convoluted math problem in their heads in two shakes of a dog's tail. But I told 'em that can't be it, 'cause you could tie your shoes real good. You just never could do nothing else to speak of."

"Ha, ha, ha," Eric said, though he grinned at the guys all guffawing at the bar. "Yeah? Well, who's holding hands with a gorgeous gal, and who's only got a bottle of beer to hold on to?"

"Score one for the big-city private dick," a man called from the far end of the bar.

"Hey," another guy shouted. "That what a *Savant* is? A dick?"

"Come on," Eric said, slipping his arm around Christi's shoulders and steering her toward the door. "This was a bad idea."

"Whoa, Keaton. Hold on. They're just having a little fun. Come on, I'll give you a table in the back of the room where no one'll bother you." He grinned at Christi, who smiled back, though she was watching Eric.

Eric winked, reassuring her. Then to Wally, "Lead the way."

Wally grabbed two menus and moved toward a private booth. "It's good to see you, bud, but I've minded my manners long as I can stand it. Introduce me to your lady, Eric."

"Wally, Christi. Christi meet Wally. Okay, now you're acquainted, can we have some time to ourselves?" His tone was light, good-natured, but it was clear he meant it.

"Pleasure meeting ya, Christi." Wally winked, winning another smile from her as he offered them both a plastic-covered menu. "I'll be back to take your order. Waitress called in sick, so I'm afraid you're stuck with me."

Eric looked at Christi. "Still got your heart set on that burger?" At her nod, he waved off the menus and placed their orders.

"Be back in a few," Wally said.

"Now that's something I've missed living in New York," Eric joked, shaking his head. "Good ol' redneck charm."

"I think he's nice," she told him.

"Yeah, he is. He and I played football together. He

was good. Had a scholarship lined up for Mizzou. Then his dad had a heart attack our senior year, and Wally gave it all up to stay home and take care of his mom. Took the insurance money from his dad's estate, moved them up here, and opened this place. Didn't know a skillet from a saucepan, his mom used to say. But he's made a good living. And you don't have to worry about the other guys either. I chose this place because I knew the folks we'd run into are mostly farmers. They're loud and rowdy, just like the name of the restaurant, but they're harmless, and they don't really care who we are. In other words, there won't be any reporters rushing the place in the next hour just because they saw my face on TV at the ball last night and probably think you're one of the contestants."

They talked a few more minutes about Wally and his good ole boy customers, and before they knew it, Wally was approaching again, their dinner orders on a tray.

"Okay," Eric said, as he salted his fries, "you were telling me all about yourself."

"Enough already!" she said, shaking her head adamantly.

"Okay," Eric said, relenting. He grinned.

"What are you thinking?" she asked.

"Promise you won't laugh?"

"Swear."

"I was remembering how you looked last night and imagining all the men who've surely fallen in love with you, and I was suddenly jealous as hell."

She laughed and bit her bottom lip as she shook her head. "Not one," she said.

"Oh, come on," Eric said. "I know you're trying to make me feel better, but no one would believe that."

"It's true," she said.

Eric raised a skeptical brow. "Uh-huh, and what

about that Italian dude you mentioned when we were talking in the driveway? What was his name?"

Christi laid her burger down and dabbed at her mouth. "Carlo," she told him. "But he wasn't in love with me. He was just a very accomplished, very persuasive liar. And now you've ruined my appetite by reminding me how easily duped I was."

Music started up on a radio in a corner of the room, and Eric grinned as he recognized the current hit. He reached across the table and wiped a dollop of mayonnaise from the corner of her lip, then licked it off his finger. "You finished? Seriously?"

"Yeah, I guess," she said, her tone suspicious. "Why?"

Eric reached in his hip pocket and pulled out his billfold. He extracted a twenty-dollar bill, tossed it onto the table, then slid from the booth and grabbed her hand. "Come on."

"Where are we—"

"Just hurry," he said, dragging her at a half run from the diner.

Wally came out from the kitchen just as they reached the front door. "Hey, where are you guys going?"

"It was great. Later," Eric called, raising a hand in farewell over his shoulder.

Outside, he opened the car door, coaxing her inside, and raced to the other side. He sat next to her and turned the key in the ignition.

"Eric," Christi said. "What's wrong?"

He held up a finger as he scanned the radio for the same tune that had been playing in the restaurant. "Shh." A moment later he grinned and turned toward her to capture her face between his hands. "Sorry. I didn't want to do this in there, and I couldn't take the chance that we'd miss it. Sometimes things happen just 'cause everything's right, and you've got to seize the moment.''

"I don't understand what you're talking about," she said, confused though excitement was beginning to replace worry.

"Listen. 'Kissed by a Rose.' It's perfect and I have to find out . . ." He didn't finish the sentence. Instead he covered her mouth with his.

His lips were gentle, questioning, until Christi answered the request by grasping his wrists with her hands and parting her lips to him. She moaned as he met her tongue with his and moved a hand to the back of her neck, drawing her closer.

The kiss was passionate and hungry, demanding and desperate. The last strains of the music were fading by the time he reluctantly ended the kiss. Another one was already beginning when he caught her bottom lip between his teeth. With a ragged groan and every measure of control he could muster, he pulled away.

"I was right," he managed on a long, harsh breath.

She pressed her fingers against her hot cheeks. "Well, whatever it is, I'm glad it worked for you, 'cause it certainly worked for me."

Eric laughed. "My God, woman, it's the crazy way we met, the murder investigation, this Rose Pageant your family hosts, those fucking flowers all over that ballroom last night, and you, the most incredible rose of them all. When that song started playing, I knew what I had to do, and I knew it couldn't wait. It had to be right then 'cause that's what the cosmos were telling me."

A slow, sassy grin spread her lips. "And?"

"And nothing," he said, as he shifted into reverse and backed out of the parking space. But as he turned the car onto the road, he was grinning. "Right now, I'm going to get you back home. And tomorrow I'm coming to interview you in my official capacity as a private investigator."

"Well, that's disappointing," she said, sliding closer in the seat and reaching a hand in between the buttons on his shirt to brush his chest with her fingertips.

He caught her hand and drew it into his lap. "God, you're not making this easy."

"You started it," she said.

"Uh-uh," he argued, bringing her hand to his lips and kissing her palm. "That wasn't starting. That was just testing. But I swear to God, as soon as I get this probe behind us, we're not only going to start, we're going to finish it."

She traced his jawline with a fingertip and sighed. "Umm, I don't know if I can wait that long."

"I'll hurry," he promised.

Chapter Twenty-three

Eric glanced at the clock on the nightstand beside his bed. Five forty-nine. Too early to get up. On the other hand, if he couldn't sleep, why lie there staring at the ceiling? If nothing else, he could go over his notes from the day before. Maybe call room service for some breakfast. Or he could just think about Christianne Anthony. No, that was out. If he spent any more time with thoughts of her, he'd find himself taking another cold shower, and hell, he'd already suffered through a couple of those. Two nights in a row was enough. He wasn't going to start his day off that way.

The phone rang, startling him for a second, but his surprise changed to pleasure as he considered the possibility that it might just be Christi. He was still grinning as he put the receiver to his ear and spoke, "Eric Keaton."

"It's Guy. You asked me to keep you posted." There was a short pause followed by a long, labored sigh. "It doesn't look good, Eric. I've been up all night."

"Just tell me," Eric said hoarsely.

"Okay, but understand, we don't have any definites yet. Just a few probables with some big holes. But we did finally hear back from our informant. He was excited and hard to understand in his heavily accented English, but he confirms that Lee and Tommy went in for the meet with Servetus as planned. Our man was there when they arrived, but Servetus told him to get lost, so he wasn't around when everything went down. It doesn't look like our guys showed up at the wrong time and interrupted a sting as we thought. 'Course the local police aren't talking. They either don't know anything or just aren't telling. Hard to know which it is, but I don't have to tell you about that. You know how it goes. Anyway, we sat up most of the night on our asses waiting for the call."

"Yeah, and who did he say it was?"

"Looks like another cartel figured Servetus was getting too big for his britches and decided to put him out of business."

Eric slammed the palm of his hand against the wall beside his head. "Shit! You telling me Lee and Tommy got caught in the middle of a war between those scumbags?"

"Looks like," Guy admitted quietly.

"But you're not one hundred percent."

"We know they were there when the shooting started, Eric. Our man just got through to us an hour ago. He says he doesn't know what happened to Thornton and Torres, but he may be stalling for time to get himself out of there before we bring the big boys in."

"If he was so tight with Servetus, why can't he find out?" Eric demanded angrily.

"Servetus got tagged."

Eric inhaled a couple of times, stalling and making sure he was getting it straight. It just wasn't fucking possible that Lee could be lost. But if Servetus had been killed, then . . . "How do you know?"

"The informant saw the body, Eric. There's no doubt Luis Servetus is dead. His brother, too."

"But they didn't find our boys?" Eric knew the sprig he was reaching for wouldn't support much hope, but it was all he had, so he waited, hanging on to it.

"It's probably no good, Eric. You don't want to accept it, I know. Neither do I, but we've gotta face facts, and facts are we may have lost them."

"When will you know?" Eric's voice was strangled with his pain. He shifted his gaze to the floor as if he could somehow deny the truth by focusing on something as unremarkable as the pattern in the carpet around his feet.

Guy didn't answer.

"When, damn it? How soon? Have you even called Glory or Marie to tell them that their husbands are missing?"

"I can't give you an exact time, Eric! I'll know when I know and you'll get it as soon as I do, okay?" He hesitated only a couple of seconds, not expecting an answer, and not getting one. Then he continued. "As for Glory and Marie, I don't have to tell you. We won't contact them till we have something solid. You know the drill. SOP."

Yeah, Eric knew. He just didn't care. Fuck Guy and his standard operating procedure, too. Glory and Marie had a *right*. He started to tell his employer just that, but he was already talking again, and Eric listened.

"We've called in Central Intelligence. I don't look to hear anymore from our informant. We'll have to depend on the authorities for answers here on out unless Lee or Tommy somehow gets word to us."

A long empty deadness filled the line between the two men. Finally, Guy asked, "What's happening on your end? Anything new?"

The question snapped Eric out of his heart-searing imaginings of his friend's body lying somewhere in a ditch along a dirt road traveled over only by murdering drug dealers or disinterested peasants. "What? Oh, the Rose Murders. Not much. I spent some time with Christi last night. Going to interview her mother at nine-thirty. Then I'm—" He lost his train of thought as as shrill beep sounded in the phone.

"You got another call?"

"Yeah, screw it. What was I saying?" The call-waiting signal beeped again.

"Pick it up," Guy said. "I'll hold."

With an irritated "shit," Eric clicked over. "Keaton," he snapped.

"Eric, Dan Small here. We've got another one, I'm afraid."

His thoughts still with Lee, Eric was a split second slower than usual. But when he got it, it slammed into his gut, taking his breath. "Son of a bitch, Dan, when?"

"I don't know. An hour ago. Two maybe. Took out one of my officers, too. Real good kid." The last word ended on a sharp catch, but the chief's voice was solid when he spoke again. "Anyway, thought you'd want to be in on it. I'm headed over to the hotel right now. I'll leave word with my people to let you in."

Eric thanked him, but the police chief was already gone.

He noticed that his hand shook slightly as he clicked back over to his boss. "You there, Guy?"

"I'm here, but listen, I'm getting off. Gonna get back to my contact at CIA. I'll let you know the minute—"

"Call me on the cell phone, Guy. There's been another murder. I'm going over to the Ritz-Carlton as soon as I splash some water on my face and pull on some clothes. Get back to me, okay?"

"That's a given," Guy said. "Business as usual." Guy's tone was gruff.

"Yeah, right." Eric muttered.

"I'm serious. Get into you work, Keaton. I'll be in touch the second I have anything."

Eric took the phone from his ear and stared at it. He didn't answer. What was there to say? *Yeah, right. Absofuckinglutely.*

Chapter Twenty-four

Road blocks had been set up with black-and-whites over a two-block area to keep traffic away from the Ritz-Carlton. KCPD cops swarmed the grounds around the hotel in a whir of blue. From rooftops on the Country Club Plaza, a sea of camera lenses zoomed in on the scene of the latest Rose Murder. Voices melded into an indistinguishable and irritating drone, and fuses were burning short.

The chaos and din followed Eric inside the hotel, though here aggravation was immediately concentrated on all the red tape that had to be hacked through. Everyone who made it that far was subjected to a request for ID, a brief interrogation, a cursory inspection with a metal-detection wand, and a more thorough, more humiliating body search. No one was exempt, Eric noticed without so much as a grain of satisfaction, as he watched the mayor being run through the exercise. Local police and FBI were working together in grim-faced cooperation, and Eric wondered aloud as he went through the ropes if it wasn't just a little too much, too late?"

The fifth floor was eerily quiet. Armed police guarded the hallways and stood in front of the elevators limiting access to the floor. Two rooms were sealed off with bright yellow tape that announced louder than a P.A. system that crimes had been committed inside.

Eric hesitated, looked around for Chief Small, then approached 502 when he didn't see the man.

Four guys were busily working the room for fingerprints, gathering blood samples, collecting hair particles, examining drawers and closets, and checking the locks on the doors leading to the room from both the hallway and the adjoining room. Two people, both dressed in dark clothing, were busy in the bathroom only partially obscuring the body of a young policewoman. Eric's eyes trailed the blood from the entrance to where the body lay. He didn't try to enter the room. Instead, he went to 518.

The scene was the same except that the murder victim was sprawled on the bed, unattended. Most of her upper body was covered in blood that had rivered along one arm as it hung over the side of the bed. But Eric's gaze was drawn to her face that had been untouched by the killer. He recognized her from the ball two nights before. Her name escaped him, though he thought that was probably because all he could see when he looked at the white-blond hair and stared into the sapphire blue eyes, was Christianne Anthony.

Hands clenching in tight fists of involuntary reflex, he turned away. He was sickened, angry. He bent at the waist, bracing his hands on his thighs and gulped back a couple deep breaths of air. A moment later, he went looking for the police chief.

He found him around the corner leaning over a young officer crouched on the floor, his hands covering his face that was tinged a waxy yellow. Eric sympathized.

He slowed his approach and buried his hands deep in his pockets, though his fingers stayed tightly curled.

Dan Small heard him, looked up. "Eric. Be with you in a sec."

"Take your time," Eric said.

Dan patted the young officer reassuringly on the shoulder, whispered some word of comfort, then straightened, his old bones creaking noisily. He cupped Eric's elbow, steering him down the hall. "Kid was on duty this morning one floor below. Name's Adam Johnson. First to hear the screams coming out of five-oh-two when one of the women went into the bathroom and stumbled over Drew's body. He did good. Radiod for backup, then went in and got the two women out of there. He pretty much fell apart after that. Can't say as I blame him. He's a rookie, but I swear it doesn't ever get much easier. 'Least not for me."

Eric nodded grimly. "Give me what you have, Dan."

"Let's go to Jillie Peters's room." He glanced at the *Savant*. "That's the dead contestant . . . Same MO. No surprise there except that this time he killed a cop, too. And of course this knocks the hell out of our Darin Woods theory." He pounded the palm of one of his hands with a fist, his face darkening with sudden fierce anger. "Drew was good, Keaton. An ace cop. Sharp as a whip. Took the test for detective two weeks ago. Passed with flying colors. Wasn't no way this bastard caught her off guard." He stopped walking, got in front of Eric, and wagged a finger in his face. "She had to know him, otherwise he wouldn't have gotten anywhere near those girls, much less inside their rooms." He started off again, this time with a spark of hope. "Guess that's something."

"What about the women in five-oh-two? Has anyone talked to them? Found out if they saw anything? Heard anything?"

Dan hunched his shoulders. "Yeah, in fact one of the federal boys is with 'em now, but he won't get any more than we did."

Eric frowned and Dan glanced his way as if reading his thoughts. "It's not Sansom. Last I heard, he's a no-show."

Eric raised a brow.

"Don't know," Dan said. "We've called his house, his office, even beeped him. Unless they got ahold of him while I was busy with Johnson, I don't have a clue."

"Huh. Well, forget it."

Dan nodded and went on with his brief. "Only one girl heard anything and not much at that. Said she heard the door open, but Officer Drew told her everything was fine, to go back to sleep, which she claims she did. The other one, uh, Linda somebody, didn't hear a thing."

"And nobody heard anything from Peters's room."

The chief put a hand on Eric's shoulder, steering him back the way they'd come. "Nope, nothing. Not a damned thing. She was awake. We know that, but she'd didn't make a sound that we can tell. There's no sign of a struggle. Poor thing didn't have time to do more than throw her arms up to try and protect herself. Come on, let's go have a look."

"No scream," Eric muttered to himself as they walked. Then louder, addressing Dan, "I don't get it. I mean, the killer wakes her up, gets her attention, and she doesn't cry out, yell, nothing? Make sense to you?" Eric asked.

"Not unless she recognized him or he somehow gained her confidence and was able to reassure her. But far as we know, none of the other Rose victims ever screamed either. 'Course this is only the second time one of them was killed while they were all together in the hotel. The other one was with our first contestant before we even knew we had a serial going." He paused, his expression far away.

"Anyway, the other contestants are being questioned downstairs."

"Wait a minute, Dan," Eric said, putting out a hand

to stop him. "You said there were two girls in five-oh-two. There were twenty-six contestants, four chaperones, right?" At the chief's nod, he completed the equation he'd been working. "Two to a room, fifteen rooms, and no one rooming alone."

"Yep, you got it, except for one thing. Jillie Peters's roommate bowed out of the pageant early yesterday."

"Huh," Eric said, a kernel of encouragement beginning to grow. "And you've called her?"

"We're working on it, yup. I'll let you know if anyone helped her along with the decision to go home to Mississippi. Natchez, that's her home. Soon as we get word, I'll pass it along."

They'd reached the slain contestant's room and Chief Small started inside. Eric stopped him. "Hold on, Dan. Our truant friend has finally shown up."

Dan took a step back into the hall and spotted the FBI agent coming toward them. "Where the hell have you been? Thought you were the case agent here. Someone change that and forget to give me the memo?"

Eric, watching Mike Sansom, saw his face redden. He had to give the devil his due. Sansom, for all his faults, was fighting hard to control his temper. Eric had no part in their disagreement, other than being right there in the middle between an old friend and an old enemy. He could help defuse the tension or aid it along. Remembering the two women who had lost their lives, he opted for the first.

"Anyone fill you in?" Eric asked Mike.

The agent nodded curtly, then turned his attention to the chief of police. "I apologize, Dan. I attended the party at the Anthonys' home last night. When I left, I realized I'd had too much to drink to be driving back to the city. I turned around and went back, asked if I could spend the night, sleep it off. I left word both at headquarters and on my answering machine at home. As luck would have it, Bonnie didn't check the machine for messages, and the guy on duty last night failed to log it in. I woke up just before seven. For some reason my pager didn't go off. I didn't find out anyone had even tried to reach me till I called in." He grimaced sheepishly and added, "My chief's going to ream me good once we get through the worst of this today."

The last seemed to appease Dan. He nodded, asking, "And where is he? Chief Callaway that is."

"Downstairs in the ballroom, supervising the interviews with the contestants."

Chief Small turned away and walked into the room where the coroner was now examining the body of Jillie Peters. Sansom and Keaton tagged after him, both of them with the same sense of déjà vu. They'd been on murder investigations before that weren't theirs until the local police turned them over. Weird how life had a way of doing one-eighties.

All of that—even the animosity that stood between them as tangible as a third entity—was forgotten, however, as Eric looked at the body of the beautiful young woman and his gaze fixed on her left hand. A knot as big as a tennis ball lodged in his throat at the sight of the fragile, pale fingers clutching a corner of blood-drenched sheet.

"How, damn it?" Dan muttered angrily. "How the hell did he get on the floor, take out one of my best officers, then slip in here without making a sound?"

Larry Cannon, the Jackson County medical examiner, shook his head. "Beats me, Dan, but I can tell you this much, he wasn't in any hurry. Very confident, this one."

Cannon expanded on his theory, uncoaxed. "Look here. See that puddle of blood and the impression on the sheet? Our killer was real casual, taking his time even after the girl was dead. Laid the murder weapon on the bed next to her, then methodically wiped it off; thus the imprint from the blade and the small pool of blood. Yessir, a real cool customer."

"We get any prints at all?" Chief Small asked a guy from forensics as he passed behind them.

"Plenty, but you know how it is. We got contestants, chaperones, hotel personnel, sponsors, family members, even media traveling in and out of these rooms a hundred times a day. I'd give you odds at a million to one we don't get a single print belonging to the perp, and that's probably generous."

Special Agent Sansom turned their attention to the murder of the police officer. "Tell me about Nancy, Dan. How in the hell did he get to her?"

Dan rubbed a hand over his balding pate. "Damn it, Sansom, you think we aren't asking the same question? The truth is, we haven't a clue. If I was guessing, I'd say she knew him. No other reason I can think of she would've opened one of the rooms for him much less allow him on the floor. At the very least, if she'd had a single doubt, she would've radioed one of the other officers. Not only didn't she make the call, we found her walkie-talkie laying on a chair in the hall along with a book she'd been reading."

"Yeah, but how come he got her to open five-oh-two instead of just coming directly to five-eighteen?" Sansom pressed.

"I'll tell you what, why don't you find him for us and you can ask him yourself. How's that?"

"That's good. Exactly what I'll do. Even take care of the paperwork for you, Chief." Mike clapped the man on the shoulder, then flashed a thin, humorless grin. "I'm going to go have a look in the other room, talk to some of our people."

Eric had been standing with his arms crossed over his chest. With Sansom's departure, he moved closer to the headboard, letting his arms drop to his sides. His wrist bumped against the cell phone in his jacket, bringing Lee immediately to mind. Not exactly a good time to remember his friend and the trouble he might have run into. Not standing in the middle of a blood-bath as he was. He winced.

"You all right?" Dan asked.

"Yeah," Eric said quickly. Too quickly. Both Cannon and Small looked over at him, their brows furrowed. Time for a diversionary tactic. Squatting suddenly so that his eyes were only inches from the hand of the victim's outstretched arm, he pointed to her index finger. "You see this? All the nails perfectly manicured except this one. Could she have broken it while scratching her attacker?"

The coroner raised his brows in appreciation. "Should have been a cop, Keaton," he said. He grinned, but his expression sobered as he turned his attention back to the girl's body. He shook his head. "I had hoped for the same thing, but it's no good. I found the broken fingernail tip in one of the wounds. Apparently, she covered he breasts with her hands at some point. Natural reflex. Anyway, the blade snapped the nail tip off, driving it into the wound." He pointed to a wide, deep cut just above the girl's left breast. "Right there."

Eric ran a hand over his thick hair as he stood up. "Shit. Well, be sure and scrape the nails anyway and bag the hands. Maybe we'll get lucky yet."

The coroner nodded, but his expression didn't look hopeful. He opened his mouth, started to speak, but a small, strangled cry from the doorway stopped him. Every head in the room turned in that direction.

Eric could feel the blood drain from his face as he found Christianne standing there, a hand clasped to her mouth, her eyes wide with horror.

Pushing his way past the coroner and police chief,

Eric hurried to take her in his arms and shield her view with his body.

"Who the hell let her in here?" Chief Small demanded. Then to Eric: "Get her out of here!"

Eric didn't have to be told. As gently as he could, he turned her from the room and guided her to the elevators. Every inch of her quivered in his arms. Dry, heaving sobs croaked from her throat. "Oh, Eric. How could . . . someone . . . do that to her?"

"Hush. Not yet."

"Where are . . . we . . . going?" Her trembling lips barely managed the words.

Eric stopped before the uniformed officer posted in front of the elevator. His eyes flashed ominously when he met the other man's. "Are you the asshole who let her up here?" he asked.

The young man's face reddened. "No, sir, I—"

"Never mind! Just get the elevator here so I can get her off the floor."

The officer jabbed the elevator button. He didn't have to be told to move aside when the doors opened.

Eric stepped in, Christi still wrapped in the protective circle of his arms. "Hold on, sweetheart, just hold on," he crooned softly against her hair. Suddenly his frustration and fury shifted and were directed at her. Why had she come?

Damn it, what had provoked her? He wanted to shake her, drag her back upstairs, and force her to look at the ravaged body of Jillie Peters. But mostly, he thought, as he pressed her closer, he wanted never to let go of her again.

"It's okay," she whispered against his throat.

He shook his head. She was wrong. It wasn't okay. That girl could have been *her.* In fact, he no longer had even an iota of doubt. Jillie Peters, Lisa Marks, all of them—they had all died because they looked like Christianne Anthony and if the son of a bitch wasn't caught, she was going to be his next victim. He was getting too cocky, too daring. How could he top this except to go for the prize?

Chapter Twenty-five

"Where are we going?" Christi asked when they stepped off the elevator on the main floor.

Eric shrugged. "I don't know. Away from here."

She laid a hand on his arm. "Eric, wait. I need to see my father."

"Okay, I'll drive you."

She shook her head. "He's here. With the contestants. Uncle Paul, too."

Eric thought it was a bad idea. All of it. He knew what they'd find in the ballroom. Tears, hysterics, frustration, guilt. Christi was only asking for more upset. He tried to tell her, but she disagreed.

"I'm okay. Really." That wasn't true. She shook her head, ran her fingers through her hair, and started again. "No, that's wrong. I'm not all right. In fact, I wonder if I'll ever know what all right feels like again. But I have to see my father now."

The contestants—all twenty-four of them—were still dressed in their nightclothes. They sat huddled together, holding hands, or closer, arms linked or wrapped around shoulders. Some wept, a few sat dazed, unmoving. Others fidgeted, chewing nails or twisting strands of hair. One woman held her knees against her chest and rocked. Each was reacting in her own way to the tragedy.

FBI Bureau Chief Cory Callaway was talking to a fortyish redhead, obviously one of the chaperons. Eric picked out the other three, two of them talking to the girls, the third one in intense conversation with Paul Anthony. A couple of homicide detectives were standing in a corner not far from the entrance, going over notes scribbled in small ringed binders. Alex Anthony was standing a few feet apart from the them, alone and lost in thoughts impossible to read.

The detectives, noticing Eric and Christi, stopped talking and turned in their direction. The attention from them started a domino reaction around the room, as one by one, everyone looked their way. Alex was the last to notice them. When he did, the color drained from his face. He hesitated only a fraction of a second, just long enough for Paul to get to them first, followed by the FBI chief.

"Christi, what in God's name are you doing here?" Paul asked, his resonant voice hushed for once. His gaze shifted to Eric. "You did this, Keaton?"

"Shut up, Uncle Paul," Christi said, her blue eyes cold and glinting like shards of shaved ice. "Eric had nothing to do with my being here. If you're looking for someone to blame, look at yourselves. This is your fault." She included her father in her glare as he joined them.

The FBI chief stepped in. "No one's blaming your family, Miss Anthony. In fact, we all—the police, FBI, all of us—encouraged—"

"*I'm* blaming them, sir," she told him. "But you're right, you all bear responsibility for those women's deaths."

"Christi, please," Alex said, working his way to her side to clasp her arm. "You shouldn't be here. Come with us somewhere private so we can talk." When she opened her mouth to protest, he held up a hand. "Please! You're only going to upset these girls more than they already are."

"Go on," Eric said, giving her hand a squeeze. "I'll

wait for you. When you're ready, I'll take you out of here."

"You promise?" she asked, her composure faltering for the first time since she'd regained it in the elevator.

He hooked her chin with his finger, raising her gaze to his. He surprised himself by kissing her lightly, then his arms circled her waist as he pulled her close and whispered against her ear. "Go on, I'll be here. I promise."

She gripped the lapel of his jacket as she pressed her face against his chest. He buried his face in her hair and they both knew that something was happening between them, something profound and irreversible.

He looked up over the top of her head, met the disapproving glares of both Anthony men. Even Chief Callaway was scowling.

Well, fuck 'em. Christi needed him and he'd just found out something else. He needed her to need him.

When she stepped out of his embrace at last, she placed a hand against his face. Tears still stood in her eyes, but the glow that had been missing from her cheeks was back and her lips tipped up at the edges now instead of down. "I'll be okay."

He watched her leave, flanked by her father and uncle. He turned to Cory Callaway. "Sorry, we interrupted your interviews, Chief. I'll just step out of your way."

"Hell, no, Eric. Come on over and listen in. Maybe you can give us some help here." The bureau chief sighed. "God knows we could use some."

Chapter Twenty-six

Alex led his daughter to a small grouping of sofa and chairs in a semiprivate corner on the same floor. "Sit down, darling," he told her. He gestured to the sofa. Then to Paul, "Take a chair."

Alex sat on the edge of his chair, his expression worried. "What's going on here, Christianne?" he asked.

Anger flared, fierce and hot. "You mean with Eric? Is that what you want to talk about? My God, two women are lying upstairs dead and you want to talk about my relationship with Eric Keaton? I don't believe this."

"Your father's just worried about you, Christi," Paul interjected.

"Worried about me? Why? I'm fine. No one butchered *me*. Just a poor woman unfortunate enough to look like me and a police—"

"You're wrong, Christi!" Paul said, shaken by her conclusion. "That woman's death had nothing to do with you."

"Then how do you explain our amazing likeness?"

He held up his hands. "We can't, of course, except for what the police have given us. It's coincidence, pure and simple. This Woods fellow is attracted to women with your general coloring. Who knows why."

"Look," Alex put in. "You've got to trust us, Christi. We don't have time to get hysterical here. We have to go back into that room and talk to those women, help them all get through this, and somehow, get them through this pageant. After—"

Christi's mouth opened in a gasp of disbelief. "*The pageant*? Is that all you can think of?"

Paul answered for his brother. "It's not our idea, sweetheart. The FBI has asked us to continue. They hope that the killer will show himself again before it's over, and they'll be able to catch him. If we cancel, we may never get this . . . this monster put away. We don't have any choice but to cooperate."

Christi clasped her hands in her lap and lowered her gaze. Maybe the FBI and the police were pressuring them to see the pageant through to the end, but they did have a choice. They could refuse. "I'm sorry, I'm not buying this. The killer hasn't ever struck twice in the same year, at the same pageant. Why would he change this time?"

"Who knows?" Paul asked. "Maybe he won't, but it's the only chance we have. If we cancel—"

"And what about those women in there?" she asked, gesturing toward the ballroom. "Has anyone bothered asking them what they want to do?"

"Yes," Alex said. "As a matter of fact, they've all agreed to stay, pending consent from their families, of course. But, Christi, listen to me. I swear, no matter what happens, this is the last one." He heaved a defeated sigh.

"I'm canceling the pageant after this year. Discontinuing it forever. I had planned to have a family meeting Sunday." His voice caught and he stopped abruptly, closing his eyes and pinching the bridge of his nose. After a moment, he looked up again and Christi was surprised to see tears standing in his eyes. He swallowed, then continued. "There are other things besides the pageant that we need to discuss."

"Alex," Paul said, a warning clear in his tone.

"Don't worry, big brother. I'm not going to get into

it right now." He looked at his daughter, found a semblance of a smile for her. "We'll announce our decision to stop the pageants to the press on Monday."

Christi looked from her father to her uncle and back again, then stood up. "I'm going to get Eric and ask him to take me home. But this isn't over. I'm beginning to understand a lot of things I never even thought about before. Like why I was sent to Europe and made a vice president fresh out of school, for one. Why you wouldn't let me come home even when Gran was so ill, for another. Even why you've insisted I work out of the plant in Anthony and never come into the corporate offices. You've been protecting me, keeping me out of harm's way. Well, that's over. I won't hide any longer. You're going on with the pageant? Then include me. I plan to attend the competition tonight and the crowning tomorrow evening. If the police want to flush the killer out, then he can come after me and not some innocent substitute."

Alex's face darkened with uncharacteristic anger as he jumped to his feet. "No! I will not risk something happening to you."

Shocked by the outburst, she took an involuntary step back, before recovering and raising a brow. "You don't have anything to say about it, Daddy. I'm an Anthony, an adult and a stockholder, and this is my decision to make."

When neither man spoke, she smiled thinly and walked away.

Eric got up to leave and Chief Callaway hurried after him, catching up just outside the ballroom door. "It's been a long time, Keaton," Callaway said. "I was surprised when Mike told me you'd taken on an investigation here in K.C. Didn't think you'd ever come back."

"Neither did I," Eric admitted frankly, "but turns

out it's true that time has the healing properties everyone claims."

"Yeah," the FBI man said, "but I gotta admit I was worried about you showing up here with Mike assigned as the case agent. I see now, however, that you've left the past behind."

Mike Sansom rounded the corner at that moment and both men turned his way. He broke a chilly grin that revealed he'd overheard. "Some things are never left behind, Chief. Ain't that right, Keaton? Some things just stick with a guy. Kind of like stepping on hot gum. Never gonna shuck it off again."

"Yeah," Eric agreed, his gaze locked with his former partner's. "There's definitely things that have a way of staying with a man. Like skunk spray."

Cory Callaway held up his hands. "Whoa, now, guys. I didn't mean to start anything up here. Tell you what, why don't the two of you talk it on out, get it settled once and for all. Otherwise, long as this investigation continues, the two of you are just gonna keep tripping all over each other."

"Not necessarily, Chief," Mike said with a smirk. "Keaton here's a private citizen. I don't have to work with him. Matter of fact, he keeps getting underfoot, I think I got the right to step on him and squash his ass."

Keaton let a slow grin spread. "Well, now, let me get my tape recorder turned on; get a record of the government threatening one of its *private* citizens. We've still got laws against that kind of intimidation, last I heard."

Callaway laughed and slapped Eric on the shoulder. "You need to ease up, Keaton. Agent Sansom was joking. Learn to laugh, my man." He turned away, disappearing inside the ballroom.

Mike picked up where they'd left off. "Look, I don't want to waste time arguing with you, Eric. I just don't need your shit right now. Not with two more murders hanging over my head." He started past the *Savant*.

"Hold on. Let's talk about that. About two *more* murders."

Mike wheeled around on his heel, grabbed Eric's jacket, and slammed him against the wall. The agent's face was as dark as the maroon flowers in the wallpaper behind his former partner's head. "Get this straight, Keaton. I wasn't responsible for what happened to your brother and your girlfriend. Wasn't me who was boffin' her right up to the day the two of you were supposed to get hitched. And I wasn't the know-it-all who underestimated a whacked-out vet. We tried everything to find you, and when that failed, I talked to Packer. Convinced him to let the pastor and more than two hundred innocent bystanders out of there.

"And then you gave some 'Howdy Doody' sharpshooter the go-ahead to take him out," Eric said, his flat tone more frightening than Mikes anger. "What did it matter if you had to sacrifice the young couple at the altar? Win some, lose some, eh?"

"Listen to me, Keaton. Pay close attention, 'cause I'm not going to say it twice. You and me were real close once upon a time, so when we lost Bryn and Dave, I let you lay all the blame on me. I took it then, and I've kept on taking it, but that's over. When you get back to your room, look in the mirror and face the guy who killed them."

A growl rumbled from some primal place deep inside as Eric pulled back his arm ready to knock off the son of a bitch's head.

"Eric, no!" Christi cried just a second too late.

Mike was down, blood spurting from his nose. He pulled a handkerchief from his pocket and pressed it over his face, before slowly pulling himself to a sitting position.

A small crowd was gathering from the ballroom. Chief Callaway was the first to get to his agent's side, warning Eric about the penalties for assaulting a federal agent, as if he didn't know. The Anthonys arrived from the other direction, demanding an explanation. Christi clung to Eric's arm, looking uncertainly from one man to the other.

Sansom, incredibly, was laughing. "You feel better now, you crazy bastard?"

And then Eric was laughing as well. "Yeah . . . yeah, as a matter of fact, I feel a hell of a lot better."

"Good, 'cause I feel like hell."

"Come on," Eric said, giving Mike a helping hand to his feet. "Let's go upstairs to the restaurant, get some ice on that."

Mike shook his head. "Naw. It'll be okay. I don't think it's broken."

"You sure?" Eric asked.

"Yeah, yeah. Besides, you better get out of here before my boss has someone slap handcuffs on you."

Eric hesitated, then put a hand on his former partner's shoulder. "Hey, sorry, man. Sorry, I lost it."

Mike shrugged. "Forget it. Anyway, it could've been worse. You could've reminded me how I've blown it with the Woods thing."

Eric stared at him for a long moment, then: "You mean because I haven't said 'I told you so?' Truth is, I was just about to do that when you pissed me off. Guess, now that I popped you, I'll have to let it go."

"Appreciate it," Mike said. Looking around at the crowd, he told them the show was over. As everyone but his chief and the Anthonys walked away, he turned to Eric again. "Your friend, Dan, told me that he filled you in. About what happened to Woods, that is. So, we're back to square one. We're going to have to go over every scrap of evidence we have from the first murder. Study everything Sci-Crime has sent, autopsies, interviews, the works. How about you come on as a consultant? Help us out?"

"Hold on, Sansom," Chief Callaway interjected.

"No, Chief, you hold on," the agent countered. "This is my investigation. I'm the case agent. I call in anyone I like, right?"

Cory looked back and forth between the two men, his overlong, homely face as woebegone as a hound dog's.

Eric saved the man the trouble of a decision he didn't want to make. "It's okay, Chief, I'm not coming to work for the FBI as a consultant or anything else. I have an employer." He offered Mike a tight grin. "I don't think you and I are ready for old times just yet, but I will take advantage of your offer to go over anything you want to share."

Mike nodded. "Sure, long as it's tit for tat. You show me yours, I'll show you mine." He winked at Christi. "Pardon me, ma'am."

"As long as I can play," she said, smiling, yet still wary.

"I'll call you," Eric said, reaching for Christi's hand. "Come on, let's get out of here." He stepped past the others with a barely audible, "Gentlemen."

Upstairs, the cops working the lobby stared curiously as the couple made their way through to the garage door. "Looks like word of your disagreement with Agent Sansom spread fast," Christi said.

"It's way more than a disagreement, babe. Way more."

"You want to tell me?"

They were settled in his car and totally alone now, but Eric still didn't want to talk about anything, much less his former lover who'd jilted him with his brother then died in a bombing meant for him. Instead of answering, he took her face between his hands. "Right this second, all I want to do is look at you. I want to touch you. I want to see how beautiful and alive you are."

She opened her mouth to respond, but he covered it with his, and when he stopped, she no longer had strength enough to say anything.

He kissed her again with a heartbreaking tenderness that almost made her weep. When he pulled back to look into her eyes, she still couldn't speak.

Eric lifted her hair and kissed the nape of her neck. "Christianne Anthony, I'm in love with you," he whispered.

She found her voice then, her eyes shimmering with tears, and her lip trembling yet smiling. "You really are?"

"Oh, yes, ma'am," he said. "And lady, when we get through this, you're going to know how much."

She kissed him, her elbows on his shoulders and her hands holding his head. "I love you, too, Eric," she said at last, and then she was crying and laughing at once. "And it feels so good and so bad, all at the same time. I mean, this terrible day . . . and I'm so happy. Oh, Lord, don't ever leave me, Eric, 'cause I swear I'll never be able to function in a normal world again. You've turned my whole life upside down, and I just couldn't face another day without you making it wonderful even when it's as ugly as it is right now."

"You always talk this much when you're in love?" he asked.

"I guess so. I don't know. I've never been in love before."

He laughed again, pecked her lips once more, then squeezed her hand. "Come on, I'll take you home, but tonight . . ."

"You know, I've got my own car," she reminded him. "I think I'd like to go to the plant, lose myself in work for a while."

"Okay, then I'll follow you part way. I have an appointment scheduled with your mother for nine-thirty. It's not quite eight forty-five. Plenty of time to make it."

Christi's eyes clouded. "Go easy, Eric. She was pretty upset when we got the call about the murders, and I know she couldn't have been happy when she found out I'd gone to the hotel. Just be patient. Mother's difficult, sometimes, but it's not intentional. She's old guard, and she doesn't know how else to be. The only thing she knows is keeping up appearances no matter what the crisis. Gran used to say that Mother might not have depth, but then, the shallower the pond, the smoother the surface, and she was definitely right about that. The world could crumple around us, and I promise you, the Anthonys would appear unperturbed and unflappable under Mother's guidance."

They got out of his car and walked to hers. He brought her around to face him. "Two promises. One, I'm going to find the bastard who killed those women. No one else is going to get hurt. Believe that."

She nodded. Of course she had to believe that. She didn't want to doubt anything he told her.

"Okay. And second, you and I are going to finish what we started. Just as soon as this is all behind us." He sealed both promises with a kiss.

Chapter Twenty-seven

Eric followed Christi to Anthony, but when she waved from her window and turned right, he continued straight instead of making a left as he would have if he was going directly to his appointment with Mary-ann Anthony.

It wasn't a calculated decision. Rather a matter of timing. He was early so he'd have a look around the town that was comprised entirely of Anthony employees and their respective families.

He cruised the streets slowly, his thoughts slamming from his probe and the early morning murders, to his friend's status as MIA, to the sudden change in his relationship with Christi. Felt like a real fierce game of racquetball going on up there. Bam bam bam. He forced the match to a stop, and focused on the town.

Peaceful, orderly, he thought just as his eyes passed over a trim little yellow house, then darted back again. Actually, it was the pickup parked in the drive that snagged his attention. Backed in so that it faced him from the front, its offending, crumpled right front fender stood out like a sore thumb.

Dan's description of the truck that had struck down Darin Woods flashed though his mind as he pulled his car to the curb and climbed out. Light blue or gray. This one was both, the metallic paint a combination of the two colors. Eric's gaze dropped immediately to the licence plate. 4JW 303. Yup. The adrenaline started pumping.

It was only ten degrees warmer than it had been the day before, but Eric broke out in a sweat. Loosening his tie, he pulled it off, shrugging his jacket off at the same time. Looking at his watch, he opened the car door and tossed them onto the passenger seat. He unbuttoned the top button and rolled up his shirtsleeves as he walked the forty or so feet to the truck parked in the drive alongside the compact yellow house.

A tall, muscular black man stepped out of the front door of the neighboring house to the west, and Eric stopped dead in his tracks. Jesus, for just a sec—Of course, that was crazy. The guy looked like Lee. Even moved like him. Only one little hitch: Levi Thornton was lost somewhere in the jungles of a tiny little known hellhole called Tingo Maria.

Still, Eric's hands trembled and sweat trickled along his brow. Reaching into his hip pocket for a handkerchief, he swabbed his face and neck, and got a serious hold on himself.

Just keep your mind on your work, Keaton. Levi's not gone till they find the body, and that they ain't gonna do. Besides, he wouldn't let anybody start the funeral for you until there was no doubt, so why you giving up on him?

Okay, back to the Ford pickup.

Squatting in front of the truck, he examined the dent from every angle. Something big had definitely collided with this truck, something big as a deer *or a man.*

Straightening again, he looked up at the house. Quiet, empty-looking, but worth a check. He couldn't be one hundred percent, but just about. It'd be easier if he could talk to the owner. If not, however, he'd just get the highway patrol out here. They'd know in a heartbeat, at least beyond a reasonable doubt, if this was the vehicle that had struck Woods. Even with all the rain, evidence was never entirely washed away. If there were traces of fibers, hair particles, or blood, they'd find them and forensics would match 'em.

He climbed the three steps to the porch, but the front door opened even before he could raise his hand to the knocker. A heavy-set man in his late twenties or early thirties with a lush beard and bleary red eyes faced him, scratching his generous belly under his T-shirt. He yawned widely before asking, "You with the police?"

Eric quirked a brow, reflecting his surprise. "You expecting the police? Because of the accident you've had with your truck?"

"I ain't had no accident, but the sheriff said he'd check with the highway patrol, find out who the hell did, and get back to me. Hey, who are you, anyway? Saw you out of my window going over it like you was a cop."

Eric didn't hesitate. Extending his hand, he told the man truthfully, "I'm a private investigator. I've been hired to investigate one of the Rose Murders. You may have heard—"

"Hellfire, mister, who hasn't heard about the Rose Murders? 'Specially here in Anthony. Everyone here works at the plant. Of course I've heard."

Eric had been about to mention Darin Woods, not the Rose Murders, but he let it go. Instead, he went with the guy, down the line he'd started along. "Uh-huh, then you may have heard there was another murder this morning. Another Rose contestant."

"No shit? I mean, no, I ain't heard that. 'Course, I just got off work. Pulled twelve hours. Eight to eight, so I'm not inclined to listen to the news, not after that many hours. I get off, all I want is something to eat, a couple of beers, and my bed." He looked past Eric to his truck before bringing his eyes back again, and giving his visitor a suspicious look. "Damn shame about that contestant, but what's that got to do with my truck?" His eyes suddenly widened and he shook his head. "Hey, it didn't run no girl down. Not this morning. This happened Tuesday or Wednesday."

Tuesday or Wednesday? "You mean you don't know which day it was you had the accident?"

The big man laughed, leaning against the doorjamb and crossing his feet at the ankles. Getting comfortable. "Hey, whoa there, fella. Back up. I ain't said nothing about having an accident, 'cause I didn't.''

Two women dead, his friend missing, and his right hand starting to throb from the punch he'd delivered to the FBI agent. Nope, Eric was definitely not in the mood for games. "Who did?" he asked.

The man in the doorway shrugged, his beefy neck all but disappearing in his thick shoulders. "Don't know. Thought it was one of these kids around here, but now I'm not sure. I work nights, like I told ya. But I'm off Tuesdays and Wednesdays. Usually a real pisser 'cause my kids are in school, so we don't get to do much together. Only this week they're out for spring break, so my wife took the girls and went to Topeka to see their grandparents. A friend of mine and me took our boys down to the Ozarks for a couple of days of fishing. Ordinarily, I woulda taken the truck, but he's got this new motor home, so we all piled in there instead. We left Tuesday morning early and just got back yesterday afternoon. That's when I seen it just like you're seeing it now, all smashed up."

"And you didn't call anyone to report it?"

"Not at first. I figured it was Jimmy Linton—a kid here in town—or one of his friends who took it out for a joy ride and hit a tree or something and didn't have the balls—er—nerve to tell me. I was madder than hell, but I asked all over town. Them kids say they didn't do it, and their folks back 'em up. So, last night I called the sheriff. He said he'd get someone over here today. That's why I'm not in bed already. Waiting on him."

Eric cut him off. "Did you leave the keys in the ignition?"

The man straightened, his small eyes darkening with defensiveness. "Sure, but the sheriff'll tell you, everyone out here leaves the keys in their cars. It's a good town. We all know each other, and ain't nothin' like this ever happened before." He took a step out of the doorway, towering over Eric as he repeated his question. "So why're you interested, anyway? What's this got to do with the Rose Murders you're supposed to be investigating?"

Eric reached into his shirt pocket to pull out his pen and notebook, not in the least bit intimidated as the other man had intended. Without answering, he quickly jotted down a phone number and name on a blank page. "This is the name of the Kansas City police chief and the number to his office. Would you call him and tell him about what you just told me, Mr. . . . I don't think I got your name."

"Webster. Gary Webster. What's this all about?"

"A man was struck and killed by a hit-and-run driver in a truck that closely matches the description of this one, Mr. Webster. He was killed around four a.m. yesterday morning less than fifteen miles southwest of here. I believe whoever stole your truck may have been the driver. I'd like Chief Small to send someone out here to look it over. Would you agree to that?"

Gary Webster's eyes had widened as Eric spoke until they seemed almost ready to pop from his head. "You think my truck hit some guy and killed him?" he asked, his tone incredulous.

Eric nodded wearily. "If you'll just call Chief Small . . ."

"Sure, sure," the other man quickly assured him.

Eric thanked him and waved, already walking away. He was homing in on the killer, but he wasn't deriving any satisfaction out of the knowledge that the trail he was blazing was taking him closer and closer to Christianne's family.

Chapter Twenty-eight

Eric arrived in front of the Anthonys' home three minutes early for his appointment. He decided to use the time to add a few last notes about his conversation with Gary Webster, but Maryann stepped around the corner of the house, apparently coming from the backyard.

She stopped short, then recovered and raised a hand in greeting.

Eric laid his notebook on the seat, taking a deep breath as he gave a return salute and climbed dutifully out of his car. Though he'd asked Webster to call Dan Small, he regretted not taking advantage of his few extra minutes to telephone him before coming to the estate. He would have liked the chief's reaction to the evidence he had uncovered before heading off on a tangent that might lead him into a blind alley. Well, he would just have to depend on his instincts for the time being. They had served him well in the past.

Maryann approached across the lawn. "You're looking very grim this morning," she observed. "But then, I suppose you've been told about the poor young woman who was killed. So tragic."

Eric nodded. "Yes, but actually, there were *two* young women murdered, Mrs. Anthony. A police officer was killed as well."

Maryann hurried forward, putting a hand on his arm. Her voice was soft and full of compassion as she craned her neck to meet his gaze. "Oh, no, I hadn't heard. I'm so sorry to hear that." She hooked an arm through his, and added, "Sometimes with all the ugliness in the world, it's hard to remember any of the beauty."

They retraced her steps slowly back around the side of the house as Eric filled in details of the murders at the Ritz-Carlton.

As they walked, she asked questions and shook her head sympathetically from time to time. After a moment, she glanced up at him with a suggestion. "I don't mean to be rude, but shouldn't you have skipped coming all the way out here to interview me, and stayed with the investigation at the hotel?"

Eric looked down at the small woman at his side. "The police and FBI are covering the crime scene. I'm better off doing the legwork."

She looked at the pruning shears she carried in her hand. "Which means investigating us," she said quietly.

Eric shrugged. "I'd call it interviewing rather than investigating." He offered a truce in the way of a smile. "After all, everyone from the chief of police to the FBI to my own boss has reminded me that your family is being victimized by this lunatic as well as the murdered girls."

She smiled, her face brightening a bit. "It's true, you know. But that's not really important, is it? We may be hurt by the scandal and damaged financially, but we haven't lost a loved one as have five, no, it's seven families, now, isn't it?" She sighed. "We do want to help, however, so let's get to work."

They'd arrived at a sprawling rose garden. Eric was impressed. Though early in the season, there were already several buds on the bushes. "Wow, your work?" At her nod, he gave her a thumbs-up. "Beautiful. My mother would have been green with envy."

"Your mother enjoyed gardening?" she asked politely, bending at the waist to snip a long stem.

Eric laughed, remembering his mother's frustration at their small plot of yard that never seemed willing to yield more than a few patches of grass. "No, but she appreciated beauty and hard work. She would have admired what you've accomplished."

"What a nice testimony to your mother." Maryann stepped back to give him an approving look. "Would you like to see my greenhouse?"

"I would. Very much."

As she led him through a brief tour, Eric listened attentively as she explained about her passion for horticulture and especially hybridization. He was astounded, not only by her extensive knowledge, but by his rapidly growing admiration for the woman he had heretofore thought of as a pampered blue blood.

Dressed in faded jeans and a well-worn sweatshirt, she looked charmingly ordinary. Her makeup was in place as he would have expected, but her chin and forehead were smudged with dirt that she might have known was there, but didn't trouble herself about. Her eyes looked tired, but her quick step and animated narration were full of vigor. Eric leaned against a long potting table, relaxing a bit. "So Alex named the beauty pageants for your roses?" he asked finally.

She cupped a dainty blossom in her hand as she laughed. "Yes. It's funny, isn't it? Most people think that it happened the other way around. I suppose it's natural. He's so innovative and clever—who would have thought I would be his inspiration?" She sniffed the air around her. "Isn't it a glorious aroma?"

Eric agreed. "So you studied agriculture in college and then married Alex."

"Well, yes, though it wasn't the way you make it sound. It isn't as if I had to give up anything. I always knew I wanted to be married." She laughed softly, as if mostly to herself. "And always to Alex, but I loved flowers, too and I dreamed of creating the perfect rose. As you can see, fate's been generous; I have both."

Eric walked around the room again, stopping every now and then to bend and smell the rich, pungent scent of a different flower. The greenhouse was a profusion of color form crimson madder, deep ruby, and poppy reds to dark golds of marigold and copper, paling to soft peaches and amaranth pinks. "They're really outstanding," he praised sincerely. "And every one of them is the inspiration for a perfume or cosmetic that one of the Anthony Spokeswomen introduces each year?"

Maryann smiled, looking down at her hands for a moment, then said, "Alex and Paul don't fully appreciate what they have in me, do they?" Her self-deprecating laughter floated around them in bitter counterpoint to the sweet scent of flowers.

Eric looked at her, his expression sober. "Probably not." It was offered as a compliment, and Maryann accepted it as such, regaining her good humor. "But you didn't come out here today to hear me prattle on and on about breeding prize-winning flowers. So, ask your questions. I don't mind. Really. In fact, I'm eager to help."

Eric turned two buckets upside down. Motioning to them, he asked, "Could we sit while we talk?"

Maryann smiled. "Certainly." She lowered herself graciously to one of the makeshift stools.

Eric sat facing her. "Do you have any idea why someone is attacking the Rose Pageant contestants?" he asked directly.

"You mean why our girls as opposed to other beauty pageants? Well, the answer is obvious. Someone bears the Anthonys—or one of us, at least—a grudge, and that person knows the way to hurt us most is by threatening our daughter. Even if she is never physically harmed, she is being seriously hurt by all of this, Eric. She is very much a victim here." Her eyes stared intensely into his.

"Has the killer made an actual attempt on her life, or are you talking about the intimidation?"

Maryann looked down at her gloves, chuckling softly as she rubbed them together vigorously, to rid them of caked-on dirt. "Oh, I see. You're asking if we've kept something from the authorities. If there have been attempts on her life that we've failed to report?" She looked straight at him, though she was obviously focused on another time, another place. "Never, Dr. Keaton. We have been entirely forthcoming. We have held back nothing. Not even unrelated incidents such as a kidnapping attempt on her life when she was only a few months old. And the vicious, horrible attacks on two of her pets."

Eric waited.

"Those poor animals. It was monstrous—someone stabbed them both—although the second dog survived, of course." She looked past him through the glass door. Eric followed her gaze to a large dog run where a handsome golden retriever sat keeping guard.

"So no direct attempts on Christi's life in the past several years, and yet you've done everything in your power to keep her out of harm's away; indeed even out of the country. Was that necessary?"

Maryann brushed a few more specks of dirt from her hands as she stood up. She walked past him to stare out the door. "I think I can best answer that with an example of another tragedy."

"It happened in the city a few years ago. A young couple just starting out had their lives ended violently by a madman with a vendetta. If I remember correctly, neither of the victims was the man's intended target, but it didn't matter. He killed them anyway in a beautiful cathedral just before they made vows to God. Destroyed them with a bomb meant for someone else." She turned to face him then, and her dark eyes shone with tears. "Such a waste. And you know, Eric, I'd bet anything if everyone had it do over again, they would have done it all differently, taken every precaution to protect that couple."

"Touché," Eric said, hearing his rage in the slight warble in his voice. "You're very clever, Maryann."

Her lips parted in a smile so benign, Eric was amazed. Not just clever, he amended. Dangerous.

"Well," she said, opening the door and holding it for him. "I really have to get back inside and get cleaned up. Work is so cathartic for me, and Alex insisted I stay here instead of going to the hotel, but I've given them enough time, I think. I must go down there and see if I can offer any comfort. After all, as sad as it is, I have been through this before." Another smile. "Maybe now we can hope the police will come up with conclusive proof against that monster, Darin Woods."

Eric stood and walked to the door, reaching over her head to hold it for her before following her out into a day that was beginning to turn overcast. "I'm amazed again," he said. "I doubt anyone else has managed to find the silver lining so soon."

Maryann's eyes flashed with clear, hot anger as she stopped and spun around to face him. "Don't be impudent, Eric. Of course I'm not making light of another murder, but where is this getting us? I'm doing only what I know how. I'm coping. Until the police or you do your job, it's all any of us can do." She sighed and rubbed a hand wearily across her brow.

"You're right. I apologize. Just one more thing if I may."

She rested her hand on her hip and met his gaze squarely. "For God's sake, Doctor, what is it?"

Hearing her own sharp tone, she stopped with a sudden shake of her head and a small laugh. "Oh, my! I'm sorry. Please forgive me. I guess I'm more upset than I thought. This has been so difficult. But, please, ask your question."

"Where were you yesterday morning at four a.m.?"

Chapter Twenty-nine

Forming a visor with her hand held over her eyes, Maryann squinted against the bright morning sun and looked up at her tall inquisitor. Laughter bubbled as if from a fountain. "I'm . . . I'm sorry," she stammered, moving her hand down from her eyes to cover her mouth as her amusement continued to well. "I know you're serious, but I can't help it, this is so absurd it's funny."

Anger stirred within the *Savant*, every bit as swift and explosive as her laughter. She was still playing games when the time for fun was long past. Two more women were dead; brutally slain. And a young man whose only crime had been a desire to be noticed by a beautiful woman. Had anyone besides Ellie Woods ever appreciated Darin? Cherished him? Given him so much as a friendly smile?

Eric kept his expression bland, his tone casual. "What is it, precisely, that you find so funny, Mrs. Anthony?"

"Uh-oh," she said, lapsing into another fit of hilarity. It seems I've mad you angry. I apologize, truly." Another smile flashed, then fell away at once. "I know what you're suggesting, and it's absolutely ludicrous."

"And why is that?" Eric asked, refusing to let her off the hook without a struggle.

But he'd underestimated her. She was good. Real good.

She shook her head and brushed a stray lock of hair

from her brow with a careless flick of her wrist. "No, Dr. Keaton, I'm not going to play these games of psychological warfare with you. They're your specialty, not mine. Besides, I've had enough of your innuendo. If the police suspect me of some kind of wrongdoing, they can come talk with me." She raised a brow, and her lips spread in what Eric had come to think of as her "consummate professional hostess" smile. "For now, however, you and I have concluded our visit. You will excuse me."

Without waiting for his reply, she turned away. Eric caught her arm, stopping her. "Thanks for your time, Maryann."

"You're welcome," she said, canting her head at an odd angle, the way one does when she's confused. "Now are we done?"

"Sure," Eric said, holding up both hands as if to reassure her that he wasn't about to grab her again. "I won't keep you for another minute. But I wonder if I could use your phone. Maybe your housekeeper would let me in the house."

"You may go to the back door. Jeannie's very likely in the kitchen right now."

Eric's answering grin was easy sliding and, he knew from experience, boyishly convincing. "Well, then, thanks again, and please, forgive me if I offended you with my question about your whereabouts yesterday morning."

Maryann didn't answer. She turned her back on him and left him standing to stare after her.

"Okay," he said. "So don't forgive me."

Some twenty-odd minutes later, the ruse of an important phone call successfully behind him, Eric sat at the breakfast bar noshing on a second slice of fresh-from-the-oven apple pie.

The sweet aroma of apples and cinnamon wafted

around the expansive room. Eric had told the Anthonys' housekeeper, Jeannie O'Rourke, as much and earned himself both the pie and a good deal of information.

Jeannie started the conversation off by admitting to a compulsion to bake whenever things were strained.

Eric nodded his understanding, putting in his penchant for working through stress, and the observation that Mrs. Anthony appeared to have found an outlet in her gardening.

"Oh, yes, indeed," Jeannie replied, replenishing his coffee, then setting the carafe on a trivet, as she pulled up a stool and dropped down beside him. "Her roses have always been important to Ms. Maryann. And it's a good thing for her to have something to turn to when times are bad." She lowered her eyes to her hands, where she worried her wedding band. "Like today, when another poor young thing has been found slaughtered."

"What about the others?" Eric asked, not really knowing why he was pressing the issue other than because there were times when the best gleaned facts came through casual conversation.

A frown settled for an instant on the woman's brow before disappearing with sudden comprehension. "Oh, you mean the rest of the family."

Eric nodded and waited patiently.

"Well, let me see. Ms. Christi usually likes to run out her pain and unhappiness. Jogs for four or five miles sometimes with her dog at her side." She smiled, as if she were seeing the two of them as she spoke. But a frown quickly replaced the momentary flash of happiness. "Mr. Alex, of course, has his apartment in the city to escape to."

Eric felt a frisson of excitement course up his spine. He was careful, though, to keep his tone relaxed. "I didn't know about an apartment. Do he and Maryann stay in the city often?"

"Him and Ms. Maryann?" Jeannie asked, the incredulity in her tone reflected in her gaze. "Good gracious, no. It's Mr. Anthony's apartment." She leaned closer and lowered her voice. "He is a very private person—needs time to himself—and Ms. Maryann . . . well, she doesn't give him a lot of room, if you know what I mean."

Eric thought he knew exactly what she meant and told her so. "Yes, ma'am, I can see where he might need time away. And I imagine there are nights when it's simply more convenient to stay somewhere nearby than drive all the way to Anthony." He raised his cup to his mouth, taking a sip before pressing her further. Their visit was proving very helpful, and the last thing he wanted to do was scare her off. "It is close to the office, isn't it?"

"Just a few miles away. On the Plaza."

"Uh-huh," Eric murmured. He hated to move away, but he didn't dare keep the conversation there too long. "What about Paul?"

Jeannie misconstrued the question, though Eric was pleased with the next crumb she dropped. "Oh, no, Mr. Paul never goes to the apartment. That is strictly Mr. Alex's getaway. Certainly both Ms. Maryann and Mr. Paul know it's at the Westmoreland, though far as I know, neither of them ever goes there. No, Paul's home here seven nights a week, same as Ms. Maryann. 'Course, there was the time that wasn't so."

Eric grinned. "Quite a playboy in the good old days, huh?"

Jeannie's face reddened and she chuckled. "Well, yes, that's exactly what he was in his youth. And today he still likes his drink, don't you know? I guess that's his way of shutting out the bad." She hesitated, then added, "Well, there's that, all right. But sometimes I think railing at the world must work better for him."

His responding laughter was genuine. In the few minutes since he'd sat talking with the woman, he'd decided that he liked her. He appreciated her candor and willingness to share her insights. And though, in effect, he was using her, he was enjoying himself.

"Now, there you go laughing at me when, in truth, you're probably thinking what a terrible person I am for speaking out about a man whose been as good to me as Mr. Paul has."

"Not at all," Eric said. "It's evident that you are very fond of him."

"Good gracious yes. Besides, underneath all the shouting and bluster, there's a man who's scared for his family. The Anthony name is more important to Mr. Paul than any of the others exceptin' for Ms. Bess, may she rest in peace."

Eric digested her words slowly. "You know, I would have thought it was Alex who cared more about the Anthony name. He is the chairman of Anthony Enterprises, after all."

"Oh, he cares about the business, true enough, but it's different with Mr. Paul. He wouldn't care a bit if Anthony Enterprises shut down today as long as their good name was still intact."

Eric shook his head, the picture of the man she was sketching for him so far from his own impression, he could hardly reconcile the two. He said, "I've seen some articles written about him. From what I read, he got into his share of scrapes while he was jet-setting all over Europe; managed to embarrass his family pretty good. Didn't sound like he was very concerned with his reputation or the family name then."

Jeannie nodded. "Yes, I remember the time well. Hurt his mother real bad and some say it was what killed his father." She stopped, inhaling sharply. Her deep-set green eyes suddenly impossibly large, she put a hand to her chest as her lower lip began to tremble. "Oh, God forgive me. This is my employer I'm going on about, and him as good to me as a man could ever be."

Eric was disappointed, but he let it go.

Following a sip of coffee, he attempted to help the housekeeper relax. "Tell me about his mother. I understand Christi was crazy about her."

"Oh, my, she was that. And vice versa, I might add. Ms. Bess and that child had a bond the likes of what I've never known in all my years. I wish you could have seen them together. Always laughing and plotting some innocent prank to tease either Mr. Paul or Mr. Alex with or just sitting in Ms. Bess's room, talking philosophy, and righting all the ills in the world." The housekeeper chuckled and rolled her eyes, obviously relishing memories of the two Anthony women together. Tears spilled over her lashes, coming out of nowhere, but the smile stayed firmly in place. "She was a lady in the truest sense. I never admired anyone so much, she was that special. Many were the times she'd come into the kitchen and sit at the table with me just like you are now and we'd talk, mostly about her husband and her daughter—it liked to have killed her when that girl died. That was a year or two before my time here, but she talked about it often enough, I felt I almost knew her."

"Paul and Alex had a sister?" Eric asked, surprised that he had not found mention of her in the news clippings he'd pored over.

"Anna Renee. She was killed in an automobile accident in Switzerland. Two weeks ago last Monday marked the twenty-ninth anniversary of her passing." Jeannie clasped her thick hands together and squeezed her eyes shut. "Oh, my, there I go again. Rattling on about things you couldn't care less about. My mother used to say I'd have the strongest back in Ireland if I worked it half as much as I did my tongue. Hurt my feelings, back then, but I suppose you're thinking the same."

Eric smiled and reached across the table to pat her hand. He was thinking that Jeannie Kathleen O'Rourke was a good-hearted, lonely woman who rarely got the chance to sit and talk with anyone. She was enjoying herself, and he was gleaning facts about the Anthonys he'd never get from newspapers, friends, or associates, and he didn't intend to discourage her. "I don't think anyone could mind what you've said. It's very obvious how fond you are of the family."

Her chipmunk-full cheeks were suddenly stoplight red, but her eyes were green and bright as she leaned closer to confide in a hushed voice. "I can certainly see why Ms. Christianne slipped out with you like she did last night. If I was a dozen or so years closer to forty, I might just give 'er a run for her money."

Eric chuckled as she'd intended him to, but his gut had suddenly twisted into a tight knot. If she saw them, who else might have been watching?

"Too bad you weren't here for Christi's birthday party," Jeannie tossed out like a baited hook.

Eric bit. "Was it special, somehow?" he asked.

"Not the day itself, no. One of the gifts." She sidled forward to the edge of her chair and looked him in the eye. "Mr. Alex gave it to her, but it wasn't from him. Ms. Bess had left it for her, had wrapped it for her granddaughter several weeks before her death. She'd instructed him to present it to Ms. Christianne on her birthday."

"Was Mrs. Anthony already ill by then?"

Jeannie's face filled with confusion. "What are you talking about?"

Eric backtracked all the way to his conversation with Christi when she'd mentioned her grandmother's illness. "I understood Bess Anthony was sick for several weeks before she died."

"Oh, no, well that's what they told her—Ms. Christianne. But the truth is, death came for her like a thief in the night. She simply went to bed same as she always did and never woke up again. The doctor called it a blessing, but I've never agreed. No, sir. I saw her face before they took her out of there, and no one will ever convince me that dear old woman died peacefully in her sleep. She suffered. A heart attack, I suppose. Or perhaps a stroke. Whatever it was, she was alone, and afraid, and in pain." The housekeeper crossed herself again, then raised the hem of her apron to dab at the corners of her eyes. "I've never forgiven myself for taking the week off to go visit my daughter in Philly."

"There wouldn't have been any way you could have known. Even if you'd been here, you wouldn't have been in her room, would you?"

She shook her head, refusing to be comforted. "I've thought about it a hundred times since then, and I just know I would have heard something. Maybe she cried out or tried to reach for the telephone. My room was right over hers, and I always heard her if she moved around in the night."

Eric recalled his mother's death in a hospital bed eight years before. She'd gone in for routine gallbladder surgery and died when an aneurysm burst in her brain. Even with a trained staff of nurses and doctors, she'd slipped away. He was virtually certain there wasn't anything Jeannie O'Rourke could have done no matter how fierce her devotion. He kept the observation to himself, however, and moved them back to the gift. "You were telling me about the birthday present."

This produced a tremulous smile. "It was a ring. A beautiful blue sapphire solitaire that had belonged to her daughter. Ms. Bess believed Annie Re would have wanted her niece to have it. She had always thought of Christianne as a gift given by God to replace the daughter He'd taken home." She sat forward and whispered, "Ms. Maryann was always annoyed by the notion, but since Ms. Christianne was born on the very day Ms. Bess's daughter died, I guess she had a right to see it that way if she wanted."

"Your phone calls all made, Doctor?" Maryann asked, surprising both Eric and Jeannie, and causing them to jump like children caught with their hands in the cookie jar.

Eric recovered first. He stood up, a smile already in place as he turned to respond. There would be no more discussion with the housekeeper. That was as plain as the dismay on her face. But the least he could do was take the blame for the impropriety of sitting in the kitchen gossiping with the servant. "No, I'm afraid I got sidetracked. Smelled Mrs. O'Rourke's fresh-baked apple pies and everything else flew right out the window." The flustered woman was now standing as well, though seemingly frozen beside her chair. "Everything was delicious and I thank you for taking the time to answer my questions. I hope I didn't ask anything that you were uncomfortable answering."

Jeannie simply smiled tightly, and moved her head in a sort of abbreviated nod.

Eric thanked both women again, then slipped out the back door. Once outside, though, it was all he could do to keep from sprinting around the side of the house and dashing for his car.

Chapter Thirty

Eric glanced at his watch as he approached Ward Parkway. Not quite noon, and the day already qualified as a royal pisser.

Levi's fate was hanging over him like a cloud of napalm.

Two more women dead, and the authorities all in a tailspin with their lone suspect resting in his private refrigerated cubicle in the county morgue.

On the other hand, if nothing else ever went right again, he had that sweet, sweet memory of Christi confessing her love in the hotel garage. That was certainly enough to put a smile on his face.

And he shouldn't forget that fortuitous moment in time when he'd spied the truck that he'd almost bet the farm had run poor Woods down. 'Course, linking it to any of the Big Three might not be the easiest thing to do, but it sure as hell ought to get someone looking in their direction.

And, too, there was the gem he'd picked up from Jeannie O'Rourke about the apartment Alex maintained on the Plaza. Eric slowed the car, looked around himself. He knew K.C. and he knew Ward Parkway. This end in particular. Not just big bucks. Money so old it crackled. And not just upscale. Top of the scale.

He was still shaking his head in amazement as he pulled into the circular drive and parked behind a refurbished Stingray. Lots of chrome on the outside. All leather interior. He'd make it 1968. Sharp car.

The door of the sprawling pink stucco mansion was opened by Bonnie Sansom instead of a housekeeper as Eric had expected. Not that he recognized her, but he knew Mike's type and she fit the bill perfectly: Long salon-blond hair, full heavy makeup, fingernails and toenails hot, hot pink, and a lot of skin above and below the white Spandex tube dress.

Definitely a knockout. Even with the scowl she was wearing. He grinned. "Mrs. Sansom? I'm—"

"I know who you are, Doctor." There was a breathless, little girl lilt to her voice that stood his nerves on end as effectively as nails drawn across a chalkboard. Her blue eyes sparked with silver as if shooting beads of boiling mercury.

Mike Sansom appeared from an arched doorway. "Okay, Bonnie. Down, girl." Then to Eric: "My pit bull. Don't worry, I've taken her through obedience school. She growls pretty good, but she knows not to bite."

"Michael," she whined, but seemed oddly pleased.

Mike laughed. "How about a cup of tea? Or some lunch?"

"No, thanks. I'm fine," Eric said.

Mike gave his wife a kiss, a quick peck on the lips, then swatted her behind, shooing her away. He stared after her until she disappeared, then turned to his guest. "Come on, let's go on into the living room."

Eric followed, noticing the tasteful decor and warm ambience. "Nice digs," he told his former partner as he circled a five-foot-square glass and brass table to lower himself onto the sofa Mike had indicated with a casual flick of his wrist.

The FBI agent dropped into an adjacent chair. "Yep, it is that. And you're wondering how in the hell I manage all this on government pay."

Eric grinned, but shook his head. "Nope. You know me, Sansom. I'm a two plus two equals four kinda guy. Figured you married money."

"You're right. I did." Mike said, leaning back and stretching his long legs out on a hassock. "When Bonnie and I met five years ago, it was perfect. It was clear she was rolling in dough and just as apparent I wasn't. So we made a deal. I promised to learn how to be a kept man."

"Sounds okay to me."

"Okay? Are you serious? It's fanfuckingtastic. I mean, I know what people say about money not buying happiness, and I can't argue with them, but it sure keeps the bill-collector blues away. Besides, she's proud of what I do. Makes it real nice to come home every night after some bad-ass days."

"And the honeymoon continues," Eric said, though not unkindly.

"You got it. Four years since we exchanged vows and sometimes I still have a hard time believing how lucky I am."

He was dressed in a T-shirt and a pair of well-worn jeans. No shoes. King of his domain and comfortable in the role. Eric was actually glad for him.

"Well, enough talk about yours truly. You want to talk Rose Murders, huh?"

"Yeah, sort of. Indirectly." He thrust his chin in the direction of his host's nose. Swollen, discolored, sore looking.

"Ah," Mike said, touching it with a careful fingertip. "Wondering about the schnoz? It's okay. Tender, but not broken. Had the medical examiner give it a look-see before he left the hotel. He said it'd be fine in a couple of days. I came home to change clothes. When you called, I decided to take some time and go over paperwork I keep here on the murders."

"I'm sorry, bud," Eric said, surprised by how deep

he reached for the words and how much apology they covered. He grinned and inwardly squirmed just a bit, not entirely easy with raking over a half-dozen years of unjustly harbored hatred with such a simple statement.

"Forget it," Mike said generously. Then, for the first time since their split, he treated Eric to the famous Sansom belly laugh. It rumbled deep inside before finally rolling out of his mouth, contagious as a yawn. Eric didn't even try to fight it.

And then an amazing thing happened. The hole that had been torn in his soul by the loss of the three people he'd once loved most in the world, began to close up, to fill in. Maybe it was the genuine laughter or the words of apology—it didn't matter which. He was healing at last.

Eric and Mike got down to business.

"Okay, shoot," the FBI agent said. "Just don't get on my back about Darin Woods. I know we fucked up there, but—"

"But what, Mike? The case against that poor schmuck went sideways the minute Hair and Fiber advised they didn't have anything—no DNA, latents, not a single hair, fiber, nothing—belonging to the suspect anywhere near the victims' bodies. Outside a hotel room, in front of an apartment, on the hood of a car—"

"Inside Lisa Marks's house," Mike interjected, though it was weak and his tone said he knew it.

Eric knew it, too, and refused to give him even that. "Oh, yeah, inside the house . . . all the way to the bedroom door. But a good twelve feet from the body. Jesus, what in the hell were you guys thinking, Mike?"

"Okay!" the agent said, throwing up his hands. "You've made your point and I get it. Look, it wasn't my case then, but, yeah, I knew it was sour. When it was turned over to me, I went over everything we had with a fine-tooth comb. Then I met with the state boys, Chief Small and his task force, and we all went over it again. Someone, I don't have a clue who, suggested maybe Woods had an accomplice and someone else came back with some wiseass remark about Dumb and Dumber. So, okay, some of us were nervous about nailing the wrong guy, but it was still possible he was the one, and we didn't have anyone else. Not even a single other suspect."

The clock on the wall clicked off a half-dozen seconds before Eric asked the question they'd both known was coming. "Why didn't you?"

"Hey, don't bother me with the 'What about the Anthonys' crap. I've looked them over from every angle and it just doesn't hang."

Eric leaned forward and clasped his hands between his knees. "Why not?"

"Why?" Mike countered.

"I don't know," Eric said, picking up his briefcase and rifling through papers. One at a time, he introduced possibilities along with documentation to back them up. "After an initial nose dive, the Anthonys' stock has doubled. In fact, as of last month, it's nearly quadrupled in value."

Mike looked over the stock reports and articles clipped from newspapers and magazines all over the world. He slid the papers across the coffee table in Eric's direction. "Shit," he said with a disgusted shake of his head. He thought about Eric's supposition, then everything he'd read and shook his head again. "Nah, that's just crazy. I don't doubt the publicity helped the company, twisted as it seems, but that doesn't mean the family's guilty."

Eric said, "Okay, let's do this. Let me tell you what I uncovered this morning. See if it starts any bells clanging for you."

Mike settled back in his chair, crossing his legs and scratching his scalp. "Let's have it."

In as few words as possible, Eric told him about his interview with Maryann. Mike didn't comment, so he went on to his talk with the garrulous housekeeper, Jeannie O'Rourke. This took a little longer, and Bonnie returned in the middle of the telling, this time settling into her own chair. "Mind if I listen in?"

Eric looked to the federal agent. Officially, legally it was his case; his call.

"Sure," Mike said. "After all, they're your relatives we're talking about."

Eric straightened to attention. "Wait a minute. What are you talking about?"

"Maryann is my cousin—fourth removed, or some such nonsense. We share a maiden name—Strauss— in common, but that's about it. She doesn't approve of me. I refused to come out as a BOTAR, went to Mizzou instead of Bryn Mawr or even Holyoke, and as you may have noticed, my taste runs counter to Maryann's." She wiggled her long, pink nails to underscore her point. "But it's okay. I don't like her either. I try to avoid her. Haven't seen any of them except once since our wedding four years ago. Except on TV, of course. Mikey sees them a lot now that he's been assigned as the case agent. Matter of fact, he was over at their place last night."

Eric had forgotten about that. He glanced at the agent, but decided to let it go for now. If he thought of any questions regarding the party or Mike's association with the Anthonys, he'd come back to it later. Right now, he wanted to stay focused. He smiled at Bonnie.

"What do you know about Anna Renee Anthony?"

"Wow, you're going back, now. I haven't even heard her name since I was a little girl. Everyone called her Annie Re, I think. Something like that.

Gosh, I was hardly more than a baby when she died. She was really young, wasn't she?"

"Yep. Jeannie—your cousin's housekeeper—told me she died in a car accident in Europe twenty-nine years ago. The anniversary of her death just passed a couple of weeks ago."

Both Sansoms exchanged confused glances, then looked back at their guest. "So?" they asked in unison.

"Probably nothing," Eric admitted. But now that he'd started it, he might as well finish it. "Just that Christi was born the same day her aunt died. I don't know, probably just another coincidence in a probe so full of them, it makes a guy start seeing cross-eyed. Like you being related to the Anthonys, even distantly. Weird."

Bonnie laughed. "No, wait, it wasn't a coincidence— the birth/death thing, I mean. I remember the story. Alex went to Europe after graduating from college. There was something of a bruhaha about it. His old man, uh, father, was all bent out of shape because they'd planned a big weeding—Alex and Maryann, that is—and then he was supposed to take his place in the family business. Instead, he announces his plans to bum around Europe, cancels the nuptuals, and before anyone can slip a word of protest in edgewise, he's outta here." Both men were leaning forward, totally involved with the story she was telling. She put herself into it. "Anyway, Maryann was mortified as only she could be. There was some sort of scandal. I don't know if she tried to kill herself or what. I think I knew once upon a time, but I wasn't even out of diapers when it all went down."

"Go on," Mike said, bringing her back on track.

"Oh, yeah. Well, let's see. I remember my mother telling me that Bess—Alex and Pauls' mother— straightened everything out."

"Alex was in Switzerland, in the Alps or something,

and Bess helped Maryann arrange a surprise visit. I
guess Alex was glad, because they got married over
there, all by themselves, no family, no friends, nothing.
Only, everyone thought they'd come home after the
honeymoon and when they didn't, after nearly a year,
Bess sent Paul and Anna Renee to visit. I don't know
what happened next, exactly, except that there was a
serious accident. Paul was critically injured, but Annie
Re was killed and Maryann went into premature labor
and delivered Christianne." Silver tears stood in her
eyes, tarnished to pewter by sadness.

"Like you said, not a coincidence," Eric said ruefully. "Just another dark era in the Anthony family
annals. I'm beginning to think you might be right,
Mike. They may be guilty of nothing more than being
the unluckiest clan since Job and his bunch."

"Well, there was something I remember everyone
whispering about when I was a little girl. You might
consider it a coincidence."

"What?" her husband asked.

"That both brothers apparently fell in love with the
same woman."

"What?" Eric and Mike protested in one loud bark.

"Yep. Or at least that was the rumor. I was five or
six, maybe seven when all the talk was going on. I
remember, though, because I didn't know how a
woman could be married to one man and get pregnant
by his brother."

"Paul got her pregnant?" Mike asked sharply. "You
sure?"

"I'm sure that's what everyone was saying. Just like
I'm sure Maryann had a miscarriage or an abortion,
maybe. Christi even stayed with us for a couple of
weeks until her mommy was feeling better. She told
me her uncle Paul had gone away 'cause he was so
sad. I don't think she knew he was the daddy or anything. At least, everyone at my house was real careful

not to bring it up in front of her. Anyway, if I remember right, he didn't come back for several years after that."

This was big and both men knew it, though they also realized something else that Bonnie obviously hadn't. This was the David Keaton and Bryn Carroll story all over again.

"You okay?" Mike asked Eric, understanding, as only friends who've gone through serious shit together can. This had to have sparked a sense of déjà vu in the *Savant*. Hell, *he'd* sure felt it!

"Yeah, I'm good," Eric told him, and it was true, though he'd felt the punch in the gut same as he had the day Bryn and Dave had told him they were in love. For a moment he empathized with Alex. In the next instant, he shoved it away. Couldn't lose objectivity. Still, it was a tad close for comfort. He turned the subject back to the case at hand. "Could we have stumbled across a motive?" he asked.

"Shit, Keaton, you're talking more than twenty years ago. How're you going to tie an affair to murders fifteen years after the fact?"

"Maybe I'm not," Eric admitted. "But try this on . . . just for size."

"I'm waiting," the other man said.

"Paul's in love with Maryann who's married to his brother. His younger brother who's also CEO of the family company. Either one might make a man mad enough to want to shake things up for the golden boy. Together they might be angry enough to try and destroy him."

"Yeah, except I don't think Alex and Maryann's marriage is exactly what you'd call a match made in heaven," Mike returned. "He keeps an apartment on the Plaza. Spends almost as much time there as he does in Anthony. And Paul was once the company's head honcho. He gave it all up when he left the country after the affair. No one asked him to. Not even Alex. He simply announced he was leaving and boom, he was gone."

"When he came back," Bonnie interjected, "Alex offered to move aside, give him back the reins. Paul turned him down. When they invited him to move back into the house, he agreed, and from what everyone says it's been one big happy family ever since."

"Uh-huh, unless the Anthonys have just gotten better at keeping their dirty laundry in the hamper."

"You're really on their case, huh?" Mike asked. "You going strictly on gut, or you got something more you're not saying?"

Eric could have told him it was a little of both, but he was already off on a different tangent. He held up a finger, suggesting Mike hold onto his question for a minute, and followed his own line of thinking. When he had it clear in his own head, he asked Bonnie, "You remember any gossip about Christi being shipped off to Italy?"

She thought about it, staring off in space and tapping her chin with a fingertip. "Hmm. Not much, no. Just the normal envious, petty kind of talk, you know? Like, how come they'd given a girl that young and inexperienced so much responsibility. And how come Bess went only one time to visit her in Rome when Maryann made an annual pilgrimage. That kind of thing."

"What about Alex and Paul? Did either one of them accompany Maryann?"

Bonnie hesitated, nodded. "I think so," she said slowly. Then with more certainty. "Yes, they did. Both of them, at least once that I'm sure about, because Mikey and I ran into them in Rome when we were there on our first-year anniversary. Remember, honey? I was so-o-o ticked off when you got called home a few days later. Another damned FBI crisis and I felt bad about that, but there's always another case, you know? And this was our honeymoon."

"Which brings us to a reality check," her husband put in. "I need to be out there investigating this one." He looked at Eric. "You got anything else about the Anthonys or otherwise?" A touch of impatience tinged his tone.

"I'm almost positive I found the truck that killed Woods," Eric said.

"Darin Woods?" Bonnie asked, her eyes owl-wide. "He's dead? And you didn't tell me?"

Neither man heard her. Eric had handed the agent something big, and they were testing the weight together.

"Where?" Mike asked, already knowing he wasn't going to like the answer.

"In Anthony, Missouri. About two miles from the house."

"Holy smoke!" Mike whispered under his breath. "No wonder you're so hot on the Anthonys. That's in their own backyard . . . And so long as we're in the neighborhood, we might as well keep digging right there."

Chapter Thirty-one

Eric slipped the phone back into his pocket as he pulled into a parking spot in the garage of the thirty-two-story granite and mirrored glass A-shaped building. A-shaped for Anthony, of course. Impressive.

In Manhattan a guy might not look twice. But this was Kansas City, the heart of the Midwest. Yes, sir, headquarters of the multinational conglomerate had been designed to make people sit up and take notice, and it certainly did that.

He opened the car door and was stepping out when a muted peal from the cellular phone in his pocket stopped the world.

Christi? Guy? Didn't matter. Had to be one of the two. Mike had the number now but had promised not to use it until word from New York came through about Levi.

Eric's heart was hammering loud and he barely caught Guy's voice when it came back.

"Pappy! Yeah, what have you got?" He slid in behind the wheel again, and slammed the car door, leaning on the armrest to steady his hand.

Guy's deep, resonant voice boomed loud now. "Slow down, Keaton. We don't have a thing on Levi or Tommy."

The day was warm, the April sun was beating down brightly on the small, compact car, but it was relief that beaded to the surface of Eric's brow. "Then why the call on the cell—" He broke off in midsentence as he realized Jameson must have gotten news of the murders. "You've heard about the women," he said flatly, the adrenaline that had coursed through him leaving him weak and nauseated as it dissipated.

"I heard. We got it over the wires ten minutes ago, but I was already on the horn with Alex. What in the hell is going on out there, Keaton?"

"What did he tell you?"

"About the contestant, uh, Peters . . . yeah, Jillie Peters, and the policewoman, of course, but also that you brought his daughter to the hotel. He's going through the roof, and threatening to pull every string he can find to get your license yanked."

"Hey! I didn't take Christi to the hotel or anywhere else this morning. What I did for that ungrateful bastard was get her out of the hotel after she had already seen too much. What's got your old pal's skivvies in a bunch is the sudden shift in the wind out here. The investigation's taken a turn toward a little burg a few miles northwest of K.C., Guy, and it's not just because I've been pointing in that direction. The Anthonys are stirring up such a stink it won't be long before a blind coon dog'll be able to follow the scent and tree the right fuck."

"And who is that?" Guy asked.

Eric muttered a curse but kept his tone every bit as even and unemotional as his mentor's. "I've got the pegs, Pappy, I just haven't found out which one fits the right hole. But I'll tell you this, you need to be more careful how you go about collecting friends."

"Eric—"

The *Savant* heard the warning, ignored it. "Listen. Alex is not exactly the Jimmy Stewart you painted him to be, and Maryann sure as hell ain't Donna Reed. As for Paul, he's a grenade whose pin's already been pulled—Jack Nicholson straight out of *The Shining*!"

Eric caught himself and sighed wearily. "Look, Guy,

excuse the blast. The shit's starting to fly out here and I'm not sure what to do about it."

"Just tell me what you've got." A lifer in law enforcement, Guy had seen too much to let an overexcited pup upset him, *Savant* or not. "And go slow, Keaton, I'm taking notes."

Eric recounted the events of the morning, checking off everything he'd picked up. He didn't leave out a thing except his growing feelings for Christi. That wasn't for public consumption . . . or even for family, which Guy was to Eric.

Guy took over when Eric finished up. "I'm sorry, but you're going to have to come up with stronger stuff than that. I agree the Anthonys sound nervous, but who knows what about. You could be right about going back a few years. Maybe your murderer hails from the past."

In other words, asshole, keep looking, Eric thought, frustrated and beginning to heat up around the collar. But Guy was right. He knew the rules and would play along. "Okay, I'll work on it, but help me out here. You got any idea why someone would hate them enough to kill innocent women just to bring them down?"

"I don't know. Just keep digging, and I'll think on it; call some of Alex and my friends from school. I've stayed in touch with a few over the years. I'll fish around. See if any of them comes up with anything."

"Okay, great. Let me know."

"Sure, but, listen, before we get off, I gotta talk to you about something else."

Eric didn't like the sound of that, but with no way around it, he went straight in. "What've you got?"

"Roni nailed her man."

Eric grinned, relieved. "Geez, I almost pity the poor slob."

Guy chuckled, but there wasn't any life in it. "Yeah,

she's on her way home from Europe tomorrow. . . .
Oh, and Keaton, about my goddaughter, Christianne?
Alex mentioned that the two of you are getting pretty
tight. That true?"

"If it is?" Eric hedged.

"Nothing. Just wondering."

"Sure," Eric muttered. "That it?"

"Nope, one more. About you and Sansom reconcil-
ing. I'm glad to hear it. Sorry you had to pop him
before you could get past all the baggage between
you, but whatever it takes, huh?"

"Yeah," Eric agreed. His boss was trying hard to
smooth the bumpy road they'd detoured onto. The
least he could do was give him a little room to work.

"Well, that's it then. Stay close to your phone."

"Will do." He started to hang up, then reconsid-
ered. "Hey, Guy, you still there?"

"Yeah?"

"It just occurred to me. I haven't heard you light
a cigarette."

"I gave it up for Lent," Guy growled.

Eric laughed. "Yeah, right."

Ash Wednesday had come and gone and Guy had
not sacrificed a single cigarette.

Chapter Thirty-two

Eric was still grinning as he stepped from the car and dropped the phone in his pocket again. "Smart-ass," he said as he headed for the building.

His good humor was short-lived, however. Alex saw to that the minute Eric was shown into his office. "You get my daughter home?" he demanded.

"I'm fine, Alex. Tired, upset that two more women are dead—senselessly, unnecessarily—but hey, otherwise I'm doing okay. Thanks for asking." He grinned. "You, too, I see. Business as usual, huh?"

Alex shook his head, exasperation joining fatigue to drain his patience. He barely held onto his temper to manage a civil reply. "No, Keaton, not business as usual. My brother and wife are on the way to the airport to meet Jillie Peters's parents. Three of my judges have backed out, and even though I wanted to cancel the pageant, the police have insisted we go ahead. So, I've been on the phone trying to scrounge up a few brave souls who aren't terrified of having their reputations irreparably sullied by a connection to the Anthonys. We've had to cancel tonight's event, which is no big deal in itself, except that it prolongs all of this—this whole terrible ordeal. . . . What do you want, anyway?" he asked in an abrupt change of subject.

"Just to ask a couple of questions."

"Okay," Alex said, surrendering. "Ask away."

"First, tell me about your sister. Anna Renee, I

think her name was." *Knew* her name was, though he thought it better to keep it vague. Less likely to tip his hand that way.

"What do you want to know?" Alex asked, clearly surprised.

"Well, I guess, I'd like to see some pictures. Satisfy myself that she and Christi looked almost identical."

Alex's answering sigh was heavy. "I don't have to show you pictures, Doctor. I can tell you myself that Christi and Annie Re resembled each other, yes, but no more so than my daughter and I. I promise you, they were not identical. For one thing, Annie Re was much shorter, and though her hair was almost as fair as Christi's, their eyes were quite different.

"Incidentally, where is my daughter?" he asked in another sharp segue, his flagging spirits suddenly evident in his weary tone.

"At the plant. At least that's where she was headed when we left the hotel. She was still upset, I think, but she insisted that her work would keep her mind off . . . everything. I didn't argue. I thought it was a good idea. Why dwell on something she shouldn't have to be a part of in the first place?"

Alex wheeled his chair around and leaned forward. His blue eyes had brightened to silver with his outrage, which he no longer even tried to disguise or control. "Just what the hell is that crack supposed to mean? I'm not the jackass who brought her into this!"

"Hey, that's good! Let's start with that; find out just which jackass you are. For starters, are you the jackass who keeps an apartment here in town for his mistresses?" Eric flared back, happy with the shot he'd fired at him.

Alex's face was suddenly blotched dark red, but he didn't flinch from the accusation. "It's no secret that I keep an apartment. It's sometimes not convenient to go all the way to Anthony. I sleep over in the city."

He paused a beat, then added, "How did you find out about that?"

"From the FBI," Eric said, not a bit repentant about crediting the government with the information instead of the housekeeper. "So, do you entertain your women friends there?"

Alex didn't answer. Instead he opened a desk drawer, pulling out his cigarette case and lighter. "Mind?" he asked, already lighting up.

"Your lungs."

Alex laughed at that, then absently focused his attention on a crystal paperweight he'd picked up from the corner of his desk. Inside, a red rosebud rested motionless and magical in midair. "Beautiful, isn't it?" he asked.

Yeah, Eric thought, but so what?

As if Eric had spoken aloud, Alex jabbed out the cigarette abruptly and returned to the question. "As I've said, I keep an apartment and on occasion, I have entertained guests there, yes." He set the crystal globe back in its place and raised his gaze to meet the *Savant*'s. "Do you now make a quantum leap from adultery to murder?"

"I don't know, Alex. You tell me. But if that jump's too big, why don't we start with smaller steps?"

Alex shrugged.

"Okay. Do you have a mistress now?"

Alex smiled and raised a brow, signaling his relief. That was, indeed, an easy step. "No. No mistress in my present or in fact, even in my past. The few women I have, uh, entertained in my apartment have been one-time guests." He tapped the paperweight, a prop to help him with the next point. "I've always made it crystal clear that I wasn't interested in more than that, and I don't believe any of my, ah, lady friends ever misunderstood my intentions."

Time for a bigger step. "What about pageant contestants?" Eric asked.

Alex grinned as he recognized the trap; the pit he would drop into if he elected to lie. "Twice," he answered directly. "But neither of them ended up dead. They were a long time back, in the first two years of the pageant."

"You got any names?"

Alex grinned, the sarcastic expression of a man who won't be pushed. "The FBI has a list of my, ah, conquests. Get it from them."

"I'll do that," Eric said.

"Look, Keaton, those girls were mistakes. I will always regret my stupidity, I had experienced some difficult times. Not a good excuse, but an honest one."

"Difficult? Like after your wife got pregnant by your brother?"

Alex's face blanched at the question. "The FBI give you this, too?"

"Your wife's cousin."

Alex frowned for a few seconds before successfully tracking that one. "Oh, you mean Bonnie Sansom. Yes, I should have realized she would know about that." He leaned back in his chair and raised his eyes to the ceiling as if he could see the past there. "God, that was so long ago. Bonnie was just a kid. Who would have thought she'd even remember." He chuckled bitterly. "I suppose it's the kind of scandal that gets talked about in families for generations."

Eric uncrossed his legs and shifted position in an impossible attempt to get comfortable with prying into someone else's soiled linens. "What about Christi? Bonnie said she stayed with her family for a while. Did she understand what was happening? Why she'd been sent away?"

Alex groaned, and for the second time in as many minutes, guilt writhed inside Eric's gut.

Alex squeezed his eyes shut. When he opened them again he met Eric's gaze, resolute in spite of the tears that stood unspilled. "I don't think so. I hope not. I pray she never does." He laughed, though there was no humor, only regret.

Eric started to interrupt, but Alex stopped him with a raised hand.

"Wait. I know this must cut a little too close to the bone with everything that happened to you a few years back, and I'm sorry for that. Fortunately for us, ours didn't have such a tragic resolution. We've been able to pick up the pieces and go on. Besides, it wasn't quite the same. I was at fault in this instance. Maryann was lonely. I'd neglected her, and she turned to Paul, who'd been in love with her since the first time he laid eyes on her." He paused, rubbed his eyes, then sighed as he met Eric's gaze again. "That's all there is. Trust me, it has nothing to do with your investigation."

Alex pushed himself from his chair and went to stand at the floor-to-ceiling window.

Eric ran his hands through his hair. "Maybe we've both had enough for today," he said.

"No. Hold on," Alex said. Keeping his back to his visitor, he shook his head, adding emphasis. "I want you to understand something here."

"Okay," Eric said agreeably.

"When Christi came home from Europe, I got real uneasy. I mean, almost the minute she stepped off the plane I had this sense of impending doom as if a black cloud had followed her and was hanging over us. Sounds melodramatic, but it's scary as hell, Keaton.

"At first I excused it to Mother's death, like maybe somehow I'd known it was coming. But when it lingered—the surety that there was still more to come, that the worst had yet to happen—I blamed it on the fear that without Mother I wasn't going to be able to keep it all together." A shrug and a grin that seemed mildly embarrassed. "She was the glue that kept me from falling apart, I can't deny it."

"Yeah," Eric said. "Mother's are like that."

Alex smiled. It faded with the return to the subject of his unease. "Then I shifted gears, blaming it on the absolute certainty that no matter what the police and FBI kept saying, somehow the lunatic who had been killing these women would succeed in getting to another."

"And you were right," Eric said.

"Yes," Alex agreed, though it seemed he hadn't really heard. He turned back into the room, circled his desk, and dropped into the chair beside Eric's. He looked lost.

"You were telling me—" Eric prompted gently.

"I was getting to the hard part."

"Sorry."

"Two women were murdered this morning and as ashamed as I am to admit it, I thought there would be relief. You know, like after the other shoe drops, you say 'okay it's bad, but at least it's over, I know what it was I was afraid of, now, and I can deal with it.' Only it's still there, inside, stronger than ever."

"The fear that the worst is yet to come?" Eric asked.

Alex nodded, then ran a trembling hand over his face. "Oh, God, Eric, I haven't admitted this to another soul."

"And you don't have to tell me," Eric said, strategically backing off.

"Oh, yeah, I do. I've waded in too deep to get out now."

Eric kept quiet.

"I'm afraid he's going to get Christi."

Eric didn't know why, but the admission made him

mad; mad enough to want to hit the guy. "Son of a bitch!"

"She's always been his real target, Keaton. And now that she's home, he's going to go after her. I know it. I just don't know how to stop it."

"You stop it by telling me who in the hell he is!" Eric shouted.

"You asshole," Alex growled. "You think I wouldn't tell you if I knew!"

Eric stood up, shoving his chair back several inches with the force of leaving it. "Yeah, that's exactly what I think. In fact, that's what I know! This killer isn't some bastard off the street who's just picked your contestants out of a random drawing. He's someone with a personal agenda that has Anthony written all over it. It's there somewhere in your past, and you'd better find out where and who and why, and then fill me in, 'cause, buddy, if anything happens to Christi, I'm coming for you. All three of you. Mama, papa, and whacko uncle." He'd gotten to the door, though he didn't remember the crossing. Turning the handle, he jabbed the air with a finger aimed at the CEO. "Count on it."

Chapter Thirty-three

Eric was on the cell phone a moment later, trying to track down Mike and coming up empty. He'd tried his number at the FBI office, his car phone, his house, and the Ritz-Carlton, all with the same result. Zilch.

He was about to punch in the agent's pager number when his own cellular squealed from the car seat beside him.

"Keaton," he said, clipped, impatient.

"Hey, Eric, it's Mike."

"Now, that's spooky," Keaton responded. "I've been calling all over town trying to reach you."

Sansom laughed. "That's what I've been hearing . . . from everyone. So what's up?"

"I need a favor."

"Shoot."

"The copies of all those files the FBI put together on the Anthonys, their friends, associates, enemies—"

"Jesus, Keaton, even I haven't been through all of them. There must be a couple hundred. You want to read them all?"

"At least scan 'em. But I'd like to go over them in my hotel room. That be a problem?"

"Nah," the agent told him. "Like you said, they're copies. Go on by the house and pick them up." He promised to call Bonnie, tell her to let him take whatever he needed. In the meantime, he was stuck out in Anthony talking to Gary Webster and his neighbors about the truck Eric had found. When he finished

there, he was going back to the Ritz-Carlton. After
that, he and Chief Small had a dinner meeting scheduled with the district attorney, the mayor, and the police commissioner. "You know that's going to be a
blast. A long night at best. At worst, a fucking finger-
pointing fest."

Eric sympathized. He knew all about trying to pac-
ify the muckamucks. Usually a waste of time. He con-
gratulated himself on the prospect of long hours
poring over the dossiers on the Anthonys and any of
their associates the FBI deemed important to the case.
Should include a pretty eclectic group; could be
interesting.

Eric was determined that before he went to sleep
tonight, he'd have one of two things: Either a solid
list of suspects from the Anthonys' 'associates' files,
or the field narrowed down once and for all to the
Trio, itself.

Back at the Marriott, he ordered room service—a
Kansas City strip and a bottle of merlot—then put in
a call to Guy; several of them, actually. Left messages
all over New York and tried to console himself with
the platitude that no news is good news.

He phoned Christi. When she came on the line, he
grinned and settled back on the sofa. Damn if she
wasn't as effective as Valium for his ragged nerves.
Definitely better than the wine he'd ordered.

"Hi," she said. "You sound tired. Long day, huh?"

"Yep, it has been that," he agreed. "How about
you? Able to get any work done?"

"Oh, I don't know. A little. Not much. Mostly I
kept doing this high-low thing. One minute thinking
about you, the next remembering that poor girl . . .
the way she—"

"Shh. Don't do that one. Push it out of your mind
if you can."

"Oh, sure."

He didn't try to convince her. He knew how impossible it was to forget something as terrible as murder. He moved the subject to neutral territory. "So, what are you doing?"

"Actually, I just changed my clothes. I'm going to go get Mustard and take him out for a run. Ground's probably still soaked from all the rain, but at least it's not pouring right now. Thought I'd seize the moment before it starts up again."

"It'll help. Wish I could join you but I've got a few dozen file folders to go through before I quit tonight."

"Oh," she said softly. She shuddered, recalling Jillie Peters's still, pale face, the fixed stare of her open eyes turned to glass in death, and her outstretched arm, veined red with her blood.

"Hey, you all right?" Eric asked.

"Yes . . . no. God, I just can't stop seeing her . . . Jillie—"

"Yeah, I know. It's awful. Go for your run, then get a hot shower and go to bed. You'll feel better in the morning."

"Okay," she said quietly. Then with more zip, "And if none of that works, I'll think about how hot it will get when we finally get together."

"Oh, shit," Eric said. "I'd better get off before we start having phone sex and I really have to get off."

She giggled. "You can call me later if you need a break and something to take your mind off work."

"Baby, I do that and I'm going to have to drive out to Anthony. The telephone's not going to do it for me."

"I never should have started this!" she said, her voice beginning to sound breathless.

"Too late, I think. I'm starting to hurt."

"Oh, wow, time to run. Talk to you later. *Ciao!*"

Eric laughed, started to hang up, then suddenly remembered something. "Christi!"

"Eric?"

"Yeah, I'm here. Sorry. You just reminded me of
something. I talked with your family's housekeeper
today—"

"Jeannie?"

"Yeah. She mentioned that your grandmother came
to visit you only one time while you were in Italy. I
was just wondering how come?"

"I don't know," she said slowly. "Why? Is it
important?"

Eric laughed. "Hell if I know. Just struck me as odd
considering how close the two of you were. But it's
probably nothing. Forget it."

"No, wait. I'm thinking."

He waited.

"You know something funny, Eric? I never thought
about it much. Guess I always just assumed it was her
age. But now that you've brought it up, maybe there
was a reason."

"Tell me," he encouraged, feeling his heart rate
quicken at the understanding in her voice.

"She and mother had an ugly argument. We were
at Alfredo's in Rome—all of us. Daddy and Uncle
Paul, too. Anyway, we were right in the middle of
dinner when Mike Sansom came in with his new bride,
Bonnie. Daddy, I think it was, invited them to join us.
Mother was unhappy and didn't try too hard to hide
her feelings. She and Bonnie are related. Distant cous-
ins or something, a fact Mother would prefer everyone
forget. Anyway, she was rude. Hostile. We all tried to
ignore the barbs she kept jabbing Bonnie with, but it
was pretty embarrassing.

"Then Agent Sansom mentioned something about
a young prostitute who'd been murdered. He didn't
go into details or anything. Just said how he wished

he could get a look at the police report, and Mother blew up. Then Gran got angry with her, and Paul got upset with Gran. . . ." She laughed. "They had a real domino thing going for a few minutes, and people were starting to stare, which is saying something in Europe where everyone expects Americans to behave badly.

"Bonnie and I pretty much stayed out of the fracas, but I remember exchanging glances. You know, silently communicating a fierce desire to get down on our hands and knees and crawl out of there.

"Anyway, that was the last trip for Gran. Dad and Uncle Paul, too, now that I think about it. I don't know if it was because of the argument as far as Gran was concerned, but probably. They were there for almost another week, and she was pretty quiet the whole time. Unusual for her. She liked to talk." She laughed. "That help?"

"Maybe, I don't know," he said thoughtfully. "One thing, though."

"Sure. What?"

"Why'd your mother get so pissed about what Mike said?"

"I think because of the Rose Pageant contestant who'd been murdered the same way—stabbed to death. It was just the coincidence of it. I mean, here they were halfway across the world and it almost seemed like the murderer had followed them."

"Huh. Maybe he had," Eric said.

Christi laughed and dismissed the notion. "That's silly. People are killed every day in every city of the world. It was just unsettling for my family after what had happened the year before."

Except that was the only year no contestant was killed, Eric thought. Besides, there's that word again: Coincidence.

*   *   *

Eric threw himself into his work, losing himself in the FBI files while keeping his mind away from the two places where it wanted to drift: His worry for Levi and his desire for Christi. He couldn't afford to think of either one. Not now. Not if he wanted to stay sane.

By one a.m. he was so tired, he had to push everything aside and get up to walk around for a bit. Stretch his legs and splash cold water on his face.

By two-thirty, he was no longer making sense of the notes he'd taken for the past eight hours. He'd made good progress. That much he was sure of, but everything was running together, making him dizzy. Time to give it up.

He wasn't even going to make it to the bed in the other room.

He'd been working on the couch and that was where he was going to stay.

Pushing the remaining file folders onto the floor, he swung his feet up, and stretched out. God, it felt good to close his eyes. The sigh he began turned into a yawn. In less than a minute, he was asleep. But just before he drifted off, it flashed clear. He was sure, now. He had 'em nailed.

Alex, Paul, or Maryann. One of them was a killer.

Chapter Thirty-four

Christi was in love.

A smile lifted the corners of her lips and color stained her cheeks. She was dreaming. Having night fantasies about him . . . about *them* together. Wonderful, delicious, wicked thoughts that had followed her from her daydreams into sleep.

But it was beginning to storm, and the sounds of crashing thunder, pounding rain, and wind-whipped trees were beginning to intrude on the happy interlude.

She woke up, grumbled, and rolled onto her side. Punching her pillow, she curled up and closed her eyes. She didn't want to lose the dream. It was too wonderful to let go of just yet.

But outside, the storm had worked itself into a frenzy, becoming loud and violent, and Christi felt the last vestiges of her naughty-but-nice dream slip away.

Flopping onto her back, she kicked off her covers and tossed her arms out at her sides with a muttered "damn."

Still, a smile spread as she recaptured bits and pieces.

They'd danced as they had a couple of nights before. And they'd made love. In real life, they hadn't gotten that far, though she was sure they would soon . . . after the investigation.

"Oh, God," she groaned, as thoughts of his body slammed into her. How could she even think of her own pleasure when the body of Jillie Peters, who had looked enough like Christi to be her sister, lay stabbed to death, cut to ribbons.

"Oh, hell," she cursed.

Outside, the wind lashed the trees and made them cry. *Scream.* A shiver rocked her. She hated the sound. Always had though she'd forgotten it in her years away. She frowned, realizing that she had never heard anything quite like it in all her years at school or in Europe. Not anywhere except here at home on her family's estate.

The crying trees. That's what she'd called them. Once, when her family had gone sailing at the lake, she'd found a comparison in the screech of the moored boat straining against its dock. But the truth was, there was no sound in the world exactly like the crying trees.

She tossed her feet over the side of the bed, and sat up. She wasn't going to get back to sleep right away, not with thoughts of Jillie Peters's death roiling through her head. She'd go downstairs and fix a cup of hot chocolate. Try to get her thoughts back on a certain gorgeous investigator. Might even get her dreaming—

Her hands stopped midknot as she was tying the sash on her robe. What was that sound?

There! The faint sound of a dog's bark. And then louder, sharper, desperate. Mustard.

Jamming her feet into slippers, she ran from the room. She dashed along the hall and down the staircase to the kitchen. As she hit the lower level, the yapping was louder, more desperate.

She punched the numbered code of the alarm system on the keypad, fumbled with the deadbolt, and yanked the door open. The wind caught it, slamming it against the wall and almost sending her back with it. She held on, recovering her balance.

As she ducked her head and darted across the terrace, metal clinked, followed by a long, labored yowl of pain.

Her chenille housecoat soaked and heavy in seconds, Christi shrugged it off, leaving it on the lawn as she ran. She stumbled and fell hard on her knees, and sobs she hadn't even been aware of racked her body as she scrambled to her feet again and flung off her slippers.

Her heart hammered fiercely in her chest, a drumroll of panic, adrenaline, and exertion. She was little more than halfway across the lawn when she was realized she didn't hear her pet. She strained her ears for his angry bark or even his yelps of pain. Nothing.

For the first time since the incident two nights before, she remembered the way the retriever's coat had bristled on his back and her certainty that she was being watched. She stopped in her tracks. Her wet nightgown slapped her skin, and she rocked precariously against the assault of the wind. She hardly noticed the storm, though, as she dashed rain from her eyes and held her long hair away from her face, trying to see the pen some twenty yards away. She could hardly make out even the shapes of the giant trees at that distance.

Moving slowly, a cautious step at a time, she silently begged for a single bark or yap from her pet.

Lightning flashed, illuminating the area as bright as a stage, and the discovery she made took her breath away.

The pen's gate had been flung wide. The grass on both sides nearest her had been uprooted in great clumps, and thick swatches of coarse, golden dog fur were caught in the chain links almost to the top of the six-foot fence.

Forgetting the danger that might still be waiting for

her, she cried out, calling Mustard's name as she dashed to the empty pen.

She didn't go inside. She didn't have to. She pressed her forehead against the fence, her fingers looped through its links. Tears spilled over her lashes and ran with the rain dripping from her hair. In the dark she couldn't see clearly, but she knew. Could tell from the ribbons running in places along the fence, rivulets the rain diluted to pink, that it was stained with Mustard's blood.

Chapter Thirty-five

Eric shut off the car lights as he turned into the private drive. He risked tearing his bumper an a low-lying boulder or tree stump. Might wind up stuck in the mud, too, but what the hell? He couldn't chance being seen.

Glancing around, he satisfied himself both with his view of the house and his cover under a low-hanging roofline of tree branches. He cut the engine, leaving the key turned to auxiliary power so he could run the windshield wipers. Without them, he'd be blind as a newborn kitten.

It bothered him that Christi had insisted he wait for her in the car. Even whispering into the phone, she'd sounded practically hysterical. He didn't like the idea of her having to sneak all the way from the house alone in the dark. Well, he'd have to keep careful watch; make sure he didn't miss her once she started from the house. Then if she needed him before she made it to the car, he'd be ready to help.

He glanced at the time on the digital clock. He rubbed his eyes with the heels of his hands. Damn, he was tired. He hadn't had much sleep since leaving New York on Monday, but he'd done with less for longer in the past. Chalk it up to emotional drain, he thought, craning his neck to try and ease the kinks from his burning shoulder blades. He should be using the time to jot down some notes. Things were breaking loose, and he knew that even one minor over-

looked fact could put the entire investigation i
jeopardy, not to mention Christi. *Especially* her.

He eased the seat back, cursing the compact car fc
its lack of legroom. Maybe he should get out an
stretch. There was no moon. No one would be abl
to see him from the house. He was more than thre
hundred yards away.

He glanced to the left, thought he made out a flick
ering, wavering light at the edge of the grove. H
eased the car door open, swearing under his breath a
the dome light came on. He pulled the door shut onc
again, and fumbling in the dark, found the plastic plat
covering the overhead light. It was a trick he'd learne
from Levi in Lebanon a couple of years back. H
could see the big, black man's gleaming smile in th
darkness as he grabbed his arm, stopping him in the nic
of time before he opened the door and lit the ca
up bright as a giant Roman candle in the middle c
a blackout.

The memory of their easy camaraderie even unde
the most trying circumstances brought a fresh sting t
Eric's eyes and the familiar burning tightness in h
throat since his friend's disappearance.

With the lightbulb removed and the cover back i
place, he pulled his raincoat from the backseat an
climbed out.

He held his coat over his head, tentlike, eve
though he suspected the rain might help wake him u
invigorate him. It was tempting, except that he'd sper
many hours doing surveillance sitting in cars soake
through. He didn't have to think hard to recall ho
uncomfortable wet clothes could be. It was the chi
that went all the way to the bone he remembered a
the worst.

He folded the coat around his head, pulling it clos
under his chin like a hood, but the rain whipped a

is face and hands and seeped into his shoes and oaked his pants legs in seconds.

He muttered another curse as his heel sunk into a leep puddle and the heavy, wet mud oozed into his hoe. He stooped to free his foot, glancing up just as . light faltered again to the north in the distance.

He squinted against the rain as lightning lit the sky, outlining a small house through the hole of vision in he winter-thinned underbrush beneath the trees. It vas the caretaker's house, he realized, and the flick-ring light must be candles. Power outage. He turned pack toward the main house, searching for Christi. Nothing.

Grabbing hold of a low-hanging tree branch, he tripped some leaves and pulled his muddied shoe rom his foot. He tried to wipe out some of the muck, out it was useless, and he succeeded only in smearing his hands and arms with the muck.

"Shit!" he said under his breath as he jammed his oot back inside the shoe and set out through the trees o the edge of the grove.

He dropped back behind a tree trunk as lightning lashed overhead again. Damn it to hell, he hated hunderstorms. Wasn't exactly the smartest thing he'd ver done either, hiding behind a thirty-foot oak. A guy didn't grow up in Missouri and not know how often trees were struck.

Oh, well, piss on it. Danger or no, he'd come this ar, he wasn't going back to the car until Christi was vith him.

Something in the distance caught his eye. Straight-ning, he squinted against the slashing rain, trying to lear his vision. Reaching for the hem of the trench oat, he wiped at his eyes. Thunder boomed overhead n the same instant. Anticipating the lightning that vould follow, he brought his eyes back fully to the awns near the rose gardens and the greenhouse where

he was certain he'd seen someone or something mov
ing in the night.

The rain was coming hard now, pelting his face. He
raised an arm over his brow as a shield. It was no use.
The storm was too intense. He darted for cover under
another tree, this one a good ten yards closer to the
place where he'd seen the movement.

He slipped, nearly falling before catching himself
with an agile snatch at a tree branch. The effort won
him a scratched palm but saved him from going down
into the muddy grass. As he reached his goal, he could
make out the outline of the person he'd seen only in
a wavery silhouette before.

Christi! Thank God.

Thunder cracked and lightning split the air almost
immediately and only a few dozen yards from where
Eric stood. Jesus, that was close. Too close.

He'd been distracted for only a fraction of a second,
yet long enough that he almost missed Christi as she
shot past. He rolled away from the giant tree trunk,
catching her around the waist. Bad move, he realized
at once as she threw her head back and screamed.

"Christi, stop! It's all right! It's Eric!" he shouted
above the roar of the rain.

She pulled away from him, tossing her head from
side to side. Her face was twisted with pain, her chest
heaving with racking sobs.

Ignoring her flailing limbs as she struck at him, he
pulled her to her feet, wrapped his coat around her,
and scooped her up into his arms. "It's all right. Shh,
everything's okay now," he promised against her ear
as he trudged across the slippery lawn that was fast
becoming a muddy swamp.

By the time they reached the covert drive, she'd
settled down. "Better?" he asked as he pulled open
the car door and helped her in.

She shook her head, doubled over, and hugged her knees.

Eric frowned. He couldn't press her until he got them out of there. He reached under his seat for the .38 he had taken from his briefcase and brought along . . . just in case.

He tucked it under his thigh as he started the engine and backed the car at a snail's pace from its hiding place. He didn't hit the lights until all four tires were on pavement. Then he accelerated, spinning the car around, shifting gears, and speeding away. He had no idea what had happened. Only that she had called, practically incoherent. He only understood that she needed him. That was enough. He'd been curious and scared shitless. At least he wasn't scared anymore. She was with him now, and nobody was going to hurt her again. His hand closed around the barrel of the gun. God help the bastard who'd done this to her.

He placed her on the bed in his hotel suite, tipping her chin up with his fingers to bring her eyes to his. "There's a fresh sweatshirt hanging on the bathroom door. I'm going to get a towel to warm you, then I want you to put it on. How about a glass of brandy? It'll do the trick."

Christi brushed the light stubble on his cheek with her hand, offering a small smile. "I'm all right, Eric. Really. I want to wash my face and get the tangles out of this mess," she said, holding out a snarled strand of long, rain-darkened hair with fingers that still trembled.

Eric kissed her, meeting her smile with his own before turning away. Then his lips tightened as anger burned through him. What in the hell had happened to her?

Christi stopped him. "Eric?"

He hung back in the doorway, looking over his shoulder. "What, babe?"

"Thanks for coming to get me."

He winked. "My pleasure." His tone was light, upbeat even, though his hands balled into fists even as he spoke. He wanted to hit something. "Go dry off, I'll fix your drink."

In the living room, he sat on the sofa and pulled off his muddy shoes and socks. Next he dipped a hand towel in the ice bucket, wetting it to clean off the smeared grime from his hands. He poured a glass of brandy for her, a double shot of Scotch for himself. He drained his and refilled the glass. His heart skipped as he noticed the red light blinking on the telephone. A message at this hour could only be bad news.

"Are you all right?" Christi asked from the doorway.

"Huh?" he said absently, then covered by picking up the glasses, taking them into the bedroom and setting them on the nightstand.

He pulled back the covers and motioned for her to climb in. "Here," he said, holding out the glass of brandy once she was comfortable against the headboard.

She took a sip, then laid her head back on a deep sigh.

Eric pulled a chair from the desk to sit at her side. When she'd drained half the glass and set it on the table again, he asked her what happened.

Slowly, painfully, she went through it all—the dog's frantic barking, the blood all around the pen—right up until the moment of her call to him.

He moved from the chair to sit beside her on the bed and pull her into his arms. She was crying again but he heard her voice against his shoulder where her mouth was pressed. "Thank you," she murmured.

"You're welcome." He released her, guiding her

back against the headrest and kissing her brow. "Now, finish your brandy and close your eyes."

She shook her head, dashing tears from her eyes with the backs of her hands. "I won't be able to sleep, Eric. Someone killed Mustard, and while I was out here trying to find him, my mother—oh, God."

Eric's jaw was clenched so tightly his teeth ached. Anger churned in his stomach and thrummed behind his eyes. Right this minute he'd like nothing better than to go back out to that house and break a certain tiny throat . . . right before he beat another Anthony to a bloody pulp. Instead, he reached out to brush a renegade tear from her cheek. "Stop crying, sweetheart. Tomorrow, first thing, I'm going out there and find your dog. I don't think anyone killed him."

She started to protest, but he squeezed her hand, signaling her to hear him out before she disagreed.

"If whoever opened the gate had killed him, you would have found him. You didn't. He wasn't anywhere around. I'm not doubting he was injured, but it sounds to me like he got hurt trying to get out of the pen. And I'd bet he's out hiding somewhere licking his wounds."

She squeezed her eyes shut, like a child making a wish and trying hard to believe it will come true.

Despite Christi's distress, Eric couldn't resist a grin. He'd fallen in love with a brave, wonderful woman, but damn if this little girl side of her wasn't appealing, too.

"I'm going to take a shower and wash the rest of this mud off. After that, if you're still not asleep, I'll come hold you until you are. Okay?"

She nodded and closed her eyes. "I'm not going to hold you to a promise about Mustard, Eric. But for right now, I'm going to believe you're right because I feel better already." She scooted down in the bed and turned onto her side, tucking her hands under her head.

Eric got up. He closed the bathroom door quietly behind him. As he stripped off his damp clothes, he caught himself in the mirror and broke a wide grin. *You are one lucky bastard, Keaton,* he told his reflection. Then he remembered the flashing message light on the phone and watched the happy smile dwindle and die. "Don't you go ruining this for me, Lee," he said aloud. "You get your ass home safe so you can meet my beautiful lady."

Chapter Thirty-six

While Christi slept, Eric had forced himself to pick up the phone and retrieve the message that came in while he was in Anthony picking up Christi. He'd been taut enough to snap as he waited for the operator to retrieve the message, but as it was read back to him, he'd sagged with relief. The call was from Guy, though not with word about Levi. Only the familiar 'no news, just getting back to you, anything wrong on your end' bullcrap that was making him crazy.

He worked through the night and at daybreak, he tossed his pen onto his desk with a growled expletive. He picked up the phone and called Mike Sansom.

Surprisingly—it was not quite six yet—Mike answered on the first ring, sounding wide awake, gung ho. He became quiet when Eric summed it all up with both barrels aimed on the Anthonys, but when he related the incident with Christi and the retriever, the agent got noisy again. "Son of a bitch!" he snapped. "Where is she now?"

"Right here."

"And does she know you've narrowed your list of suspects down to her family?"

"No," Eric admitted. He almost told Mike the rest of it, what Christi had stumbled across after finding her pet missing. Somehow, though, he couldn't, not without feeling like he was betraying her trust.

"Don't you think you better warn her?" Mike was asking.

"Yeah, damn it," Eric snapped. "I'm gonna tell her, but not till after I go out there and look for her dog."

"Okay, listen," Mike said. "I was headed out to Anthony this morning anyway to talk to the sheriff. I'll call him and see if we can't get some of his men out there beating the bushes with us. The Anthony Estate covers a lot of ground. You could still be looking on your own come Christmas."

"Thanks, Mike. I'll tell Christi. I know she'll feel better."

There was a brief silence, then Mike asked, "Hey, bud, this thing with you and her, is it getting pretty hot and heavy?"

No reason why the question should irritate him, but it did. Maybe because 'this thing' was so new, so perfect and untarnished, he didn't want to lay it out, expose it just yet. *Probably* because Eric had a bad feeling that if he let Mike in on the inside with him and Christi, it would all go sideways like it had with Bryn. Superstitious baloney, he knew, but that's the way he was. Nothing he could do about it. "Listen, thanks again for the help. I'm going to fill Christi in, make sure she's settled here, then I'll hook up with the rest of you."

If Mike was offended, he covered it well. "See you at the OK Corral," he promised with a short sardonic laugh.

Eric arrived at the Anthony Estate less than an hour later, but he didn't see any evidence of his dog posse. He decided to start on the inside and work his way out.

Jeannie answered the doorbell, her face brightening at the sight of him. "Why Dr. Keaton, how nice." She stepped aside for him to enter. "Miss Christi's not come down yet—probably taking advantage of the plant being closed and all—but the others are at breakfast in the dining room. May I show you in?"

A crooked grin flashed, then disappeared. "Christi isn't upstairs, Jeannie," he told her, handing her a small envelope. "She's spending the day with me, but she asked that I give you this. It's a list of clothing and personal articles she'd like for you to pack for her."

The housekeeper's eyes darted from the paper pressed into her hand to the dining room.

"Don't worry about her family. I'm here to explain it to them. If you'll get her things, I'll show myself in."

Jeannie nodded, her eyes twinkling with her delight at helping the handsome young private investigator with the devil-take-you look in his eyes.

Eric could hear the volley of voices as he approached the dining room. The sound of their easy conversation pissed him off. At the very least they were guilty of unconscionable neglect.

Maryann and Alex saw him first, their surprised expressions cluing Paul in. His knife clattered to his plate as he started from his seat. "What the—"

Eric waved him back into his chair with a gesture. "Sit down, Paul. I've come to disrupt your morning family social hour, and I don't have time for your bullshit."

Maryann's face blanched as her hand fluttered to her lap, but her eyes seemed to grow brighter as if all of her energy had been drawn there. "How dare you come into our home like this!"

Eric yanked a chair from the table, bouncing it to the floor again several inches back, then dropped into it. His dark eyes flashed with hostility while a grin played across his face, hard and mocking. "You'll have to forgive me, Maryann. I never give etiquette much thought when I'm wading neck high in sewer muck and dealing with the subspecies that feed on it."

All three of them made noises of protest. Eric ignored them and went on, his eyes fixed on his hostess. "Maybe you would have been more receptive to an impromptu visit last night, just as you stepped into your brother-in-law's arms before disappearing into his room. Perhaps I would have appreciated the romance of it that somehow eluded your daughter. What do you think?"

Alex dropped his fork. The heavy silver clanged against his plate before plopping almost soundlessly to the thick carpeting. "Where is she?"

Eric rocked his chair onto its back legs, enjoying the cockfight he'd started though unsure which Anthony to put his money on.

Maryann rallied first. "Don't be ridiculous, Eric, Christi simply misunderstood what she saw. Misread it completely."

"Hmm. That's exactly what I told her," Eric said agreeably. "But after she told me where he was touching you, and how he picked you up in his arms, Maryann, I didn't believe it myself. Gotta admit, though, I am impressed by your nerve."

Alex's gaze had turned to silver with outrage. He looked back and forth, wife to brother, brother to wife, as if unable to decide which one he more wanted to strike. He jumped to his feet, sputtering with frustration as he struggled to articulate his incredulity. In the end, he gave it up and looked down at Eric instead. "Where is she?" he demanded again.

Eric narrowed his eyes as he met the other man's gaze. How much of this was real? How much for his benefit? Certainly seemed sincere. Even his hands were trembling. Was it possible he really hadn't known his wife was still boffing his brother after all these years?

"Let me go talk to her," Alex said, quieter this time.

Eric felt sorry for the poor bastard. He really hadn't

known they were still carrying on. But that didn't necessarily mean he was innocent of murder.

"You might as well sit down, Alex. I will tell you that Christi is safe. She's not coming home for a while. The danger's too great."

Silence.

Eric grinned. "What, no argument?"

Suddenly Paul's chair fell back against the wall as he knocked it away jumping awkwardly to his feet. "I'm going to tear your head off, Keaton!"

Maryann held out a hand in her brother-in-law's direction. "Please, Paul." To Eric she said, "We've already talked to the police and told them we were here when that poor girl was killed. We were all asleep, in separate rooms, as a matter of fact."

Eric ran a finger around the rim of the plate that he guessed had been set for Christi. He sat forward, preparing to leave. "Fine. So you two can't give each other an alibi for the time of the murder and leave poor Alex here out on a limb by himself."

Maryann got to her feet with him. "What are you going to do?"

"Do? Why, I'm going to join the search for Christi's dog. The sooner we find him, the sooner I can get to the nitty-gritty of my probe." He stood up, walked to the door, then turned and looked back. "I asked Guy to have some of our people dig around for a picture of Anne Renee. He's also checking into the Strauss and Anthony families about the time they merged. We've got a guy in Rome looking into the murder of a prostitute that went down about the time you all were there visiting Christi a few years ago. I wanna find out if her killer was ever apprehended. If not, it might explain why that was the only year a Rose contestant wasn't murdered. Asked him to fax me a photo of her, too, if he can come up with one. See if she was as blond and blue-eyed as the victims here."

Paul's fist slammed down into the middle of his plate with enough force to shatter it and rock the entire table, upsetting glasses, and salt and pepper shakers at the same time. Even Eric jumped with surprise. "Goddamn you, Keaton! Why do you keep insisting that one of us is a murderer?" The tiny capillary veins in his face that had burst with time and too much drink, fused together to create an ugly, red rash of fury.

Eric's grin spread easily, though there was no warmth in his eyes. "Why, Paul, I haven't *kept* insisting anything. In fact, I wasn't even sure until last night."

There was an audible gasp around the room, and Paul's red face went white.

Eric seized the advantage. "It's nothing conclusive, you'll be relieved to know. But in a couple of hours, perhaps even as we speak, Chief Small will be showing your pictures to guests and employees who've been staying at the Ritz-Carlton. He'll be asking, of course, whether anyone remembers seeing any of you. He'll be checking to see if any of you requested a key to the rooms on the fifth floor. And at the same time, one of his officers will be showing the same pictures to Darin Woods's mother to find out if she remembers seeing you at his hearing before the Grand Jury and to see if she recalls if Darin received or made any calls last Tuesday night to arrange a meeting. Someone else is getting a court order to look at your phone records—all of them, including your offices and apartment. In the meantime, I'm planning a trip to the morgue today to talk to Larry Cannon, the coroner, and get the results of the autopsy and lab reports. He and his staff are looking very closely for fiber evidence and I expect the police will be here anytime to take samples of the carpeting in your house as well as from your automobiles." He started to walk away, letting the weight of his words fill the silence, then went on. "Oh, yeah, one more thing. Did I forget to mention I've asked Dr. Cannon to talk to your mother's physician? Your housekeeper tells me her death was sudden. Unexpected."

He looked around him. Yep, they looked pretty stunned. Good. Let 'em worry. That was when they started making mistakes.

"You bastard," Paul whispered.

The soft words provoked a raised brow above Eric's obsidian eyes. He'd expected Paul's usual loud arrogance or booming indignation.

"You've been gunning for us since the day you arrived," he said, coming out of his chair and taking a couple of steps toward the investigator.

Eric surprised him by closing the gap between them. "You're wrong, Paul. I was bothered that your family wasn't under closer scrutiny, but I was prepared to accept whatever the evidence turned up. That's called doing my job."

He turned to go, but Alex stopped him. Grabbing Eric's shoulder, he forced him around with such violence that both Paul and Maryann gasped in amazement.

"Look, you arrogant fuck, you may have Chief Small in your pocket, but I've still got some very influential friends. I want you to back off and do it now. And then I want to talk to my daughter. Now, unless you want to be slapped with kidnapping charges you'd better tell me where to find her and then get the hell out of my city!"

Eric rubbed a hand over his brow thoughtfully. He had been sure that Alex was innocent, but the menace and uncontrolled anger he'd just demonstrated was characteristic of a man who usually kept himself well contained and didn't know how to deal with frustration.

Maryann opened her mouth to speak, but Jeannie appeared in the doorway with a garment bag draped over one arm and a small matching suitcase in the other.

"I found everything she asked for, sir," the housekeeper said to Eric, her eyes passing over her employers uncertainly. "Oh!" she said, suddenly remembering something. She leaned toward the investigator as if to confide to him alone. "I couldn't find her earrings. I looked everywhere."

Eric thanked her and took the bags.

He'd just pulled open the door when Mike raised his hand to ring the bell, Both men stepped back, surprised.

"Geez, Keaton, I guess we still got it," Mike said, laughing. "The timing," he explained to the Anthonys standing several feet back.

No one spoke, and Mike, not sure what was going on, chuckled uncomfortably before remembering the news he'd come to the house to deliver. "Hey, Eric, tell Christi we found him. The dog, Mustard."

"And?" Eric asked impatiently.

"And good news, he's alive. Banged up, but otherwise okay. Looks like he might've gotten hurt trying to get out of the pen. The caretaker said he came scratching on his door early this morning. He called the vet, and that's where the dog is now."

"What about the open gate?" Eric asked.

"Hell if I know. Looks like he was jumping all over the fence trying to get out. Maybe in the process, he somehow unlatched it." He looked down at his shoes and pants legs, which were splattered with mud and grass-stained.

"Well, I'm glad about that, but I'd still like to look around the pen. You mind?"

The agent shrugged. "Me? No. I'll go with you. Already ruined these slacks, so what the hey?"

"Let me put these bags in my car and I'll be right with you," Eric said. Then, shifting the two pieces of luggage, he grinned at the Anthonys. "If I had a buck for every time I've wished an animal at a crime scene could talk, I'd be as rich as you folks. What do you say? Think we ought to take a ride over to the vet's, see if he reacts to the sight of any of you?"

No one answered.

Chapter Thirty-seven

"Well?" Mike asked after Eric had walked the perimeter of the dog pen a couple of times. "You see anything I missed?"

Eric didn't answer. He was crouching down, peering in front of the retriever's house. Sun had broken through the cloud cover, and flashed on something laying in the grass a few inches away.

Eric held up a ring.

"Damn, Keaton, how'd you see that?" Sansom asked as he took the ring from Eric and wiped the mud and grass against his pants leg. Holding it a few inches from his face, he inspected it carefully. "Looks okay. Bonnie'll clean it up for me. I'm grateful you found it. I don't have to tell you about the value."

No, he didn't, Eric thought, twisting a similar ring on his own finger. It wasn't the monetary value he was talking about. They hadn't been expensive. Simple gold rings bearing their initials and a couple diamond chips on either side. Their 'class' rings. Of course there was no such thing. Candidates might go through official training at Quantico, officially graduate as FBI agents, even celebrate an unofficial brotherhood, but there was no fancy ceremony and certainly no fraternity pins or class rings.

But Eric and Mike had been more to each other than classmates. They'd been guys from the same hometown, assigned back to that city, and good friends right from the first. There had seemed a need for omething special to commemorate both the event and he bond. So they'd picked out the rings.

Funny, Eric thought now as he watched Mike slip is back on his finger, how neither of them had topped wearing his, even after all that had gone down etween them. Maybe, subconsciously, they'd both eld onto the hope that they'd one day find their way ack to the friendship they'd shared.

His eyes burned suddenly. Too little sleep, he hought, though he knew it was more. He was wearing is emotions on his sleeves too much these days. He ubbed his eyes hard with the heels of his hands, but he ache remained and even spread to his throat. Couldn't do this. Emotion shot perspective all to hell. He brushed it off, no big deal. "Yeah, lucky I saw it. How'd you lose it there, anyway?"

The agent shrugged. "Must have come off when I lug out the button."

Eric looked at him strangely.

"Just a little silver button," Mike said. "Had an eagle or something on it. Who knows, could be a ead."

Christi was sitting on the edge of the chair facing the loor when Eric returned from Anthony. She wore his athrobe and looked almost as pale as the white erry cloth.

"Great news, babe," Eric told her. "They found Mustard. He's okay."

Her bottom lip quivered and tears filled her eyes.

"Hey, don't cry. I swear to God, he's safe. He's anged up, but the vet has guaranteed he'll be good as new in a day or two."

Tears spilled over her lashes, but she managed a shaky smile as she jumped up and half circled, half climbed over the edge of the coffee table in her hurry to get to him. She hugged his neck and buried her face in the hollow of his throat.

Eric let the bags drop to the floor as he wrapped his arms around her, drawing her even closer.

"This isn't just about your dog, is it?" he asked.

She didn't answer, and he heard a dry sob.

He squeezed her to him once more, then stepped back, catching one of her hands to lead her to the sofa. "Come on, we're going to talk."

"But—"

"No, I have to tell you about your folks," he said, gently pushing her to the sofa, then dropping down beside her. "I told them what you saw, and—"

Her hands over her face, she rested her elbows on her thighs and leaned forward, shaking her head. "I don't care. It isn't important."

"It is to you," he said.

She looked at him then, tears running down her face. She laid a hand against his cheek. "Guy called."

"Eric?" Christi asked several minutes later, after he'd broken the connection with New York.

He didn't answer right off. His head bowed, he was trying to sort through the long series of revelations he'd made during the past five days. *Five days!* Had it really only been that long sine he had held his best friend in a bear hug, come to Kansas City, fallen in love, and into a web of deceit and horror so complex even he had trouble believing it?

Christi had stood on the far side of the room, her hands balled tight behind her as she waited. She knew it was bad. She'd heard the truth in Uncle Guy's voice when she spoke with him a half hour earlier. Saw it in Eric's slumped shoulders and the taut muscle in his jaw.

She came to sit beside him, leaning her head on his